No Alligators in Sight

A Novel

Kirsten Bloomberg Feldman

Cover design ©George Restrepo

Cover image ©Didy van der Veen / Alamy

ISBN-13: 978-1492792192

DEDICATION

For my family, the near and the far,
The big and the small,
You know who you are.

I don't believe an accident of birth makes people sisters or brothers. It makes them siblings, gives them mutuality of parentage. Sisterhood and brotherhood is a condition people have to work at.
~Maya Angelou

PROLOGUE: MY LIFE BEFORE MY LIFE

"What's this?" Venezuela holds the slim book up by its corner as if it might contaminate her. She acts this way about anything that came before she did. Her head tilts slightly to one side like the goldfinches listening for danger before they take seeds from our heavy nodding sunflowers.

My heart began to thud. "Oh, Zuzu, light of my life! Wherefore didst thou find such stuff?" We have taken to speaking in faux Shakespearean since she is doing *A Midsummer Night's Dream* for her eighth grade play, or at least I have. Her father had been a mighty fine Oberon back in the day. It still made me smile to picture him in tights.

"I told you. I was up in the attic looking for wings for my costume. You *said* they were up there." Sunlight glints off her shiny new braces, so much metal for one gap-toothed mouth, blurring her s's as they had been when she was learning to speak. Wisps of hair escape her braid and float around her ears. My eyes follow their lazy flight until they tickle her and she corrals them behind her ears.

"So many things up there, the wings amongst them, I trust. Thou art merely lucky they have nary a tooth to bite you with, so poor art thou at seeing what lies right in front of thy charming face." I hold out my hand for the book, hoping that we can put it aside and go search together. No such luck.

Now she is holding the book clasped against her chest. This will be harder. The truth, that's the answer. Because that's what we do in this family, no matter how hard; I was just dazed for a moment. I take a deep

1

breath.

"Momma, did you write this? Because I started reading this, and it's, like, so sad..." She doesn't call me that much anymore; now it's mostly Mom in that emphatic tone of teenagers everywhere, every statement hovering between demand and whine.

I clear my throat. It has somehow gotten clogged, though the pollen count isn't bad today, and the sky is clear as watercolor. "Yes. Yes, I did. What you have there is the story of the summer before I went to high school, just the age you are now, or will be in a few months, and I was having a hard time. That was the worst time of my life." Her brow furrows now. I hate to see that. She has always been empathetic, feeling for others even when she is hurting herself. It makes her father and me want to wrap her up and hide her away, always, but of course she'll have to go out in the world, just as we did. "But then it was the start of the best times, too." When her face clears, she smiles; I am blinded by the glare. "Would you like to take turns reading it out loud, you know, like we do sometimes?" We had alternated our way through *Frog and Toad* and *Little House* and *The Hobbit* and too many others to count since she could first read at age four. This helped with the tricky parts, the pronunciation, of course, but later with can all frogs talk, why Ma hated Indians, and was Frodo going to die.

"Is it true?"

"Pretty true."

"All true?"

"'Pretty all true.' As true as one person's version of things ever is." My apologies go out to Ian Falconer's *Olivia*, who has become a part of our family vernacular. "Should we start now?"

PART ONE: HAVE YOU SEEN MY LIFE?
PROVINCETOWN, LATE JUNE INTO JULY

1 SQUELCH

I was seven when she left us. That was six years ago. I could iron by then, so I guess she thought I was set. My brother though, he was three. He has a heart-shaped birthmark right between his eyes. If that couldn't keep her here, what could? She moved to Florida with a man who sucked his teeth. And that was that.

I scratched the newest mosquito bite on the back of my hand. The scratching made my pen go all crazy so I could hardly read the last *that*. I scowled and erased, but erasable pen was never as good as they said. You could always still see the mess-up. That was true about most things. People kept trying though. Maybe that's what all those whiners were doing on the morning talk shows, trying to fix the stuff they'd screwed up.

My seventh grade social studies teacher called mistakes a learning opportunity, but that was crap. Grownups never learned anything from their failures. Take my father. He'd gone right out and started drinking again a few months after our mother left, even though that was why she said she'd had to go, or at least that was what *He* said she said. As for why she had to go alone, I couldn't say. I'd tried asking, but adults didn't answer questions they didn't like.

Like the counselor, Candace Stopper, who came to my school two days a week and thought she knew everything about everyone. My friend Mayes and I called her Whopper, not terribly original, but true since she probably weighed in at about three hundred pounds. It was her idea—the Whopper's, not Mayes's—for me to write this journal, to try and "cope" with my anger. She even gave me spares, just in case. When I asked her how it was supposed to fix something I didn't have, she just sighed and said I was in denial. I guessed she'd know a lot about that, since every time I'd seen her she was eating candy bars, but her tote bag said Jenny Craig. Where did she get off talking about my anger? Like I yelled at the walls or went around wearing all black and dying my hair. Not that I could even if I wanted to since that takes bucks.

Mayes had lived near us when we'd had our own house, before we had to move into this piece-of-you-know-what apartment. Too bad Mayes was down at her grandma's in North Carolina now. Her mom had gotten a new job in Boston since she didn't want to work with Mayes's dad anymore, so they'd packed Mayes and her brother off to some camp down there, and now all our plans for the summer were shot. I *was* angry about that; maybe I should write about what a loser Mayes's father was.

I heard a clank. What was Bert doing out there? He was probably making some kind of dessert, since Bert was only interested in foods with sugar. Not that I could talk, really. I'd eat a whole pint of ice cream right out of the carton. I should get up and look, make sure he wasn't setting the place on fire or cutting off his fingers, but I just lay there thinking about Mayes. She'd left a few days ago, but it felt like a month. That was one of the problems with only having one friend. Now that summer was finally here, other girls were out screwing their boyfriends and working on their tans, and I didn't even have Mayes to do stuff with.

I used to have other friends besides Mayes. That was before I was Bert's permanent watchdog, and who wants to hang with a kid who always has to bring her little brother? It's not Bert's fault, not really. He was a pretty good sport about it. He even used to let my friends and me dress him up like a baby, a girl baby, of course, and wheel him around in a stroller. But then I started thinking about how my life sucked and how I wasn't fun anymore. A real sourpuss, that's what He called me, our father that is. We never called him Dad or anything like that when we talked, even to His face. He didn't really need a name; He just was, with a capital H. To other people we called him Joel. Yeah, maybe I was a sourpuss, whatever that was, but it sounded grumpy. Well, there was something pretty seriously messed up with my life, and I was only recognizing that.

"Let? Let? Where are you?" Bert called.

"Like I could go very far in here," I grumbled. The apartment had two microscopic, no make that *infinitesimal* rooms—good word, huh; this bedroom that was pretty full with the bed and the living room with the kitchenette at one end. I didn't count the bathroom as a room really, because what could anyone do in there besides the obvious? When I sat on the toilet, I could hold onto the edge of the sink and stick my arm into the shower stall. I dreamed about bathtubs. Then louder, "I'm in here. And I told you at least a bazillion times, my name's Annie now. Annie." I closed the bluebook and slid it beneath my pillow. I could tell I hadn't been quick enough.

Bert leaned in the doorframe, something slick and brown ringing his mouth. "But, Let, I mean Annie, that's been your name my whole life. I don't hafta throw away almost nine years because you got crossed, do I?"

"Confirmed. I got confirmed. When Sister Yvy gave me my new name, she gave *me* a whole new start, nothing to do with *you*." I squinted at his face and sniffed. "Pudding?"

He nodded and licked at the sides of his mouth. He came and stood by the side of the bed. "What're you doing in here? I saw that book."

"It's none of your business, nosey parker, but I'll tell you. It's for school." I meant to put him off with that since he couldn't stand school, too much sitting down.

"But it's summer, Let, I mean, Annie. Why're you doing school stuff in the summer?"

"The Whopper said I should."

"Should what?"

"Write about her."

"Write about who?"

"Gertrude."

"Who?"

"Don't play any dumber than you already are. You know, the egg donor."

"The what? The Easter bunny?"

"Not quite. The birth mother."

"Oh, her." His voice reminded me of when they wrote in books about telegrams, full stop.

"Doesn't The Whopper talk to you, too?" I knew damn well that she did. If you're going to be the perma-sitter, you might as well enjoy the snooping part.

"Yeah. So what."

"So what'd you tell her?"

"That I don't even remember what she looked like. Or anything about her." Now he sounded like our old dog Maggie had when she wanted to get in out of the rain, desperate.

"Nothing?"

"Nothing."

I sniffed again. "What'd you want, anyway?"

A *crack-bang* from the kitchen made us both jump. Something was definitely burning.

"You remember the emergency plan?" When the fire truck had visited our school in fifth grade, the speaker said to make a family emergency plan in case of, well, emergencies. Like everything else, this got left up to me.

Bert shrugged.

Okay, so he didn't remember. I sighed my best put-upon sigh. Bert didn't even notice. "Let's see what happened and if it's a fire or just a mess. I'll go in front of you and check, and if I tell you it's a fire, you head out to the sidewalk quick as you can without running. I'll be right behind, and then we can call 911 from the liquor store. Got it?"

Bert nodded solemnly and got in his "let's see" stance, on tiptoes in a little crouch. I shook my head and smiled a little. I rolled off the bed and took the few steps to cross the room and then one to cross the hall. I stopped in the kitchen doorway, and Bert bumped into me from behind. "It's the second."

"But it's only the first time I made pudding by myself—"

"No, stupid, I mean the second thing I said, a fire or a mess? Damn, is it ever a mess."

Bert poked his head around my side and looked.

"It looks like the blood in that horror movie we watched a few weeks ago, you know totally fake?" Everything came to network TV eventually. With my finger I swiped some from the linoleum that peeled up on all sides of the room like it was trying to outrun the adhesive. It blanketed every inch of the apartment, though the patterns were worn clean off in some places. "Ouch. Hey, there's glass in here. What broke?" I scanned the room and saw bigger chunks of glass.

Chocolate dripped down the one small window near the sink like thick, seriously polluted rain. It clung in places to the fake stucco ceiling, already grimy with grease and cobwebs. Shards of glass had stabbed our two sad bananas.

"Damn. This is going to take freaking forever to clean up."

"Sorry. I didn't mean to," Bert whined.

"Doesn't really help us, does it?" I paused meaningfully, though really I could pause until doomsday, and it wouldn't matter. "We have to put shoes on before we do anything. I'll mop, you can wipe. No, I'll do it. It'll be faster. You'll just screw something else up." I started to go for my shoes where I'd left them by the front door, but then I turned back. Bert was still standing there, so I ran into him again. "Quit that. Hey, Bert, where's the pot? Did it vaporize or something?"

"What pot? I didn't use any pot. I 'mixed' in a bowl then I 'heated.'"

"In a POT. You heat in a pot. Don't you know anything, you dumb ass? I—"

"That's what it said," Bert's eyes were brimming, and his heart was bright red.

"Never mind. It's fine. Get me the mop from the closet. Let's get this place in shape before He gets home."

I could hear Bert rattling around in the closet with the tools and the shoes and the broken badminton rackets from when we'd had a yard. We'd be lucky if He put in an appearance before we went to bed. Even then, it would be safer to pretend to be asleep, certainly less slobbery. I put on my shoes, grubby tennis sneakers that I also had to wear for gym class, and tried not to mind the slick feeling under my heels.

Bert came back with the mop and triumph on his face. I ignored him and got to work removing all signs of what we would call "the sweet ga-bang". Would it have been better if he'd made vanilla? Not likely. Rotten hidden stuff smells even worse than rotten stuff right in front of you.

"Hey, Bert."

"Yeah."

"Why were you calling me?"

"I wasn't calling you."

"Not now. Before. Before the bowl blew up."

"Oh." He scrunched his face. "Oh, yeah. I wanted to know if I could still have pudding after dinner if I had some now."

"Had you already had it when you called me?"

"A little."

"Maybe next time, maybe try and ask before you do it."

"Okay, Annie. Annie." He looked at me with squinty eyes, like he was trying to line me up with the name. "It's a good name. Think I should change my name, too? I could get crossed when I was thirteen, so long as I didn't have to wear no jewelry."

"Any jewelry. Well, you'd have to be older like you said, but most of all you'd have to want to. You aren't my shadow, you know. You don't have to do everything I do. Jeez, Bert, you don't even seem to like it when we go to mass."

"It's so lo-o-o-o-n-g…"

"I know. It gets a little easier to stay still when you get older. Haven't you noticed how grown-ups mostly sit around on their asses all the time?" I smiled at him, and he smiled back. That was us, in league against the adults of the world. "But Bert, your name, it's you. You don't need a new name. I just never felt like a Lettie, never mind a Leticia." I said the old name like it left a bad taste in my mouth. "I'm still the same person inside, and an Annie on the outside. Okay?"

"Okay." His grin split his freckles and made his heart puff up, something about how the muscles in his face worked together. Maybe I'd find out in biology when I got to high school. "What's for dinner?"

Like that should be my freaking job. "I think you mean what's for dessert, don't you? I'm about to get the rest going."

"Will He be home?"

"Not 'til late, I'm guessing." I started for the cupboard we euphemistically—another good word—called the pantry. My absolute favorites though are contranyms, words that can mean one thing and the exact opposite of that or something totally different, like squelch.

I turned back and saw Bert still standing in the doorway with his 'what can I do now' look on and reminded him about his model airplane. "You still have the wings to put on that plane, right? And put newspaper on the table this time." The fun never stopped in my life.

I put *Blonde on Blonde* in my CD player and cranked it, like that mattered since it only had one speaker that worked anyway. It was always the right time for protest music; I had so much to protest. Since I hardly ever got to get new ones, I had to go for the classics, none of the rap crap kids at school liked. Bob, Neil, and Bruce were my friends. Who cared that they were old now? They were young when they wrote their songs, the good ones anyway.

I took a can of Beefaroni out of the cupboard, opened it, and dumped the contents in a saucepan. Bert liked the squelching sound it made as it fell from the can; he thought it sounded like farting. I looked at the contents of the produce bin for a minute, not that there was much to look at, before I took out a limp carrot. I slammed the drawer on the rest of the moldering mess, such a cool word. My English teacher last year said try to use good words, you know, make them your own, and you won't sound like all the idiots out there. I'd heard enough idiots in bars in town to know what she meant. I scraped the carrot and put half on each plate, knowing Bert's would still be there when dinner was over. I'd found the plates at a yard sale for a quarter each. One had a blue flower and one had a red. The last one had a yellow flower. I'd noticed that yard sales often sold sets of three, plates or chairs or glasses, with the fourth one lost or broken or whatever. Just like us.

For dessert, with the pudding out of the question, all that was left was my secret supply. Checking to make sure Bert was still gluing, I reached up to the top shelf of the cupboard and took down a package of chocolate chip cookies. Someone had discovered them though, but it wasn't Bert, or they'd all be gone. That left Joel. Sometimes I thought all He ate was booze and sugar. He certainly left most of what I made behind on the plate, and I'm not a bad cook. I knew I could be a better one if I had something decent to work with. Mayes and I had made some awesome dinners at her house, and her family raved. Of course they had a ton of money, so a trip to the store was no biggie, even for the gourmet stuff. I put out two cookies for each of us and set them aside. I slid the rest of the cookies back up on their shelf.

"Dinner."

I watched Bert leave his airplane on the coffee table, one wing dangling precariously near the edge, but I didn't say anything. He slid into his seat at the table and looked at me expectantly. Our game was the same every night.

"Did you wash your hands?"

He slid away again without answering and returned from his trip to the bathroom faster than any human could have even turned the water on and off. I ladled the food onto the plates, set one before him and one on my side, and added cups of milk and forks. That was the last of the milk. I'd have to get more tomorrow, if I could get the money out of Joel. That was always a joy. It was like He was constantly surprised that we needed food again since He ate so little of it Himself.

The evening passed the way most of our evenings did, a little television, a game of cards, a squabble or two. Not even a telemarketer called to shake things up. Bert was yawning too much to protest my announcement of bedtime. I tucked him in, making sure Mousie was within easy reach, and lay down on my own side of the bed. I waited until his breathing steadied and then reached for my flashlight and the bluebook.

I don't know what she looked like either. Not really. I have a few photos hidden away, but I just have those images in my mind, I can't picture any others. They're just of her, not with us. I never found any of those. Joel, He'd shred them if He knew I had them. I think about shredding them, too, because what's the point? It's not like she cares. Obviously. Everyone says I look like Joel, but they're just saying that. You'd have to be blind. But looking like her and being like her are different. That's what I tell myself anyway.

His truck made the only sounds outside; all the other drunks had already gone home. I flicked off the flashlight and slid it and the book under the pillow. I heard Him stumbling His way up the front stairs, fumbling His key into the lock, and making His unsteady way into the living room. Good thing the new lady across the hall seemed to be a heavy sleeper; the last one had called the cops more than once when He was really raving.

Whack. "Damn." I hoped the refrigerator door hadn't swung right back open. The last time that happened, the milk was spoiled in the morning. Then I remembered the milk was gone anyway, so what the hell.

He'd be coming this way any minute. He always went to the left first.

"Bertie, Bertie, you awake to say g'night?" His voice was jarring in the quiet that blanketed a room where someone has been sleeping for a while.

I heard wet smacking sounds and a few rustlings but no words.

"'Night, then, Bertie." Thud. Click.

There went the nightlight in the wall. Bert would be sorry the little glow was gone. I'd called him a frigging baby once during a fight because he wouldn't give up the nightlight, but the truth was it was kind of comforting.

"Hmpf." He navigated the slim alley around the bed like a man who'd never been aboard a ship, when I knew He had. He seemed to have forgotten a lot of things. Like I have a photo of me up on His shoulders. I remember I used to sing "Lucy in the Sky with Diamonds" up there, except for some reason I thought it was about a guy named Michael who had diamonds. He was my imaginary friend for years. In the picture He is holding onto my calves with His hands and smiling at the camera like He owns the world. He'd forgotten that feeling, too. "Lettie, I know you're awake. Say 'ello to your old man." The alcohol fumes ran off Him like water. They were lighter and sharper than the cigarette smoke that lived in His clothes.

I might as well get it over with. "Hello." My voice sounded thick after hours of silence, thick and cold.

"You don't sound too happy to see me. What's eatin' you? God knows it's always something."

"It's late. I'm tired."

"Yeah, well I'm tired, too. I just wanted to say g'night."

"Good night then." I couldn't resist. "I thought you said you were working the afternoon shift."

"Well, missy, aren't you the smart one. Yeah, I worked the afternoon shift; then I stayed for a few with Al and Gene when I got off. You got a problem with that?"

"No problem. I was just wondering. Never mind."

"You aren' the only one that can ask questions. I smell choc'late. You made somethin' and din' even save me none? Tha's not very daugh-ter-ly." He drew out the word in His effort to say it clearly.

"Bert made pudding. But it's all gone. It spilled." He seemed to be waiting for more. I gave it. "Sorry."

"Yeah, we're all sorry. I'm goin' to bed. You sleep tight; don't let those June bugs bite." I tried to bunch myself up in the pillow to avoid it, but the big wet slurp came anyway. It was like with a dog, but His breath was worse. I steeled myself to wait until He left. "Bed bugs," I mumbled into the pillow.

"Always the smart one." The door banged against the frame.

I wiped my face vigorously with the back of my hand and fanned the air to break up the smell. At least Bert had slept through it this time.

She always liked Bert better than me. It's probably because I can't keep my mouth shut.

10

I was probably telling her things like I had to get to school on time and could we eat something besides cinnamon toast for lunch. Bert was only a baby though. She was always Engie this and Engie that. You'd think I'd hate him after a few years of it. But that's all it was, a few years, because then she was gone. Even Engie wasn't cute enough to keep her here. Engelbert and Leticia. Good God.

2 PINCH

As usual His rumbling snores alternated with wheezy sighs like the bus on its way through town. On the rare day He was awake before ten, He would flip eggs onto our plates from across the kitchen, but it wasn't dependable, and it wasn't today. I used the last of the eggs and scrambled them the way Bert liked. We had "fruit drink." Was actual fruit in there, watery like that? Store brands sucked. I'd have to ask Him for money for groceries, but I dreaded it. Maybe He'd be too hung-over to get going on Grandma E and how she'd saved rubber bands and tinfoil during the war and couldn't we make the money go a little farther? It wasn't like I was out buying Cocoa Puffs (or beer). It made me burn inside.

After breakfast He was still sleeping. I'd wanted to take a shower but I'd forgotten we were out of shampoo. While Bert was in the bathroom, I reached into His pants and extracted the first two bills my fingers came to. That was my rule, the first two, whatever they were. This time it was a ten and a five. I hadn't spent any of it yet, but it felt good to have it, a little emergency fund. I slipped into our room and tucked them in with their relatives under my socks. I took my change purse with me.

When Bert came out, we crept past Him on the pullout sofa that blocked our path to the door. Bert sucked in his breath prior to a yell when he saw his airplane lying crookedly on the floor beside the coffee table and its reeking ashtray, but I clapped a hand over his mouth. I didn't take it away until he nodded. After I checked my pockets for the key and gave him the thumbs up, Bert edged the door closed behind us. Takeout flyers and old newspapers littered the hall. The front door took the two of us to pull it inward past the dreck. It was too early for the mail. Who was going to write to us anyway? Oh, yeah, maybe Mayes, that would be cool. I'd already written her once and had another one started even though there was nothing much to report. We went down the front steps and around the side of the building to the narrow parking lot made from broken clamshells, the Cape's own version of recycling.

We got our bikes and rode into town. Our bikes were someone's hand-me, hand-me-downs that a guy at the bar had given Him. Mine was black, a dirt bike kind of thing. I didn't know anything about that, but I knew it wasn't a girl's bike. Not like Bert's. Now his was a girl's bike, screamingly pink. Bert had done his best to cover the pink with stickers he got at the gas station, the grocery store, wherever. Bumper stickers were the best because they covered the most. One said, "My other car's a broom." Another said, "Vote for change, Vote for McNamara." He'd won his selectman seat, but he hadn't changed Bert's or my life that I could see.

It was a hot day already, one of those days where nothing moves that doesn't have to. It felt like pushing the pedals of the bike through something solid instead of through air. A few people were out cleaning the sidewalks in front of their shops, but not many. The town's big summer beautification effort, barrels of red geraniums set here and there, looked like they hadn't been watered since it rained last week for a minute. At least rain wouldn't ruin the fireworks. Probably the drunks would do that, if the selectmen were serious about canceling if the rioting didn't stop. Big muscled guys unloaded trucks with dollies; I knew better than to look in their direction.

"Wanna look at magazines?" I called over my shoulder.

"Yeah, all right."

We stopped in front of the drugstore that was still Adam's but looked like a chain like the circulars stuck in the Sunday paper. I remembered the ladies in their hats who had cried when they took out the ice cream counter because of some new government law, HIPA or WIPA or something. Old timers in town used to sit there for hours drinking cheap coffee and watching kids come in for cones and candy after school. The same people worked there: they just wore different smocks, and they made you take the receipt. We slid our bikes into the bike rack, empty at this hour. The tourists were late risers for the most part. We didn't lock the bikes and wouldn't have even if we'd had a lock. We'd had a cheap combination one for a while, we'd gotten it for Christmas, but then two weeks later Bert had wanted to unlock it himself out on the wharf and it fell in the water, so goodbye lock.

When we pushed on the bar, the glass door opened inward slowly, grudgingly, like it was loath to part with the cool air inside. We went in, turned right, and again down the third aisle, for some reason called aisle twelve now on the sign above. I couldn't see how there were even twelve aisles in the store unless they counted half aisles or something. We only ever went in a few of the aisles, this one with the magazines, six with the shampoo, and three with the kids' chewable meds.

I picked up *Seventeen* and began to flip through the pages, looking at the clothes for fall, for back-to-school. Some of the skirts were so cute with the lace. I tugged at the collar of my alligator shirt I'd found at the thrift shop, some golf guy's who probably wore it once, and looked down at my pink plastic belt that I wished was a ribbon one. It was tough to be fashionable with no money, since having money seemed to be one of the main parts of fashion.

Bert studied a racing magazine, no doubt looking for articles on his hero, Dale Earnhardt, Jr. Why Bert was fascinated with auto racing when he'd never seen any race but go-carts I wasn't sure. It might have had something to do with His not even having a car, just a ratty, rusty pickup that if anyone else was with us we had to ride in the back.

"This here isn't the library. You plan on buying those?"

I looked up, startled to find the clerk's face inches from me. Her dark eyes behind her glasses were huge, magnified so many times I thought she must see things huge, too. Was my head big, like an alien head? Probably. That would figure since I felt like an alien in my body half the time. I'd been reading about when to wear a shrug and when to wear a sweater. I guessed I wouldn't get the definitive answer. "Yeah. No." I put the magazine hurriedly back in the rack. "Come on." I tugged on Bert's sleeve and headed for aisle six. Out of the corner of my eye I watched Fly Eyes smoothing the corner of the magazine like I'd soiled it in some way. That pissed me off. Pegging her with the nickname helped a little; it usually did with strangers who bugged me. Bugged me, ha, I was a riot. Still, I bet she didn't do that when tourists looked at stuff, but they probably just bought it.

I grabbed the only bottle of shampoo that was on sale for ninety-nine cents and headed for the front, Bert in my wake. On the way I passed a display of nail polish I'd just seen in an article called "Foliage for Fall." In a flash I grabbed Cheers, Chestnut and stowed it in my shorts pocket. At the counter I made sure I looked Fly Eyes full in the face and plunked down the shampoo. I reached into my other pocket for my change purse and counted out the plus tax.

"That it today?"

Beat, beat. "Yeah."

Fly Eyes rang up and bagged the shampoo, counted the quarters and dimes and pennies again, and gave me my receipt. In less than a minute we were back out on the sidewalk.

Bert walked to his bike and grasped it by one handlebar and the seat, but then he just stood there looking down at it like a new bumper sticker had appeared while we were inside. "You shouldn't have done that, Let. What if you got caught?"

"I won't get caught. I'm too fast. She just made me so mad. She didn't think we had any money."

"We don't."

"I know. But we bought something, didn't we?" I brandished the bag like it proved something.

"But—"

"But nothing. I've got it covered. Not to worry." I reached out and touched his shoulder briefly. "Want to go the beach? Before it gets really hot?"

"Sure. Yeah. We need our stuff." We backed out our bikes, mounted, and set off toward home. "You think He'll be awake when we get back?"

"Who knows? Why?"

"Just wondering."

"We'll see."

He was. He sat at the table in a straight-backed chair looking down at His hands like the answers to life were written on them. I hadn't ever seen anything there but calluses, but He looked a lot.

"Where're you two squirts coming from?"

"The drugstore."

"What for?"

"We were out of shampoo."

"You buy some fruity smelling kind again?"

No thanks, huh? It figured. "Just 'fresh.' Here, see." I dropped the bag on the table.

He pulled out the bottle and squinted at it. "Huh. Costs more every damn time I turn around."

Sometimes I wondered what century He lived in. Obviously He hadn't look at the prices on the other options. "We need milk. And some other stuff."

He rubbed a hand back and forth across the stubble on His jaw. He was still in His underwear. I looked away.

It was better to try and stay on track, away from whatever bigger questions He might be considering, like the big WHAT WE NEEDED. No, that was me thinking about that. "Milk and cheese and bread. Some cereal. Twenty ought to do it."

With elaborate care He withdrew His battered shiny wallet from the pants slung over His chair and pinched out a ten-dollar bill, its face crumpled and careworn. Like His.

No point in saying anything else, so I said, "Thanks." I pocketed the money and turned to go, and Bert did, too.

"Hey, little man, you her shadow or what? Where you two running off to now?"

"The beach," he mumbled.

"Tough life you two have. Me, I'm going to take a shower and head into work." He slapped the table with two hands, the sharp sound making us jump, and stood. He picked up the shampoo. As He passed, He brushed the hair on the top of our heads with His hands, one hand to one head like we were dogs or something. I willed myself not to jerk away.

The whole ride through town we dodged tourists hell-bent on crossing the street no matter what was coming. They plowed on toward ice cream or dolphin key chains or whatever they had to have right now like waves rolling toward the shore, relentlessly, that was the only word for it. Fat men and even fatter women clenched cameras in their hands, clicking, clicking but not seeing. It was beautiful here, and all they saw was themselves, them and their fat kids.

"It's a good thing cars only go one way, or there'd be a lot more flounder in the street." I laughed a little at Bert's joke, even though it was an old local one I'd heard a million times.

While Bert and I were waiting at the crosswalk, I saw Camilla and Justine, my grade's version of popular girls, walking down the sidewalk, their heads together, laughing. What's not to laugh about when one of your fathers owns half the town, and the other one's father owns the other half, including our dumpy apartment building?

Camilla had these eyebrows, dark and straight like bird's wings stroked across her olive forehead above her perfectly almond eyes. It sounded corny, but they were really like that. Boys wanted to eat her up with more than their eyes when they passed her in the halls at school. If you watched their hands as she went by, you could see them wanting to reach out and just touch her. Justine seriously looked like a movie star in one of those windblown shots where her hair bobbed softly around her face and never tangled. She had dark blue eyes, clear skin, and long legs that ended in tiny feet she kept nail polish on even in the winter. I didn't even shave my legs yet. What was the point? Boys who square-danced with her in gym bragged that they could fit their hands around her waist with room to spare, like that gave them some kind of ownership claim. She said she was going to stay a virgin until she got married or famous, whichever came first. The second seemed like the winner to me, since I figured some model scout for one of those TV shows would be spotting her any minute. Now me, since I wasn't winning any beauty contests, I was going to use my words to get out of here.

I used to be friends with Camilla back when we were little kids, but after Gertrude left, somehow that ended it. I couldn't bring myself to keep hanging out with her when her life was so awesome and mine so wasn't. It was different with Mayes, because everyone knew her parents could barely stand to be in the same room together, especially since he'd gotten this other woman pregnant and the woman had stayed in town, not going home to wherever she was from, flaunting it, it seemed like. Yet there they were, still married, hating each other's guts maybe, but still together for their kids. There wasn't a flaw to be seen in Camilla's or Justine's lives. If there *were* flaws, they were doing a bang-up job hiding them, which kind of made me hate them even more. I kept my head down in case by some miracle they were going to say hi to me while I was looking this nasty in last year's bathing suit on my ratty bike with my little brother. Like that was going to happen anyway.

At his signal we pedaled past the dancing policeman, surely captured on film worldwide, turned, and coasted up to a bike rack. This one was jammed. We propped our bikes on the end and headed for the beach right beside the wharf. I liked to go there because it had the least chance I'd see anyone from school since everyone cool went to Herring Cove or to Race Point for the waves. Here in town on the bay it was mostly young mothers with babies and toddlers or else tourists who didn't know any better.

We've had the same phone number my whole life. Someone is always calling and hanging up. I bet it's her because if Joel answers, He swears more than usual like He does when He hears her name. What would I do if she called and I answered and she didn't hang up? He says to hang up right away if no one says anything after I say hello. I'm sure I'd say something else she didn't want to hear, something like, Why do you bother calling when we are not interested in you here? When she'd probably rather I just asked is the weather nice down there in Florida, like normal people making conversation.

"You gonna write in that book all the time now?"

I hadn't heard him come up behind my shoulder. I slapped the book shut and slid it into the nylon carryall I'd brought as a beach bag. They'd been giving them away last summer at the grocery store with one hundred dollars in purchases. I'd saved the receipts after He'd seen them for most of July, afraid that the bags would be gone by the time I had enough. The bag was a nice color blue, but it said the name of the company on the side. I always put that side face down in the sand. I so would have rather had one of those cute straw ones like in the magazines in the spring, but that wasn't going to happen.

"Don't be a spy. No one'll like you."

"I have more friends than you do."

"I have Mayes."

"She's like a sister or something. I mean other kids."

"Yeah? Where are your buds then?" I scanned the horizon with my hand shading my eyes, pretending to look hard. "I don't see them."

"I told you. They went to soccer camp this week."

"Oh. Yeah. Sorry." Bert had wanted to go; Joel had said it cost too much. It wasn't so much that it wasn't true; it was just that Bert had wanted to go so badly. Bert didn't seem to want much really, at least that he said out loud.

"Want to go in the water?"

"Race you." He was off before he even got out the "you."

"Cheater! No fair!" I wrenched off my tee shirt that I always kept on unless I was actually going in. My legs churned to catch up with him; with almost five years' growth on him it wasn't hard.   I wasn't the tallest kid in my grade for nothing, even when I slouched, which was all the time. The new problem was, since I'd stopped growing so much, I was getting wider right where I already hated, my thighs.

"I deserve a head start. I'm younger," he panted from the water's edge. The waves lapped at his toes like kittens batting at yarn.

"You deserve a lot of things. Like this." I kicked water at him. "Last one in…" there was no need to finish our usual dare; we were about equal on the rotten egg front. I had longer legs, but he was closer to the ground. Also, I stopped a lot just before I dove in, feeling the last bit of heat before the plunge. It was one of the few times I stood up straight, with the sun on my face and my legs spread just wide enough that my thighs didn't touch. He always took advantage of my hesitating, like he did today.

We stayed in the water until the tide pulled back, exposing the sand in ridges that rubbed against our stomachs. So many crabs had nibbled our feet we lost track. With the bottom revealed, we collected large unbroken clamshells. It took us an hour to find a dozen. I had heard people who grew up here years ago say that the haul now was pitiful. I knew the shellfish had gone with the fish, into the nets of the trawlers that raked the bottom of the ocean. I'd heard people say it was more like rape than like fishing.

"Let's go paint these. Today's a good day to build up our stock, with the festival coming and all."

It used to be the Blessing of the Fleet; now that there was no fleet really, it was the Portuguese Festival. The tourists didn't know the difference. Or care. They still spent the day gorging themselves on fried dough, fudge, and penny candy. If we were lucky, the women would drop a few of their dollars in Bert's outstretched hands in exchange for the shells we'd painted. They all thought Bert was so cute. Bert usually made ocean scenes with stiff sails on his boats and spouts on all his whales. I went for sky scenes, full of clouds and wheeling birds. I liked to draw and paint stuff, no big deal, not like I was going to be an artist. Artists were nuts. I'd seen enough to know.

"I don't have any more blue," Bert whined.

"I'll share," I grumbled. "Maybe we can make enough to get some more paints." I thought of the money I'd been taking from His pockets, like He'd ever even notice. I had two hundred twenty-seven dollars now.

Chickenshit that I was, I hadn't spent even one. "Let's lie in the sun first."

We walked back to the bag, and I put my shirt on first thing and then pulled out our towels, one from a cigarette company and one that had no edges left, only raveling, and no color either. I spread them in the sand and pulled out my book. Movement caught my eye, and I looked toward the wharf at a blonde woman on a rental bike pulling a kiddie trailer with two little ones in it. I looked back down at my book.

3 BAR

She used to ride me around on the back of her bicycle in a little seat. My aunt told me that. She said we were "a picture." She used a lot of funny expressions like that. She's dead now. Other people He knows, people He probably doesn't know talk to me about her, say guys used to check her out when we rode around on that bike. She was a real looker, they say, like they can't figure out how she ever got together with Joel. I bet He can't now, either.

"Annie."

"Yeah?" I slid the pen into the book, knowing what was coming.

"I'm hungry. What can I have?"

"You're always hungry. You want these crackers?" I held up a package of Saltines that came with chowder at the cheap restaurants.

Bert snatched the package and ripped it open, stuffing both crackers into his mouth at once and chewing rapidly. "Nothing else? We didn't even have any lunch." He spewed cracker dust as he talked.

"Chew and swallow. We have peanut butter at home."

"I'm sick of peanut butter. Can't we get minute steaks? He gave you money. I saw."

"He didn't give me enough money for those." He didn't give me enough for even the things we needed, but Bert didn't need to know that. At least when we got back to school we'd get two free meals a day, that is if I snagged the forms out of the mail and forged His signature again, which I would.

"What can I have then?" His voice rose into a wail; he got this way when he was really hungry.

I tried to fend off the full breakdown I knew he was capable of. I was so not in the mood for that. "Jesus, Bert, hold it together. Let's put our shoes on and get our bikes. I'll think while we're riding."

He seemed to calm with the movement in the direction of food. We sat on the curb to put on our shoes. My eyes rose from the street and settled on the red building behind the bike rack. The neon sign for Budweiser didn't glow yet in the still bright sun. Cigarette butts littered the brick step. Why were smokers such pigs? Then again, I'd watched tourists throw bigger trash than that on the ground when they were right next to a garbage can.

"Want to go in there for something to eat?"

"Last time though…" Bert looked down at his feet, still sandy in their socks and sneakers.

"That old biddy wasn't a regular, just some tourist. It'll be all right." I hoped that was true. Most natives worked in the tourist industry, so that meant lots of restaurants and bars. Kids in town knew their way around those places as well as they did around their own houses. The town had gotten stricter about kids in bars since some guy gave his son a sip of his beer right as one of the new cops came through the door, but you still saw lots of kids in and out of bars. The lady who had spooked Bert wasn't a cop though; she had been old and wrinkled but her outrage was shrill. Why she cared that a kid was watching her guzzle down chardonnay like it was lemonade, I don't know, but she sure did.

I took another look around. It was pretty early on bar time and plenty light, so most of the customers stood on out the deck, drinks in one hand, cigarettes in the other, and admired the few remaining fishing boats and the lighthouse in the distance. They all said the same corny things every summer, so charming, so picturesque. It made me want to gag. If it was so charming, why were they trashing it and buying up all the houses for millions and not even living in them more than a week or two a year? Gay, straight, bi, I couldn't have cared less, but they could have bought us one of those houses and hardly even noticed the missing cash the way they threw it around. I made up my mind. We headed for the door to the interior, its glass panels tinted dark, and no bouncer yet. We would have known any of the bouncers by sight at least anyway, but I didn't want anyone to alert Joel to us until one of the servers saw us.

I pulled the door outward, and we both slipped inside. We stood a minute to let our eyes adjust to the dimness and the shock of cool after the hot, dusty street.

"Well, look who's here. Come give me a hug!" Martini Tina was all over us, enveloping us in her warm arms, her dense perfume, and her high heavy hair, before we even took a step forward. She'd known us our whole lives, and she didn't care that I was kind of skittish about hugs since my chest had gotten sensitive. Not like I had any boobs to speak of, but I guessed my body was getting ready. I didn't have the nerve to ask anyone about it, if I could even think of who to ask. She just barreled right in, no matter if I resisted, and I kind of had to admire her. People put me off so easily, at the slightest glance or word, but she wasn't put off by anything. "Been at the beach, I see. Water nice? I ain't been in ta-day."

We nodded. I could tell Bert felt a little shy, too, though not because of his chest, just because Bert wasn't the most trusting guy. It was like if he didn't see someone for a few weeks, he thought they'd gone and left him. Could you blame him really? Even if he said he didn't remember Gertrude, he lived with her actions every day. We both did.

"Youse want somethin' ta eat? He's here all night, double, huh?" We nodded again silently, knowing that she already knew the answers to these questions. All three of us turned together to look toward the bar. His head popped up from below right as our eyes reached the dark, shiny wood.

"Well, look what the cat brought in. What'd I say about coming in here? You know I don't need the trouble."

"They ain't never been no trouble in their whole young lives. They can jus' sit right here and have a bite to eat and then be off. It's early." Her tone said discussion closed, and I wished I could master it. No one gave Martini Tina trouble, not even Joel. She pushed us down into two chairs and patted the tabletop. "Your order?" She flashed us her big grin so full of teeth it was a miracle her lips could close. We looked from her to Joel and back and decided to go with her. She was offering the food.

"Can I please have a hotdog? With chips? And no pickle?" Bert asked.

"Can't have no pickle juice messin' up the chips, makin' 'em soggy, am I right, my man?" She chortled deep in her throat where she could lodge the smoke from her cigarettes longer than anyone I'd ever seen. Once when she had exhaled, I had counted three breaths of my own. "What about you, missy? You're gettin' prettier ev'ry day."

I looked down at the table. Compliments made me nervous. I'd rather hear an insult any day; I knew how to deal with those. Plus, she had to be lying or just being nice. I looked in the mirror every morning, and what I saw there was no great shakes. Obviously no boy in town agreed with her. "I'd like grilled chicken fingers, please. Salad? No fries?"

"Watchin' the figure, huh? Good idea. Tini should think about that one a these days." Her laugh said that day would be a distant one. I had seen how men's eyes followed her, back and forth, almost reaching out to pat her ass then thinking better of it.

"Won't be two shakes, and we'll have you two fed and home." She glided off to the kitchen to place the order.

She stopped back on her way to the bar. "I told you it'd be all right, din' I?" She smiled at Bert, and when he smiled back he had his tongue in the gap where his teeth had been. "Comin' in yet?"

Bert shook his head.

"They will. It takes more time than you'd think. That's true about most things." She looked around.

The place was still almost empty. Billy Joel was singing about the regular crowd shuffling in. It seemed like all his songs were about drinking, but they were pretty good anyway. Two old guys sat at the bar pushing a dish of peanuts back and forth while they took tiny sips of their beers, eking them out. Joel was cutting lemons and limes, getting His set-up squared away before the rush. He did not look our way again, at least not when I was checking. A couple sat knee-to-knee at a square table like ours but more prominent. The man raised one finger and waved it in the air, clearing his throat at the same time. Martini Tina swayed over. She had a walk that seemed slow while you watched, but before you knew it, she was there.

"Somethin' else I kin get youse?" She stood with her hand on one hip. Martini Tina never wrote down orders or got one wrong that I'd seen. When she brought the food to a table, she always set the right plate in front of the right person. I'd seen locals switch seats while her back was turned to try and mess with her. It never worked.

"It's these clams. There's something wrong with them. She says they taste funny." He hitched a thumb at the woman in question. The woman said nothing, didn't even nod her head.

"Do they. Well, I'm real sorry to hear that. How 'bout some nice nachos? They got beef and cheese." The teeth flashed.

"That sounds great."

"And another g-and-t here. Another die-kri." Martini Tina made it sound like she was confirming an order, not suggesting one. No wonder her tips were putting her kid through college.

Martini Tina took the offending clams and headed back to the kitchen. On the way past the bar, she quipped, "Another go-round on three, hon." At the order window she placed her new order and then motioned for a clean plate, her back always to the room. She slid the eleven clams onto it, added new cocktail sauce and lemon, and turned.

She sidled over to the table with her usual swagger. Was she nervous about getting caught? I doubted it; nothing made Martini Tina nervous. The chief of police was in here every night of the week, and she always waited on him. "I know youse love these. Those bum'kins wouldn't know a fresh clam if it squirted 'em. Whitey Under the Lobster Trap raked these this mornin' early. Can't get no fresher than that. Enjoy." She was gone, back to the bar before we could even thank her.

The clams were wet and curled in their shells, like the pictures of kidneys in health class. I could almost picture them breathing, way down underground, just a little bubble on the sand to let you know they were there, all mouth and stomach. Like Bert. I laughed a little to myself. We'd been eating them raw as long as He'd worked here, which was as long as we were, pretty much. There was nothing I'd tried like a cold, slick clam combined with the bite of the cocktail sauce and the squint of the lemon. Afterward, I'd clamp the lemon wedge between my teeth and siphon out the rest of the juice, not caring that the dentist said it was leaching the calcium off my teeth, but not now. Clams first. Bert loved them as much as I did, which surprised me when I thought about it since he was kind of a picky eater. We ate in silence, in reverence, since we hadn't had them in so long and kept on eating when our order came, extras of everything and no pickles in sight, until the last chip was gone.

"Thought you said you didn't want chips or fries."

"I changed my mind. I can change my mind, you know."

"Sure, except they were *my* chips."

"You didn't really mind, did you?"

"Naw. We're in this together."

We stuck our fingers in the chip salt and then our mouths, knowing His eye was on us as the bar filled. People we knew, other locals, came by our table and said a quick hello or patted our arms then moved toward the bar, drawn to it like ants to apple cores.

Bert licked the sides of his mouth and stared longingly at Martini Tina's broad backside. Like she felt his stare, she came our way when she was done setting down a new round for a raucous table of six, all but one of them spilling over the sides of the chairs.

"Think I forgot?" Her grin revealed her gold tooth two back on the left. Bert once speculated that she was a pirate at night when she closed up. I said I guessed she hadn't found gold yet since she was still working here. She pulled two lollipops, one yellow and one red, from her apron pocket. They were the good kind, the ones with chocolate at the center, not like the lame ones they gave away at the bank, those thin disks that didn't even have a flavor really, just sugar. "Youse be good now. Head on home before the crazy drivers hit the streets." She planted a kiss on top of Bert's head and held her hand on the back of my neck a minute longer than someone outside the family would.

Bert grabbed the red and left me the yellow. "What do you say?"

"Thanks, 'Tini Tina." His words slurred around his sucker.

"I tol' you, no thanks. Git on outta here now."

As we passed the bar, we hesitantly raised one hand each in Joel's direction. "Give a ring when you get home so I know you're not roadkill." He inclined His head, the lights bouncing off His glasses and obscuring His eyes, and then turned back to His customers.

"Careful now; it's hard for cars to see us at dusk. You go in front, and I'll follow." I held my bike away from his so Bert could maneuver off the curb and into the street. Cher was handing out flyers for her evening performance, and so was Barbara Streisand. Judy Garland was a fixture in town and waved at us as we wheeled by. We waved back.

We had to stop at Cumbie's. They had the cheapest prices besides the supermarket, but Bert wasn't going to make it there and back. There was a fire truck parked in front, and it made me think of Ralph, this guy in my class that I'd had a crush on since I was in diapers, even though it was his dad who was the firefighter. Lots of things made me think about Ralph that made even less sense than that. We went inside, and I told myself get over it, but that's hard after so much repetition. I focused on money. That always brought me right down from the clouds. I had enough for English muffins and corn flakes if I bought the small box but not for the coffeecake Bert wanted. He pouted but didn't freak; maybe his stomach still remembered dinner. Bert was dragging when we got back to the apartment, so I put his bike away behind the building while he sat on the front steps. When I came back around and climbed the stairs, he reached for my hand.

"Let's get you into the shower, big guy." I kept his hand while I shouldered inside the heavy entryway door and put the key into the lock.

"Do I hafta?"

"You'll be up all night itchy. Just a quick one."

"Hair, too?"

"Hair, too."

"Will you do it?"

"I will."

What does she do all day down there in Florida? It can't be nicer than here. This is the most beautiful place in the world, and I haven't even been anywhere else. I don't have to. I just know. She must like it though; she never comes up here. Maybe she's busy. I know she's some kind of artist. The artists I see here are painting, painting all the time, looking so hard at things I think their eyes are going to fall out on the sidewalk. I hear all the tourists talking about the light here. It can make a heap of dead fish look like glistening treasure at the right time of day, late in the afternoon or early morning. I'll bet they don't have light like this down in Florida. So how come she's an artist there, then? And how come being an artist is more important than being a mom?

4 DUMP

We woke to a bedroom full of the smell of warm butter. Usually on a Saturday we ate cold cereal and watched a couple hours of cartoons before He even stirred. Bert was out of bed in an instant; I wasn't far behind. We went toward the kitchen in our pajamas.

"You two are looking a little groggy this morning. Have some breakfast, and then we need to get cracking." Eggs and toast were already sitting on plates.

"Where're we going?" Bert sat down and shoveled in a forkful of eggs.

"'Where're we going?' It's moving day. Pack up your clothes, and then you can help me with the dishes and the rest of the shit."

We stared with forks back down on our plates.

"What? You think we were going to live in this dump forever? Right here on the street and me in the so-called living room on that god-awful couch? Not likely." He slugged back the dregs of His coffee and refilled His cup. He lit a cigarette and walked over to twitch back the curtain at the window. "I'm going to pull the truck around front so we can load up." With a bang of the front door He was gone.

"Lettie, what's He mean, moving? Like, out of town moving?" I glanced at Bert. His heart was bleached out.

I didn't correct him on the name. "I don't know, Bert. I don't know every damn thing." I left the rest of my eggs and went back to our room. I sat down heavily on the bed. What the hell? I could go ask Him what was up, but that was risky. It obviously didn't matter what we thought, so I might as well start packing. The yelling or worse would come too soon otherwise.

I picked up the bag from the beach and dumped the sandy towels on the floor. I took them into the kitchen and told Bert to shake them outside.

Then I opened Bert's two drawers in the dresser and put in his raggedy collection of tee shirts, shorts, sweatshirts, and pants that would be too short for him in the fall. I added his other pair of shoes and looked for Mousie. When his purple Highness rested securely in the bag, I zipped it shut. I pulled our other bag, a camouflage duffel from the army/navy, out from under the bed and started on my own two drawers. A dress that I never wore from the closet, a windbreaker, my ballerina jewelry box, and a few paperbacks filled out the bag. Under my pillow I found the bluebook and my pen. I looked under the bed. There were Bert's playing cards, hopefully all fifty-two, some jacks, and a comic. I thought of our paints and paper and Bert's shovel and rake and our shells. I'd have to use a bag from the grocery store.

He'd brought some cardboard liquor boxes from the bar. The pots and pans and plates and silverware took one; the food from the cupboard and the refrigerator took most of another. The glasses I wrapped in our towels and filled another grocery bag. I pulled the sheets off the bed and balled them up before adding them to the next bag. His sheets He hadn't thought to pull off before He folded up the pullout for the last time. I yanked it open, pulled off the sheets, and clanged it back shut in long-practiced moves.

When we were done, the truck was only about half full. The apartment looked the same as it had when we'd moved in, like the bigger motel rooms around town with the stained, pilled couch and glass coffee table, the double bed and battered dresser in the bedroom, and the unmatched table and chairs beside the kitchenette.

"Climb in. Why the long faces? Where we're going, it's going to be great. Much better than this. You'll see."

We did as we were told and then sat leaning against the door, Bert against me, me against the frame. I cranked down the window, and the heat coming in was just as heavy as the heat inside. Joel gunned the engine, and with a roar we were off up Bradford Street. No one said anything, but He whistled. He hadn't whistled in a long time. Shortly He turned right, and I assumed we were headed for Route Six and out of town. It surprised me when He quickly turned again into a shell driveway, backed up, and headed back the way we had come. At the intersection He turned left, and now we were almost in front of our old apartment. I felt Bert stiffen beside me, leaning in that direction like a dog near its home, but then the old truck pulled past. Bert sank back against me. Still no one said anything, though the whistling continued.

"You two are a quiet bunch this morning."

I couldn't think of anything to say besides it takes more than two to make a bunch.

In less than a mile He turned left into the opening in a gateless split rail fence. A little sign said Tapper's Cottages. I'd noticed it in our travels around town on our bikes; I'd thought they were tourist weekly rentals. Maybe they were, ones that were too run-down to rent even when people were desperate to come to the Cape. Hell, *we* were desperate. He drove to the back of the oval of macadam and stopped in front of a weathered shingle cottage with red trim around the door and the window frame.

"You can get out. We're here."

Bert and I looked at each other and back at the cottage. We climbed out and stood beside the truck.

"Here's the key. Take a look."

We tore off for the door. I pulled open the screen and put the key in the lock, and it turned with only a little resistance. I pushed the door open, and we both squeezed through the doorway at the same time and stopped. Before us lay a small living room, and beyond that, two small bedrooms, a kitchen, and a bathroom. You could see it all from where we stood.

He'd come up behind us and put an arm on each of our shoulders. "See?" He steered us toward the first bedroom. Two twin beds stood waiting for sheets and blankets. "You'll have your own beds."

"There's a window!" Bert exclaimed and darted to it. "And a yard!"

"The old man did pretty good, huh?" He looked smug, His whiskers bristling in His unshaven face. "Give me a hand getting the shit out of the truck." He turned and strode back outside.

"It's pretty nice," I began.

"PRETTY nice? This is awesome!" Bert ran out the door after Joel and returned with the duffel bag, one handle coming loose from the stitching. He dumped it on the bed and rooted around until he came up with a purple fuzzy lump. He held this squeezed between his two hands and pointed it around the room. "Mousie has a new house," he declared and propped his old friend on the worn dresser that sat between the beds.

"Mousie used to have ears and a tail, too, before you sucked them off," I commented. "At least now I'll have some space between us before you start on my toes or something, you sicko."

I hadn't seen Joel so perky since He read they were reinstating Tuesday two-for-one beers night at the "A" House. No, seriously, He reminded me of the way He used to be, joking around instead of scowling. And the house, cottage, whatever, is pretty cool, a lot better than the apartment, just like He said. Maybe this will be a new start for us. God knows we could use it.

5 STRAY

We got a package from Gertrude today. I could hardly read the writing on the brown wrapper; I don't know how the postman could. She sent Bert some old jean shorts and a tee shirt that said THE GAP on it in raised letters; it looked like it used to be blue until somebody washed it with something red. They fit pretty well though. She sent me a sundress that went down to my ankles and was missing a button for one of the straps. I stuffed it in the bottom of my drawer. Why was she sending us stuff anyway? We hadn't heard from her in months, unless you counted that postcard that had the wrong zip code. It had a picture of a sunflower, and it said (He said, because we couldn't read the writing), Have a great day, you two. Thinking of you. Love, Mommy. He snorted when He read that. Why the hell did it sound like she just saw us yesterday? But then nothing she did made any sense to me.

I sat on the two steps leading into the cottage, and Bert sat down in the dirt and grass. He'd dumped buckets of water from a plastic pail onto the bed where flowers might grow if anyone planted some and then mixed it around with an old wooden spoon. Now he was scooping the muck into some aluminum trays that had held pot pies, one of our staples.

"Who's the fourth one for?"

"It's for her."

"Who her?"

"Oh, I mean him. Mousie, I mean."

"You're lying. Who's it really for?"

He was stubbornly quiet filling the fourth tray.

I relented. "Want me to help decorate? You know I love that part."

He looked up at me, his eyes bright. "Let's look for stuff."

We collected seedpods and pebbles in silence for a while. Some weedy Johnny Jump-ups grew by the foundation; I picked a few of the little

31

flowers. "These can go in the center of each one, if you want."

He nodded but still said nothing. That was his way of punishing me, I knew. It wasn't that I minded silence, I liked it actually, but he was only silent when he was angry. He edged behind the scrubby bushes along the left side of the cottage. I heard him draw in a breath sharply, and I was there before he took his next one.

"What? What's the matter?"

"Look. That yellow cat must of got him. He's still alive." He crouched down and scooped a tiny ball of gray fur into his hand. He held it out for me to see.

"Ooo. He doesn't look so good. He didn't even try to get away. Maybe you'd better leave him."

"Can't we try and help him? Please?" His anger had gone from his face, replaced by the deep worry crease he got between his eyes over all small, helpless animals.

"Oh, all right. Bring him in the house."

I spread antibiotic cream on the bite marks and unwrapped a knock-off Band-Aid. "It's gonna go all the way around him. Like clothes." I laughed a little.

He sucked in his breath again, excited this time. "You could make him some clothes. Like you did for those other mice of yours."

"Those were stuffed. I can't sew on him. It'd hurt."

"Maybe wrap him in something?"

"All right." I went out and came back with an old blue bandana He used as a handkerchief, a pair of scissors, and the box from some tea bags. None of us drank tea anyway. "Put him in here."

Bert did as I said without hesitation. He waited, watching intently, while I cut the bandana in four pieces and used one to wrap the tiny scrap of fur.

"Let's leave him inside while we're decorating. I don't want that cat getting him again."

We returned to the pies, working steadily until it was time for supper. We set the pies to one side of the warped wooden step to dry. Bert wanted to put them in the oven.

"They'd burn, you idiot. Leave them."

When we were hungry and He didn't come, I made a box of macaroni and cheese and sliced an apple. I cut away the brown bits and the skin, knowing Bert would reject it all if he saw anything but pristine white. Pristine. I loved that word. It sounded like the life I wished I had. We ate quietly, glancing occasionally at the door when each thought the other wasn't looking. When Bert began to yawn, I helped him find some nearly clean pajamas. While Bert snuggled into his, I lay on my bed and listened to him breathe. I was impatient but trying not to fidget. When his breathing was good and steady, I turned on my flashlight.

Bert's always begging Joel to let him have a pet, but sometimes if feels like Bert's the pet we don't have: walk him, feed him, put him to bed. Once he showed Joel a flyer for a dog someone needed to find a home for. Could we take him? Joel had said no we couldn't, of course, but then He had more to say. He sneered, 'There's not a snowball's chance in hell of anyone taking that mutt, face like that. People want cute little puppies, and most times, once they're half-grown, they throw 'em out in the street. Not cute anymore.' I remember thinking His eyes looked a little misty, which was weird. I remember I nodded vigorously. It made sense in a way that I couldn't explain. When Bert lets in strays, He never lets them stay, saying they're too much work and plus lots of landlords don't like pets, one more creature to beat on their already beaten-up properties. Properties. Such a fancy word for most of the dumps I've seen in this town. This place, the cottage, I mean, is a million times better than the apartment was, but He's pretty much back to same old, same old, staying out drinking half the night and hung-over like crazy the next day. The stray thing though. Maybe Bert's attracted to strays because we're strays. I mean, we're not orphans or anything, but sometimes it feels like we are. It feels like Joel thinks His life would be a whole lot easier if we weren't around. Then He could just work and hang out with His friends or whatever. He could drink Himself into the ground, and no one would give a flying. I guess this isn't really writing about her and why I'm angry, but it kind of is. Is writing in here like talking to myself? That's what they say crazy people do. I know I'm not crazy. Actually, I feel like I'm one of the sanest people I know, me and Dory and Donnie. I know they're His friends, and they were Gertrude's friends, but they're my friends, too. A kid can have grown-up friends, right? As far as I can remember, they've been there for pretty much everything that has mattered in my life. Time for some shut-eye. Now that we've established that I'm not crazy, I can say, Night-night, journal. See you tomorrow.

"What in hell is that smell?" This was the first thing Joel had said that morning. He moved slowly, like even walking pained Him, and He spoke slowly, too, like His brain ricocheted with each syllable.

"You mean, besides you?" I wanted to say. From the fumes that it had been a Ballantine night instead of a Scotch night.

"I mean it, you two leave some food in the couch or something? Jesus. Help me look."

We got up and began looking around, under cushions and even picking up the edge of the rag rug. I looked in the fridge. We didn't find anything.

"I'll be damned. Is this some game you're playing?" He held the tea box by one of its flaps, peering down into it and then looking at us like maybe a dead mouse dressed up in His handkerchief could be a hallucination.

"That's Gray. He's sleeping!" Bert whispered, the whisper louder than his usual voice. We both ran over and looked in, crowding each other for space.

"Sleeping my ass! This thing's dead, and Christ does it smell." Joel sniffed and looked closer. "What the hell? What'd you put on it?"

"Just a little powder 'cause he hasn't had a bath in a while. He's resting, he's not dead. We fixed him." Bert was reaching for the box, but Joel held it out of reach.

Joel poked His finger in the box. His eyes narrowed. "You fixed him, all right. Son, he's as dead as they come. I'm sorry, but it's got to go." He walked unceremoniously back toward the bathroom. And I'd thought Bert had let go a bad one this morning like he sometimes did.

"No! He's mine! Let me have him!" Bert was shrieking now.

He turned and eyed me steadily over the top of Bert's head. "You're the older one here. You'll help him take care of this, no monkey business?"

I came forward and took the box from Him. "Don't worry. I got it."

Joel went into the bathroom and closed the door. He sat down heavily on the toilet and took a crap, a long, loud one. That one would smell. The post-drunk ones always did.

"Come on, Bert. We did the best we could. We'll make him a nice grave in the yard."

Bert looked at me for a long minute to see if it was any use arguing. I had on my grim face, lots of practice with that one, so he swiped at his eyes and followed me outside. Someone had tripped on the pies and sent one of them crashing into the dirt below. Bert was too focused on our mission to notice.

"You want to do it, or should I?"

"You. You do it." He picked up the wooden spoon abandoned yesterday and shoved it toward me forcefully.

"All right! Take it easy." I took the spoon and looked around. I rejected right in front. My glance settled on the scraggly bush to the side of the cottage. "How about there, where you found him?"

Bert only nodded, his eyes brimming.

I dug a small hole, the sandy dirt coming away easily, and looked at Bert again. "In the box or out?"

"In."

I dug a bigger hole. "There. How's that?" Without waiting for his answer, I nestled the box in the hole. "Come see. You can say goodbye."

He sidled over and stood behind my right shoulder, looking down at the hole. "You know all that prayer stuff, say a prayer for Gray, so he, so he goes to the right place." His voice was thick now.

I thought a minute then spoke solemnly, "Jesus, if you could please find a place in Heaven for this little mouse, Gray, we'd be grateful. He was a good mouse. Amen." I looked over at Bert.

"Not like that mean ol' cat." I *ah-hemmed*, and he added, "Amen. 'Bye,

Gray."

"Okay, you close the box now."

"No, I can't! You do it!" His voice verged on hysteria.

"All right, I'll do it. 'Bye, Gray. Rest in peace." I gently closed the lid and then quickly spooned the dirt back into the hole. The extra I mounded on top. Then I put a stone as a marker. "Let's go make a tombstone. We can use popsicle sticks." I laid the spoon to the side, stood, and held out my hand.

He took my hand and went with me into the house.

I rounded up two sticks, some yarn, and a colored pencil. "What do you want it to say? You want to do it?" I held out the pencil and a stick.

He took them and sat on the faded red couch. He put his tongue in the space where the tooth had been and pressed his finger into the tip of the pencil. Satisfied with its point, he held the stick in place against the scarred table with his other hand and wrote laboriously and carefully Gray. RIP. Love, Bert. He looked at his handiwork for a minute and then added, & Annie. The Annie was scrunched at the end of the stick.

"That's great. Let's put it together and then put it up."

He held the stick out to me, and I took it, crossed it against its partner, and bound them together with the yarn. It reminded me of making god's eyes in girl scouts when I was little. I hadn't liked it much. It was in the basement of the church in this room that smelled like sewer, and you only got two stale graham crackers for snack, but you did get badges. I practiced sewing them on so no stitches showed. Some of the girls' badges hung half off their sashes, where's your scout pride, Missus Foster would scowl, but not mine. I loved the tiny embroidery, the paint set for arts and crafts, the log and flames for when you could light a fire. I tied off the lashing and looked up. Bert was watching me intently, like he did when he didn't know how to do something but I did.

We headed back to the side of the house and squatted together. I held the stick in place for his approval. He nodded, and I sunk one end into the soil behind the stone. Joel came up behind us.

"You got everything squared away? No more mystery meat?" Joel laughed a dry, hard laugh. "You're seeing Donnie and Dory. Put some clothes and your suits in a bag."

"Yay!" Sadness turned to elation and then dismay as Bert's face skidded faster than clouds across the sun on a windy day. "Where are you going?"

Since we'd been in the cottage, it seemed like Bert had been on a run of concern about Joel's whereabouts, like a return to the days of two-year-olds that don't want a beloved parent out of their sights. When I wasn't thinking what a pain in my ass he was, I thought it might have to do with his feeling that this was really a house, and a house ought to have parents in it. Me, I didn't trust the house or the parent(s). Back to Bert: to me he'd always clung like a periwinkle to a rock, but this fascination with Joel was new.

"I'm going up to Boston. Told the boss I'd take care of a delivery problem, broken down van or some goddamn thing. People gotta have their fish, and Christ knows they ain't catching it all out here no more."

"Oh."

"Why, did you think your old man was running out on you, too?" He cast a look at Bert with one eye; Joel called that the hairy eyeball. Sometimes He missed the most obvious things, but sometimes He surprised me with His perceptions. Like now.

"No, I just—"

"That's not a thought to concern yourself with. I ain't goin' nowhere that I ain't coming back from. Now the sooner I get out of here, the sooner I'll be back, the friggin' traffic aside. Get your things." He ruffled Bert's hair on His way to the kitchen.

"Why'd you get upset? Have you been thinking about her?"

"No. You're the one who's always writing about her. You and that book, you're like best friends."

Now my grim face was for real. "Have you been snooping?"

Bert's indignation swelled almost too large for him to contain; he looked like he'd burst quicker than an over-inflated balloon if I touched him. He clamped a hand over his mouth and looked at me defiantly over the fingers.

I reached out and tickled him hard beneath his arm, right in the pit. He wrenched away, screaming. I followed, wagging my fingers in the air. "Have you?"

When I had him pinned beneath my weight on the couch and helpless with laughter so hard it made no sound, I asked again. "Have you? Just say it."

Bert nodded, once, small.

I felt my anger drain away. I shrugged. "Who cares anyway? She sure as hell doesn't."

"I don't hear any packing going on out there. I'm making myself a sandwich for the road. We're on that road in five minutes, packed or not."

True to His word we were, a minor miracle in itself. People always told Him to come an hour earlier than the real time so we had a chance. Of course I didn't know what time we were supposed to be there.

He pulled into the shell drive and left the motor running. We sprang out immediately.

"Joel, I was just making lunch. Can you stay?"

"Now, Dory, I told you. I have to go." He looked at us, already at Dory's side. "I'm sure these two'll do their best to eat you out of house and home. How about a hug for your old man?" A bleak grimace went with the question like He wasn't sure we'd comply or maybe whether He deserved it.

We sidled over and offered one-armed hugs, His thin frame barely accepting those. "You be good, now. I'll see you tomorrow." He spat once off to the side, lit a new cigarette, and was gone.

6 CUSTOM

"Now we have you all to ourselves. Let's see about that lunch I promised, shall we?" Dory giggled, and it sounded like a sunbeam dancing on the water would if it sang. Her long reddish braid swung down her back. The three of us hiked up the winding white stairs to the second floor entrance into the kitchen.

Their son Danny, the same age as Bert except for a month, sat at the kitchen table reading a comic book, his brownish hair on fire in the slant of sun coming through the window. "Hey," he cried, "I hear you guys are staying tonight. That's so cool. You can sleep in my room." He looked only at Bert when he announced this.

"And I have your special little nest set up for you, my dear," Dory interjected smoothly, because this wasn't a house for hurt feelings. The comfort ran too deep. "So, I have a job for everyone. Bert and Danny, you'll be splitting the muffins. Take these forks; that's right. Now, with five of us, I'd say we'll need eight. Two for each of you, and one each for Donnie and me so we can still fit in our bathing suits.

"Lettie, if you could unwrap these minute steaks, I'll get the butter going in the pan again. I had it heated, and then I turned it off."

I pursed my lips and shook my head. We were supposed to be here earlier.

"She's Annie now, you know. Since she got crossed, while you were gone to Mermont." Bert announced officiously; he loved when he could one-up a grown-up.

I was so embarrassed that I didn't jump to correct him on Vermont. In the hustle and minor death of our morning, I'd forgotten how hurt I'd been that Dory and Donnie hadn't come to my confirmation. We weren't really related, but it felt like we were, we'd known them so long. When they

39

didn't show up, I'd focused on my slight and conveniently put aside that Donnie's mother was sick. I blushed and stammered. "It's, it's… all right."

"Crossed? Oh, confirmed, you mean. You must have been disappointed we couldn't come. I have a little present for you, and I will try to remember, Annie. I want to respect your wishes. But I'd like it if we could talk about why a bit, maybe later. I do love your given name. Could we do that?"

I nodded. I would have jumped out the window if that was what Dory wanted. Of course, that would never be what Dory would want. She wanted the best for everyone. Even on my dark days, I didn't think jumping out the window was the answer. Throwing up once in a while if I was feeling fat, or biting my nails until they bled and I tasted the salty blood on my tongue—that *could* be the answer, but so far not jumping out the window. Anyway we'd never lived higher than the second floor and never been anywhere high but up the Monument. No one could jump from there though, with the bars on all the windows.

"I have the butter going nicely here, and now I need those steaks. Really, I think they should call them second steaks, don't you?" She moved them in and out of the pan with easy practice. The smell was overwhelmingly wonderful. "I have some nice pineapple here, too." She put a yellow glass plate brimming with pineapple cubes on the table. "Oh, wouldn't you know it? I forgot to ask you boys for those muffins. Bring them over here and we'll get them toasting quick as can be. The oven's all ready." She held the oven door open while they slid the muffins onto the tray.

"Annie, if you could call Donnie. He's sitting out back reading the paper."

I went through the tiny living room and out onto the tinier porch. Donnie sat in a deck chair with the sports page in his hands. I'd never seen him read any other section. When I'd asked him why one time, he'd said, "At least in the sports pages, the bad news makes sense. The other team played better, we lost. Simple." He'd jabbed a finger at a prime example, another Red Sox loss. The headline read, "Boys of summer blitzed again."

"Donnie, lunch is ready."

"Hey! I didn't hear you come in! Your father here, too?" Donnie stood and enveloped me in a bear hug, his red beard grazing my forehead as he went by. It tickled. I'd heard that redheads couldn't grow a beard; I guessed Donnie was the proof against that. Were there any absolutes in this world, and if so, what were they?

"No, he had to go. The fish're waiting."

"He went fishing?" Donnie looked genuinely puzzled, maybe thinking, why wasn't I invited? I wouldn't have been surprised if he'd said, did I ever tell you about the time we tried to go clamming? He'd told me that story about a thousand times. It was still funny though. Donnie had gotten there, raked up his bucket of clams, and was getting ready to go home when Joel finally showed up. The tide was in. Of course, Donnie version took a lot longer to tell.

"No, he went to pick up fish in Boston. Someone's truck broke down."

"Oh, that's right, Dory told me. Did you say something about lunch?"

"It's ready."

"Let's get to it then." He took a big, showy sniff. "Let me guess, minute steaks?"

"Yeah, but it's not like it's so hard. We have them every time we come."

"That's right, we do." He put his arm around my shoulders and tried to lead me inside, but we couldn't fit through the screen door together. He stood back and extended his arm forward. "Ladies first."

This made me giggle, though, or maybe because, we'd done this many times before, too.

"What's so funny, you two?" Dory said this in a way that everyone knew she wasn't jealous about missing the joke but rather was glad that everyone was happy.

"He said 'ladies first.' It always makes me laugh."

"Well, you are getting to be quite the young lady. Any day now you are going to be getting breasts and all kinds of other womanly things, and I want you to be sure and know you can ask me anything you like, anything at all. You are bound to have questions."

I liked how she said this like it was perfectly natural that I would have questions, rather than the annoyance that Joel always seemed to feel when I asked one, though not about anything like breasts, obviously. It was a little embarrassing, but still I was glad Dory had said it. The lunch was like a hundred other lunches we'd had in the white kitchen, full of good food and laughter and conversation, and completely unlike our meals at home. I helped Dory wash and dry the dishes. I knew where every dish went on the shelves. I even had my own bowl with Peter Rabbit on it. After lunch Danny and Bert hunkered down for a game of Battleship; the living room rang with cries of hit and miss. Donnie returned to work. Dory was on the phone with one of her many relatives; everyone always wanted Dory's advice. I could understand that. I snuggled into a corner of the couch and pulled out my bluebook.

When we talked about my name, Dory asked if it had anything to do with my mother, so that's why I'm writing about it here, in the book about me and why I'm so mad. That's what I'm going to call it when I'm rich and famous, The Book About Her and Why I'm So Mad. Then she'll be sorry she ditched us, and not just because of the rich and famous part, though that won't hurt. Huh, that's the first time I've said I'm mad. I think at the beginning I said I wasn't mad. Yup, I checked. I did. Well, that's a lie. I am mad. Other people have mothers. Danny has a mother; he has the best mother in the world. Why couldn't she be my mother, instead of freakin' Gertrude? Now there's a name. So yeah, that's why I want to get rid of Leticia, and that's what I said, because she picked it. And if she can ditch me, then I can ditch me, my stupid ass name she picked anyway. Plus, could it be uglier? It's like she tried to pick a name as ugly as hers. All the pretty names in the world, she gives me Leticia. Dory said she likes it, but she has to be lying. Not that I can think of a time Dory has lied to me, but still. How could she not be? She did say though that if Annie was what I wanted to be, then Annie I'd be in this house. Gertrude must have not liked me from the get-go. Otherwise my name would be Shelby or Lindsey or Elizabeth or something good and pretty. I don't know though. She did like Bert, and his name is god-awful, too. But then again, she ditched him, too, so I guess she didn't like him as much as I always thought she did.

One of the great things about Dory and Donnie's house was that it seemed like we were always eating and that there was always more food coming. At home I always felt a little nervous about eating, like maybe I should stretch it out (not that I actually did). I never felt nervous in this house. Like with my name, after we'd talked, Dory had reminded Donnie about my confirmation and my new name, and we went from there.

I asked Dory one time what she remembered about Gertrude and me. She said she always thought of this one day she was at our house on Bradford Street. She said Gertrude, she always calls her your, my, whatever, mother, let me feed myself, that she didn't care about the mess. Then she'd carried the high chair out onto the deck behind the house and hosed me off. Dory said that impressed her, that Gertrude was so relaxed as a mother. Me, I'm thinking that must have been so scary, getting hosed off, like people hose dog poop off their sidewalks. Did I think it felt great, or was I scared? Dory doesn't think I was crying. I don't cry about lots of things now, and that doesn't mean I like them. And another thing. Clearly Gertrude wasn't as cool with mess as Dory thought, because look what a mess she left behind. I wish we could stay forever at Dory and Donnie's. Their life is so normal. Donnie goes to work in the morning, he usually comes home for lunch, and then he comes home for good by early afternoon. He doesn't come home stinking drunk. When he has a beer, he just has one. When Danny is in school, Dory works at some counseling place, but when he isn't, she's mostly home. Danny hardly ever even has a babysitter, not that we did anymore, that was my job like every other thing. Dory and also Donnie make great food, and they all sit and eat it together. How was I supposed to be turning into this rebellious teenager who wanted nothing to do with my family, when my family wanted nothing to do with me? I couldn't even really count Bert, because he had no choice. It wasn't like he had anywhere to go if I got sick of the sight of him, which was often. He was going suck me dry with those helpless eyes one of these days, and when his heart started to glow or sometimes bleached away entirely, MY heart started to pound. I couldn't fix everything though, I mean, I was only thirteen. I didn't know enough stuff. I didn't know what to tell him about Gertrude. I didn't even know what to tell myself. I know he thinks about her, what kid wouldn't, but he won't ever say anything, even when I hold Mousie hostage. And for Bert, that's something. He was always saying something about something, until I thought my head was going to explode if he didn't stop. But not about her.

7 STICK

"Get your stuff. The old man's got a day off, and we're heading out to the Point."

The shrieks of Bert's excitement filled the cottage. I took a chance that Joel might see me writing and ask what it was and turned back to my book. He was soon banging around in the cupboards.

I've heard I almost died out there. The story went that Al and Gene saw me floating face down and fished me out. They did mouth-to-mouth, managing the breaths and the compressions like in health with those creepy bodies – they're called Annies, what a bummer – even though they'd been drinking all day. I threw up enough seawater to fill a bathtub, give or take. What were THEY doing while I was drowning? This was back when they were together, when everyone's parents were together. Other kids still had their mothers though. Gertrude couldn't wait to see the back of us. Isn't that a great expression? I read it in some book. Although really I guess it was the other way around, that we saw the back of her. Were we standing there, and she just walked away? Or was it the chickenshit way, in the night while we were sleeping? It seems like a good thing to know, how such an important event happened, but probably there are different versions. That's what our social studies teacher last year was always saying, that there isn't just one history. Probably Joel would say one thing, and Gertrude would say another, and what actually happened was totally something else. Dory said it's better I can't remember too many things, she said it's the mind's way of protecting itself. She says maybe when I'm older I'll be ready to let myself know. She knows everything it seems like, so she must be right about this.

I got my bathing suit, scowling just looking at it, and put it on. It was pilling on the seat and pulling up in the rise. I twisted around trying to see my ass in the bathroom mirror, like it was hard to miss. We hadn't seen anybody at the beach the other day, but today though probably some kids would be there, Ralph at least, since Joel and Al were such great friends. I tried to decide if that was good or bad. I looked back at the mirror and scowled some more. Bert's suit wasn't much better, but at least with trunks they didn't show your private parts to the whole world, not that Bert cared. I wasn't sure I wanted anyone to see my parts, such as they were. My chest was pale and flat with two tiny nipples like mini pencil erasers, not like Dory's, large and dark like pepperoni. The hair that had recently grown in my crotch itched, and I didn't like how it stuck out the sides of the elastic of my underwear and my bathing suit. I pulled my longest tee shirt over my head and packed a sweatshirt that would hang even below that and one for Bert in case it got cold when the sun went down.

"Can we ride in the back?" Bert demanded.

"Not 'til we let the air out of the tires. I don't want no cop bustin' on me for 'endangering youngsters.'" It didn't sound like He minded the endangering, only the busting.

We climbed in front, Bert in the middle with the hump and me against the door, leaning as far out the window as possible to get away from the smoke. That always made me feel like the dog we didn't have. He pulled out of the circle and into the street in one steady swing. A blue sedan too close behind us now honked.

He flipped His hand holding the cigarette at the car and shook His head. "Frigging tourists, driving' too fast." He chugged down the road slower than usual, put on His signal, and maneuvered the old red truck around the corner and out toward the highway all with one hand.

"Who else is coming?"

"The usual." He left it at that, and I didn't pursue it. It was no use trying to get Joel to talk when He didn't want to; that only led to anger and maybe the belt later for "mouthing off," He called it. Why could He say whatever He wanted, including a swear word at least every other minute, and we couldn't? People thought kids' lives were so easy, but they must have forgotten what being a kid was really like or else their childhoods were different from ours.

In a few minutes He pulled into the sandy parking lot beside Pilgrim Lake and rolled to a stop. My science teacher had told us all about how the lake had been reborn, filled with mussels and other creatures, once the tide broke through and made it salt again. Nature was stronger than most of what people could dish out given enough time, and nature had time on its side. That's what Mr. Smith had said anyway, but if you looked at the headlines in the paper, it looked like nature better get a move on. The old truck rattled for a minute deep in its engine after Joel shut it off, like it was thinking of settling here permanently and telling Him so. He climbed out, tire gauge in hand. I noticed we weren't the last ones to arrive for a change.

"Hey, Al. Pam and Ralph coming?"

Al waved a hand in greeting, keeping his other hand on the tire gauge letting the air out of his tires to get ready for the sand. I looked out the window like I was bird watching or something, but I wasn't fooling myself.

"Joel. Kids. Yeah. Pammie'll be here any minute. She had a stop to make on the way, some church thing." His eyes scanned the lot and brightened when he saw the green Pinto pull in. Mine probably did the same, but also my stomach lurched this weird way like it did when I saw Ralph at school, which was often. "Here she comes. Looks like Suze and JoJo are right behind them with their gang."

Joel turned to the other truck preparing for our expedition. "Vin, Alice. You check the tides this time?" It was a running joke that Vinnie had been a little one-eyed two times ago and gotten us all stranded until the wee hours waiting for the tide to turn.

"Yeah, Joel, we're set. I got that six here we owe you. Want one now?" Suze was already reaching behind the seat, knowing the answer like everyone did. Their twins, five-year-old girls with blonde curls, were blowing bubbles in the back of their truck, one of those ones with the extended cab. After they'd shown up in it the first time, He'd said why not get a frigging car, that looks so stupid.

"Don't mind if I do." When Joel heard the sound of the door handle ratcheting down, He looked in the window at us. "You two stay put. We'll get going a lot sooner if I don't have to hunt you down looking for birds' eggs or whatever foolishness you had in mind. Let me get to these tires."

When Dory and Donnie and Danny arrived, Dory came right over to the window to say hello while Donnie worked on their tires. Like he sensed our imprisonment, Danny hopped into the bed of the truck and began making faces on the rear window, smashing his lips and nose against the glass in grotesque shapes. Bert laughed out loud. I decided I was too old for that and ignored him. I focused on Dory. She was talking about the food that she'd brought, always something I wanted to hear more about.

When He finished, He stood with a grunt and lit a new cigarette, cupping His hand around the flame the way I'd seen Him do a thousand times. He exhaled a long plume of smoke that the wind whipped away and climbed back in the truck.

Since I couldn't write or else He'd see me or I'd get carsick, I didn't know which one would be worse, I wrote in my head instead. I'd started doing this more and more since Bert kept bugging me to see the bluebook again. I was always having to find a new hiding place, which was tough in a house as small as ours. So now I'd write in my head and only write for real after He went to sleep, trying to hold onto what I'd wanted to write during the day. I thought it was a good test for my memory. That's what they said about Alzheimer's, that you had to play memory games to keep it sharp, so

I'd have a head start there, or else maybe I could make up for all the stuff I couldn't remember from before Gertrude left.

My English teacher was always saying how a writer has to show their readers, not tell, and the parts I liked best about a lot of books took you away somewhere. Even though it mostly felt regular to me, a lot of people thought Cape Cod was pretty cool. They sure came here from all over. Since I didn't seem to be going anywhere else anytime soon, I tried to see it their way in my head.

There were five trucks today, all with their over-sand permits on their bumpers. We moved off slowly into the dunes, the sand making a slishing sound almost water-like against the soft balloons of rubber. The well-worn tracks led toward the horizon and looked like they'd remain into eternity. In reality the restless wind would scour them clean overnight, as it did most every night. As long as those on the move kept their pilgrimages to the paths, the dunes did their ceaseless dance meandering up and down the coastline with remarkably little permanent wear.

A flock of seagulls flew over laughing loudly. What did the trucks look like from above? Maybe a line of beetles or sand crickets inching their way along the water's edge where the sand was firmest. I'd come out here once on horseback when there was still a stable in town with a friend and her mom. I wasn't friends with Opal anymore because she had a mother and I didn't. No, that wasn't it exactly. It was that I didn't like people feeling sorry for me. She'd told me once when I slept over that I could share her mother, and I knew right away that was it. I hated her. I hated everyone who had a mother, except Danny. Who could hate Danny? He didn't feel sorry for me. He'd known me his whole life like some kind of big sister since he didn't have any sisters or brothers. But at least he acted the same all the time, never looking at me like I was missing one leg.

About the horses though, I remember feeling so small way up on that horse, different than how it felt in a car. On the horse I'd been able to hear the peeps of the sandpipers that scuttled out of the heavy hooves' way and the suck and roar of the waves as they threshed the sand and rocks at the tide line. I put my head out the window, but there was only the deep moan of the engine. I saw Al's dog Clover with her head also sniffing the air, her tongue lolling. I put my tongue out then quickly back in.

The line of trucks drove far enough out on the sand that no signs of human habitation could be seen, unless the little artist shacks counted. They didn't even have electricity or water. The Park Service was trying to get rid of them, let the land be natural, but I thought that was a joke, tacked together piles of driftwood nestled in the sand, more like birds' nests or animal burrows than houses really.

Like they'd agreed ahead, the first truck stopped and on down the line, evenly spaced. The drivers pulled into a horseshoe shape and turned off their motors. A few engines coughed for a minute, Joel's of course and maybe another, and then went silent. People piled out of doors and truck beds like water overflowing a barrel.

"You kids go collect wood. Dry stuff, none of that wet crap you brought back last time that smoked up the joint." I didn't point out that it was tough to smoke up the outdoors. He seemed like He was in a good mood; I'd try not to spoil it like I usually did.

Other kids had gotten the same instructions. The twins Moon and Beam seized a piece of wood and began to pull it back and forth to shouts of, "Mine!" and "I got it first!" Their fighting was nothing new. The two looked nothing like either parent; in fact they looked like the fire chief, a burly guy with blond curls who locals called Prince Charming. If five-year-olds could look burly, these two did. Bert and Danny ambled past them in search of unclaimed sticks without a glance in the twins' direction, little girls that they were. Suze and JoJo's three boys had big armloads of wood before I even had one good stick.

"Hey."

I turned to see Ralph, a red bandana tied around his dark hair, pulling a log stripped of its bark toward the campfire site. I wanted to touch his hair, like they said about crows that can't resist shiny objects. It looked so soft. I must have touched once, since we'd been playing together since we were little kids. We were in the same class most years in school. I liked being able to watch Ralph in class. He never said much, but he always paid attention. He was quiet in a good way. Not like me, who was quiet because I couldn't think of the right things to say, I felt like he was quiet because he was content with himself.

His head was down now, looking behind him at the log that held back in the sand like a kid trying not to leave the beach, dragging his feet every step of the way while his father tugged and swore under his breath (or not). His father and ours were shoveling out a pit in the center of the horseshoe.

I was pretty sure it had been too long for a casual response, but I said it anyway. "Hey yourself. What's up?"

Ralph didn't mention the time lag. "Not much. Got a dog."

"Yeah? What kind?" I looked around for a dog and saw only Clover.

"Saint Bernard. Dad wouldn't let me bring him though. He didn't want him peeing in the truck."

"That's too bad. He's home alone? Is it a he?"

"Yeah, a he, Boner. He's at my aunt's. It's her litter." His aunt used to baby-sit me and Bert and Ralph together. Once I'd made her throw up over the side of the car of the Ferris Wheel. I'd been trying to make it swing higher so we could see the moon behind us.

I snapped out of my carnival reverie, unsure if I'd heard what I thought I'd heard. I colored a bit, could feel the flush creeping up my neck to my cheeks. I kept my eyes down. "What'd you say his name is?"

"Boner."

My eyes snapped up to his face. "They let you call him that?"

"You've got a dirty mind! His one sister's named Mouser, and his other one's Slipper, on account of the toys they like the best." He smiled that slow smile that I thought about on bad days, which meant I thought about it a lot. Was I glad or not that now Ralph thought I had a dirty mind? I decided I was glad. It was better than Ralph thinking I never thought about sex or anything else interesting.

"You two think we got all day? Get your behinds over here with that wood. We'll be eating' on frigging Tuesday."

I didn't look at Ralph as I grabbed a few sticks and started toward the hole. I looked around for Bert and Danny. They each had a bunch of sticks and were headed in the same direction.

"Who's got the dog sticks?" Al bellowed.

"We do!" the three Santana boys bellowed right back.

"Good green ones?" Al continued the ritual.

"The best green ones!" The youngest, Luke, ran for the hole. His brothers, Mark and Matt, were right behind him. People had been asking Suze for years now when John was coming. She still laughed.

Al doled out hotdogs to each kid who had a stick. The twins fought over which stick was better, and one hotdog fell in the sand.

"Uh oh, dog down, dog down. Better swab it off before the crabs set in." Alice was a paramedic and Vin a cop; they talked like an accident report.

"I'll do it." I was up and out with the sandy hotdog before anyone else moved. I walked quickly down to the water, shiny with the reflected colors of the sunset. The lighthouse flashed its light at me as I bobbed the hot dog up and down a few times. I let the water chase my toes along the edge of the tide line.

"How late you think we're staying' out?" I startled, unaware that Ralph had followed me down. He held up another sandy hot dog. "Those twins can't keep a dog on a stick," he murmured, when I didn't answer.

"Huh. They're a little wild, I guess. What'd you say before that? I didn't hear."

"Oh, I asked how long you think we're staying out here this time."

"Don't want to get swamped?"

"Not so much," he grinned. His teeth were square and very white. I was sure mine were not as white. I smiled back with my lips covering my teeth. "Not that I mind a little work with a shovel now and then, but my back was killing me the next day. Sand is brutal."

"At least your father's truck wasn't made in the last century. Joel's, it's a good day it starts, never mind digging it out of the sand." I felt a little disloyal saying this, because really the truck ran pretty well considering, kind of like Him actually, but it seemed like the right kind of teenagers-against-parents thing to say. I was never sure what was the right thing to say with kids my age, except Mayes. Maybe I'm out of practice, or maybe I wouldn't have been any good at the banter anyway, even before.

Ralph laughed, even though I didn't think what I'd said had been that funny. With someone else I would have thought that was dumb, but not with Ralph. With Ralph it made my heart happy. "What've you been doing since school let out?"

"Just hanging around. Watching Bert mostly."

"He's getting to be pretty big for watching, isn't he? I think you and me were racing around town on our bikes when we were his age."

"Yeah, you might be right. Bert's not like we were though. He's always getting himself in trouble. First kids are different."

"Only kids, you mean."

"Yeah, that, too. Do you ever wish you had a brother or sister?"

"Naw. I got the best deal. My mother lets me do whatever I want, and my father's too busy to notice."

"Tell me about it."

"Your mom isn't... oh, hey, I'm sorry. I wasn't thinking. I didn't mean—"

"It's all right. Forget it. How many kids live with only their fathers, right? It's easy to forget."

"I didn't forget. I was just being stupid. Sorry."

"We should get back."

Ralph nodded. He moved a little closer. "I was wondering, maybe some time—"

I didn't get to find out what Ralph was wondering because just then came the cry, "You two on a hot date down there? Bring back those dogs. Food's not getting any warmer sittin' on your plates."

I colored and turned away. I hoped Ralph hadn't seen or else thought it was the sunset reflected or something. We trudged up the incline together but not, a space between us as each swung an arm clutching a hot dog.

I know this book is supposed to be about her, but how much can you write about someone you never see? I'm not even sure the things I remember are right. Like I think she liked Nestlé's Crunch. Why that? I don't know what her favorite color is or if she has a sense of humor. I remember some music she liked, Simon and Garfunkel, that song "Cecilia," or was it just that I liked that song, and the Supremes, "Stop, in the Name of Love," but she didn't stop. She kept going. Anyway, I want to write about some other stuff that's happening because I like writing in here. When I started I didn't, but now I really do. Maybe it's because I don't really think of it like a school thing anymore. I like school more than not, I like learning new stuff, not doing the same stuff over and over, and I like getting good grades as much as anyone, maybe more. But I'm never going to show this to the Whopper. Or to anyone. This is for me. So anyway, I've been thinking about what Ralph was going to ask me. A lot. I can't wait to hear back from Mayes so I can find out what she thinks. I'd really like to call her and speed up this process, but two things keep me from doing it. First there's Joel who told me when Mayes left that He'd better not see any calls to North Carolina (or anywhere else) on the phone bill or I'd be paying for a long time to come, method unspecified. Mayes's grandmother said the same, cheapskate that she is, and Mayes's father wouldn't get her roaming minutes for her cell phone that's only for emergencies. We are stuck with letters like Jane Austen or something. Then there's that I don't even know what Ralph was going to ask me, so maybe I'm making a huge deal out of absolutely nothing. If Mayes was here, we'd have spent hours already debating it, nothing or not, but the phone has too high a price, whatever the price actually is. Mayes and I always tell each other about stuff like that, or at least she tells me because I never have any guy stuff. I still don't, not really, but I think maybe I was going to. Maybe he was going to ask me to go somewhere, like a date. Yeah. And maybe he was going to ask did I think he could borrow my, my, I don't know what. Okay, so I don't have anything Ralph would want to borrow. Something else then. Sometime I could help him with his summer reading essay. That's probably it. Kids are always asking me that.

8 STRIKE

"Why don't you go outside? Tommy and Michael are in the lot with a ball. I bet they'd let you play."

"What are you doing?"

"I don't know. What's that got to do with it?"

"I might want to do what you're doing. Are you gonna write in that stupid book?"

"I already wrote in there today, thank you very much. I might go for a bike ride."

"Can I come?" His finger sidled to his nostril, in and out quick.

"Maybe I want to go by myself. Just once. Would that be all right with you, you little nose picker?"

His heart was dark red like a bruised strawberry long past good eating. "Go ahead then. Who wants to go on a stupid bike ride with stupid old you anyway?" He slammed out the screen. That we had a screen at all was laughable since the mesh had more holes than not. The funniest part was that someone had taken the time to sew in one of those screen patches over a hole in the middle near the door handle. Maybe they thought bugs liked that one best.

I followed him out, grabbed my bicycle, and rode off without looking back, but not before I'd made sure that Michael and Tommy's mother had registered my departure. Her black eyes had narrowed, and a frown had appeared between her eyes. Missus Tosca wouldn't leave now without taking Bert with her, not that I'd be gone long enough for it to matter, not that he was a "strike out on his own" kind of guy. I wanted a little air, a little of my own air. Joel would hear about it, there's nothing I did or didn't do that Missus Tosca didn't find worthy of reporting to someone, so I'd have to make up something later, but it would be worth it.

I rode to the center of town and parked my bike among the many others on the rack. I had taken nothing with me from the house, no bag to check, nothing but a ten from the money I'd been filching and my change purse. Ten was my limit to spend the first time out. I went straight to Strangeways and started browsing CDs. I spent the longest time in the used bins, hoping to get lucky like I'd heard people did, finding a hot CD that someone with bucks had bought, burned, and resold the next day. Flip, flip, flip. It was all trash that no one should have wanted in the first place, never mind paid full price for, ever. It wasn't even worth the bargain bin prices, except this. I held *The Best of the 60s* close to my heart and smiled. I flipped it over and scanned the songs, great, great, and great. I flipped back. No. It was misfiled, wasn't really used at all with a price like that. It was so unfair. All I wanted was a little break once in a while, but no, not Annie, all right Leticia, Leticia Irene Endquist. My monogram was LIE. What kind of parent does that to a kid? I had to admit Bert's EWE wasn't much better. It was a good thing kids in town probably didn't know what a girl sheep even was.

I don't know how long I stood there scanning back and forth from the songs to the price, the songs to the price, but nothing changed. I looked down again at the bins. I picked up *The Best of the 70s*, and it was really used, beaten on even, like someone wanted to punish it for sucking. I had the money for that, but who wanted it? Without noticing, I had slid down the face of the bins until I was sitting on the floor. I wasn't alone in this; other people who liked cover art or lyrics from the play-station selections sat in similar poses, pouring over song titles and times. They were engrossed in the music. No one would care. I dislodged one corner of each price sticker with my nails, chipping the polish in the process, of course, pulling slowly and carefully, until each thumb wore a sticker. Then I switched them.

I stood and replaced *Best of the 70s* in the used compilations bin. I click-clacked through a few more CDs, pushed the pile backward into place, and then made my way to the front counter. My heart hammered, but no louder than the deep beat of the store's music that began at full volume when it opened and never lowered even when people screamed in the paper about it. It's funny, but my heart didn't pound this much when I flat-out took stuff, so why the fuss when I switched the tags? I put my selection on the counter and made a study of digging in my front pocket for my money.

"Good find," the clerk announced. I heard the admiration in his voice, and I liked it. He wore a Lynyrd Skynyrd tee shirt, so yeah, he would say that. Somehow I was glad he wasn't a rapper or a metal fan. He had a thin face and long, jet-black hair pulled into a scraggly ponytail that blended with his black store vest. He reminded me of pictures I'd seen of Alice Cooper.

"Huh? Oh, yeah," I put the ten on the counter.

"Got fifty cents?"

I added two quarters.

"Need a bag?"

"No, that's all right."

"Here's your receipt then."

At the door I felt a hand on my shoulder and turned, my feet dragging like they were packed in wet sand. Maybe it was someone from school or someone Joel knew. People were always coming up to Bert and me.

"Miss."

Not someone from school then.

"Miss, I'm going to have to ask you to step back inside."

Not someone He knew, or hopefully not. That would make it worse. No, probably nothing would make it worse than it was going to be. I turned to face him in his rent-a-cop uniform.

I hated the fact that I smiled, or tried to anyway, even though it was sickly, and I was probably green or red or some other awful color. "Hm?"

"Come on. I saw you switch the prices. The manager's in her office. Let's go."

I saw the clerk's face as I went by, not such a good find after all.

The sort-of-cop told his story to the manager, a saggy woman full of folds of flesh and fabric with a face set like concrete. She didn't even ask me for my side of the matter, like they do in those after-school specials; she just asked if I lived here or not. I nodded, unsure of my voice.

"How old are you?"

I didn't have enough fingers to hold up or I might have tried. I felt like a golf ball was wedged in my throat. "Thirteen," I croaked. On a good day I would have said almost fourteen, but I thought younger might play better. At least she wasn't saying she was calling the police yet. Maybe for a minor you had to wait until a parent came. When I closed my mouth, she asked for my parents' names and number. I opened it again.

"Couldn't I just give it back?"

"No, hon, it doesn't work quite like that. Didn't you see the sign that said we prosecute all shoplifters? Let's give a call and get things rolling."

"But I didn't steal it. I paid. Some. If someone brought it in really used, that's how much it would be. That's not the same, is it?" It was like someone else, someone much bolder, had taken control of my body, or at least my mouth.

"Do you understand this is real serious here? I could call the cops and you'd be ridin' in the squad car in a few minutes, but I'm tryin' to cut you a break here, young as you are. Not that that excuses anything. Not that half the thieves in here aren't young, just like you, but what the hell. I'm thinkin' lookin' at you that this here is enough to scare the crap out of you. You wettin' your panties yet?"

The manager looked at me steadily and reached for the telephone. Her long, stringy hair looked like it had been slicked to the sides, but I thought it was probably just dirty. I gave my home number and His name, knowing of course that no one was there. I tried to think of what my next step was, but my mind was whirring so fast I couldn't hear any of the thoughts go by. The three of us, me, Greasehead, and Rent-a, listened to it ring and ring. "All right, now, enough of this, where's dad or mom work? We'll try that."

"The Surf Club. He works there."

"You know the number?"

I shook my head, even though I did.

Greasehead sighed, and the cop guy shifted from foot to foot. She waved a dismissive hand at him, like go catch me some more and earn your keep, loser, and he went. He looked back at me, I thought his eyes said sorry, a lot of good that did me now, and then he was back on the floor. Greasehead heaved herself out of her chair and went across the small office in search of the phonebook; she found it buried under a pile of old newspapers. Even though the office was tiny, it took her some time to plod her way back to where I still stood, my hands clenching and unclenching. There wasn't an empty seat even if she'd offered me one, and I hoped my legs would hold up. I had this lurching kind of feeling that I got from boats.

"The Surf Club, you said?"

I nodded, as small as possible.

The big woman dialed, her fingers surely pressing the wrong buttons they were so wide, but no such luck.

"Surf Club. Help you?"

"Joel Endquist, please."

I could hear the other half of the conversation as well. Was that because the office was so small or The Surf Club was so loud the person would have to shout or what? It was Martini Tina.

"Who's askin'?"

"That's private. If you could just get him?"

"Oo hoo, someone's a fancy pants. Joel got an admirer?"

"Really, ma'am, could you bring him to the phone? I don't have all day."

"Well, all right then, hold yer horses." I heard the phone smash down against something hard; maybe it was broken.

"What's this all about? I'm working here. It's lunch rush." His voice was harried, like He sounded when Bert and I were fighting and He wanted to read the paper "for five goddamn minutes." Wait 'til He got a load of this.

"Sir, I'm calling about your daughter," Greasehead looked at me significantly, one eyebrow raised. I realized she hadn't asked my name.

"Annie," I mumbled.

"Annie. She's gotten herself into a bit of trouble here—"

"I don't have a daughter named Annie. Mine's named Leticia, for chrissake. Think I could forget a name like that?" Another bang of the phone, and He was gone, back to the lunch rush.

She turned back to me. "Want to tell me the deal, or do we need to call in the cops? I'm losin' my funny here."

"My name's Leticia, but I hate it. I got a new name, Annie, when I got confirmed. He didn't want me to do it."

"Huh. You know I'm going to have to call him back, right?"

I nodded miserably, picturing the wrath that was coming my way, building with each passing second, only compounded by the timing of it all. Only I would be stupid enough to get caught during lunch rush.

"You want to do it?"

I nodded, sort of grateful for what I knew was a break and sort of resentful that this was all still going on, like I hadn't had anything to do with it.

The phone in my hand felt wily and slick, like some kind of skinny fish. I swallowed and dialed the number the manager marked with her finger. I was too nauseous to even pretend to need it.

"Surf Club. Help you?"

"It's me. It's Annie, you know, Lettie."

Martini Tina brushed right over the Annie. With all the noise in the background she probably thought it was the connection. "Well, now, Lettie, what're you doin' callin' during the lunch rush?" She sucked in her breath, it sounded like a wind tunnel in a cartoon. "Something wrong? Bert all right?"

"Yeah, no, he's fine, it's, it's me who's not so great. I need to talk to Him."

"Sugar, you jes' tell me what's goin' on. It'll be better that way."

I couldn't picture much better in this scenario other than blinking on out of here like in "I Dream of Genie" reruns, but what the heck. "Well, I... I got caught."

"Caught on what? You stuck?"

I pictured a giant fishhook swooping in through the back door and lifting me out. No joy there either. "No, caught, caught stealing." There, it was out.

"Oh, sugar, what'd you go and do that for? I'd a given you the money. What for?"

"A CD."

"You all even have a player? I guess that don't really matter. Huh. Well. I don't see how I can not tell him. I sure wish I could."

"I know." The manager raised her eyebrow at me again, like I don't have all day here. "I'll wait."

To my way of looking at it, the wait wasn't nearly long enough. "What in the hell were you thinking? Where are you?"

I forced the words out. "Strangeways, you know, near the Penny Patch."

"I'll be there as soon as I can. I got to get 'Tini set up to cover. Just what I fuckin' need." Joel was gone, back to the bar.

"Well?"

"He's coming." I said a little prayer that time would stop or I would sink through the floor or something.

He came sooner than I would have expected, much sooner than I had hoped or prayed. Clearly I had no more control over time than I did over anything else I wished for. I heard the door bang, and I knew it was Him. Not that it was so great here in the office with Greasehead, but I wasn't looking forward to leaving either. He'd be meaner then. I bit my lower lip and my thumbnail alternately until both were bleeding.

9 SKIN

"So what happened here?" He looked straight at me, not noticing the manager as much as He would have a mosquito, had they ever bothered Him. They didn't bite smokers, He'd said when I asked, as surprised by the answer as the fact that He had answered one of my questions at all. He was so skinny, really His pants would have fallen past His hips if it wasn't for the belt, but somehow He filled the doorway. He'd left His vest at the bar. I looked at His belt again, the leather shiny in places, the buckle dull brass.

"I told Martini Tina." I squeaked on the first "i."

"Now you'll tell me." His voice was dead level, no variance of pitch or real volume to it. A mouse cornered by a venomous snake couldn't feel worse.

I looked at my shoes and kicked the back of one against the front of the other. "I switched the prices."

He made this sharp sound in His throat that I knew meant He thought I was trying to make it sound like nothing much, sugarcoating shit, as He'd say. "What did you want so bad?"

"This." The manager dangled the CD in His face, like maybe she was trying to get His attention. Would He swat it away like a fly?

His eyes darted to it and back to me. "How'd you pay for it?"

I kept my mouth shut. Lying would be another crime, digging the pit deeper when the waves were already coming in.

"My money, I'm guessing. A frigging thief two ways, eh?" He turned from me, done with me for the moment, and fixed His gaze on the manager. "What are we going to do here? She's never done anything this stupid before, and I'm betting she won't again when I'm through with her."

Greasehead started back with a grunt like He'd threatened her instead of me. "Well, sir, we do have a company policy that we prosecute all shoplifters. If we let one walk—"

"She paid something, right? So she's shifty as hell, but she's thirteen. How about you cut me some slack, and I pay the difference? Hell, I'll pay the difference, and you can keep the piece of shit."

The clerk from the front came to the door and put in his Alice-like head. "Delivery. I need your signature."

"I'll be right there, Nick. Go on back to your register." She waited until the clerk had gone. She faced Joel again. "Look, duty calls. Get her out of here. Keep her out of here. Tell her next time, no deals." Greasehead ambled out without looking back. I felt invisible and very young, but I knew that wasn't going to help me either.

He turned to face me. "We're not done here, miss. Not by a long shot. But I have to get back to work." He put His hand on my arm and steered me to the door, through the store, and out to the street. His grip cut into my skin, bruising it in line with His fingers. The bell jangled harshly on the door. Like it was some kind of signal, He let go. I could still feel the pressure. He started to go toward the wharf and turned back. "Where's your brother? At least tell me you didn't drag him into this fucking mess."

I blushed at my other transgression. I saw Him take note of it. "He's with Michael's mom. He's fine."

"You get your butt back home. I'll see you tonight." The undercurrent ran deep and ugly. I thought about His belt and the welts it would leave, wider than the stripes on my arm. I shivered and did as I was told.

When I wheeled my bike into the circle, pushing it from the handlebar and the seat because my balance had left me, Bert came running from Michael's. His mother looked out the kitchen window and gave me a small nod. I felt like she knew already, like everyone knew.

"Where were you? You were gone such a long time."

"Get out of my face." I slammed into the cottage and our room and retrieved my bluebook and pen.

"Now you're gonna write in there?" His eyes widened, and he moaned. I knew he had seen the glowing marks on my arm. "What happened?"

"Nothing. Now leave me alone."

"Did He do that?"

The reverent, scared tone of his voice jarred me out of my sulk.

"Yeah, but it's my fault. I did something stupid, and now I have to pay for it. Huh. If only."

"What'd you do?" The fear was larger now.

"I switched the prices on two CDs. I got caught. He's pissed."

"Is He gonna…" His voice trailed off, out of power to put his fears into words.

"We'll see, I guess, huh?"

We waited out the evening like prisoners on death row. I'd made chili from a can; it still mostly sat on the plates when Joel came through the door. His face was set and gray. His eyes were hard behind His glasses, the frames always reminding me of Elvis Costello without the singing. I could smell the beer from where we sat, but He walked steady and even.

"Let's get this over with. You know the drill."

I got up from the table and went into the bedroom. I sat heavily on my bed.

He came in, His hand on His belt buckle. "Where's the money?"

I swallowed hard. "That manager lady still has it, right?"

"Don't give me that shit. Where's the rest of it?" He turned around and wrenched open the top drawer. He dumped it on the floor and kicked at the contents. When He didn't find what He wanted, He went for the next one. Bingo. He held up the wad of bills like it was contaminated, waving it in my face. "So now you're a liar, too."

"I didn't—"

"I don't give a rat's ass what you didn't. I got plenty of what you did." He started to unbuckle His belt.

"I'm too old for that!" My voice had a screech to it, like it needed oil.

"I'll be the judge of that, I guess. You may think you're all grown up, but you've got another thing or two comin'. Now turn around."

I breathed out raggedly and turned over on the bed, my face pressed into the bedspread, my arms beside my head, my feet flexed against the floor. I vowed I wouldn't cry though, at least that He could hear. He probably knew it, too.

He set His glasses case that hung on His belt to one side. Then He held the buckle in His hand and swung the leather through the air. Whack. Again. Whack. Again. He grunted with the effort. Whack. Again. Whack. I jerked each time and my eyes watered, but I didn't cry out loud.

I stayed still when more didn't come because it would make Him madder if I moved before He was finished. The tears leaked out of the corners of my eyes and slid down into the wet patches on the bedspread.

"You stay in here awhile and think about what you've done. I'll let you know when you can come out." He left the room, and still I stayed on my stomach. He swore at Bert, telling him to stay the hell out of there, and then went into the kitchen. He took a glass from the cupboard and the ice from the freezer. I heard the wrench of the tray, the click of ice on glass, and then the crack of the cubes as the liquid thawed them. I heard the rattle as He raised the glass to His lips. Then I slid down onto my knees. The force of the pain made me yelp, but I stifled it. By inches I lay myself down on my stomach on the bed.

When I opened my eyes, it was dark. I looked over at the other bed and saw Bert's crumpled form under the covers. He must have come in quietly, trying not to disturb me. That thought made me want to cry. I didn't. I inched my way to the edge of the bed, wincing at the pain and my stomach heaving, and decided to take it all in one lunge. I nearly flung myself off the bed, the back of my hand glued to my mouth, and into an upright position. I opened the bedroom door and peered into the dark living room, not lit by even the blue glow of the television. It must be late if He'd gone to bed. The way clear, I walked to the bathroom bending my knees as little as possible.

I clicked on the light. The sudden, harsh yellow made the dark rings around my eyes jump at me. I blinked rapidly to get my eyes adjusted. It would be hard to see my ass with only the mirror on the medicine cabinet above the sink. I bit my lip. Gingerly I felt around the back with my hands, one on either side. There were four strips of pure pain, two of them overlapping, but only one had broken the skin, the lowest one. That one had missed my shorts and struck my bare legs right below the hem. The welt had bled, I could feel the rawness, but had stopped now. Someone else seeing it might think it was a scrape. I didn't know how someone would get a scrape there, but someone might. I wanted to see it, all of them really, just to know. I opened the medicine cabinet and scrabbled among the combs and ratty hairbrushes until I came up with a yellow plastic hand mirror. I remembered taking it from the Little Store. I remembered the feel of it in my back pocket, thinking the clerk might see the outline then pulling the tail of my shirt lower.

I held the mirror behind me and craned my neck, but my shirt was in the way. I held my shirt aside with the other hand and craned my neck again. There they were, the four marks of shame. Where had I heard that? I didn't feel ashamed actually. I was just sorry I'd gotten caught. Other people did far worse things.

I reached back into the cabinet for the first aid cream. I put down the mirror because it would be impossible to hold my shirt, the mirror, and the cream. I squirted a line of cream on my finger and tried to apply it by feel, following the sear of the pain.

"Can I help?"

I started in surprise and fear at a voice, and then tried to calm my heart when I registered who it was.

"Hey. It's late. You should be sleeping."

"I looked over and you weren't there. Is it bad?"

I laughed mirthlessly. "It could be better."

"Let me help."

"I can do it."

"I can help. I'll be careful."

I handed him the cream and tensed while I waited. He must have squeezed at least half the tube onto his hands, and then he applied the tiniest of pinpricks onto my skin.

62

"You may have to put on a bit more for it to work. Thanks for being careful though."

He didn't answer or pause in his painstaking application until he was done. "There. Now it'll get better, right?"

"Eventually, yeah."

"Does it need a kiss?"

I hesitated a minute then thought of the many times I'd kissed his hurts. "I think it does."

His kiss was as gentle as his cream application. He was right; it did help a little. I put away the cream and the mirror, wiped his hands with a tissue, and took his hand to lead him back to our bedroom.

I lay in the dark, the pain rising and falling with each breath I took. I knew that was it for sleep tonight. I pulled out my book and pen, wincing with the effort.

I was hoping Martini Tina would have calmed Him down some when He went back to work, kids will be kids and all that. Guess not. Does Gertrude hit, too? I do remember this one time them throwing things at each other. I think they were plates. Bert and I sat on the stairs in our old house and tried to look down through the banister, but we couldn't see anything. It was like the time Bert and I were watching this scary movie on TV, and the picture went out. It was scarier to just hear it. Does she think about us? And why did she leave? The guy with the teeth must be pretty persuasive. All I know is one day he came to our house, and when he made that squelching sound, I asked were we having clams. She shushed me and sent me to my room. I can't remember how far before she left that was, but I was always sure they left together. No one ever said that; I was just sure. It was probably sex. It seems like sex makes people put everything else out of their minds, like what happened with Mayes's father, except he didn't leave. People leave behind things they don't want. Weren't we good enough? Did we make too much noise? What? Adults are always saying it wasn't our fault, but if that's true, why doesn't she want to see us? Do I want to see her? Yeah, I guess I do. I'd like to ask her why. I'm sure she wouldn't answer, because adults don't. Like the time I asked Him why He drinks so much, and He told me it was none of my damn business. He said I'd know sure enough when I grew up and saw what life had to offer. Well, that was encouraging.

10 BREAK

"I've had about all the shit I can take, from your mother and from you." Joel looked meaningfully at me; I looked at the ground. This was new, but I felt already I didn't like being lumped in the same category with Gertrude. "Seems you can't keep it together here as well as I thought, might as well give it a try in Florida. I know you think about her. Kill two birds with one stone."

My stomach fell. The phone conversation I'd overheard this morning, full of swearing and references to computers and tin cans with wings and thieves, began to make sense, but Bert was shocked. "It's not fair! Bobby and them just got back from soccer camp." Bert could get righteous when he thought someone wasn't playing fair. He didn't seem to get the idea that the world wasn't ever fair, but the world kept trying to teach him.

"Well, pal, beach there, same as here, I guess. Flight's tomorrow morning. I'm gonna go pick up the tickets then head into work. Pack your things. See if you can stay out of trouble."

The rest of the day passed in an agonizingly slow haze of pain. I managed to get our clothes packed into bags. Bert was not much help; in fact whenever I turned my back, he took stuff out.

"I don't want to go to Florida. I want to stay home."

"I know you do, Bert, but we don't have a choice. I have to get these things packed, or He'll be mad. I know you don't want that either." It hurt to bend to get the things out of the drawers, hurt so much I had to hold my breath. The circles around my eyes were darker than they'd ever been. I hadn't been able to find any way to sleep that didn't hurt.

"But why are we going? After all this time."

"He says it's because of what I did."

"What do you say?"

"I think He was looking for an excuse."

"He wants to get rid of us, you mean?" Bert's voice rose into little-girls-scared-of-spiders range.

"He wants a break."

"But we're coming back, right? I mean, like, to this house and everything."

"Yeah, I think… No, yeah. We'll be back."

Bert chose to ignore the hesitation. "What do you think it'll be like? What's she like?"

"You really don't remember anything?"

"I *was* only three."

"Oh, I know, believe me. I don't remember so much about her either. Dory says that's normal, that it's your brain protecting your heart."

I'd thought and I'd thought, but it just gave me a headache. I still remembered hardly anything about her. How could you forget someone who gave you half your genes? You'd think she'd be imprinted in there somewhere, tapping me on the shoulder while I'm brushing my teeth or whatever just to say hey, I'm still here. But no, no tap, no nothing. I thought she liked scarves. Wow. Score one for memory lane. It was enough to get you all choked up, wasn't it?

"This heart?" He touched his forehead. "But it's on the outside."

"Yeah, that one, and the one inside. It's like it's all hooked together, like a puzzle."

"But we're missing some of the pieces for our puzzle."

"What are you talking about?"

"Our family. It's broken, and you can't put it back together 'cause she ran away. How come she doesn't get in trouble?"

"It's different for grownups. Almost everything is. Plus she is still our mother. It's not like some special offer, and time runs out. She still is."

"Not to me, she isn't. I hate her. Don't you?"

"Sure, sometimes. Who wouldn't? But what can we do?"

"We could run away."

"To Dory and Donnie's?"

He nodded vigorously, obviously pleased that I'd understood his plan. His eyes shone like he'd come up with the best idea ever, like some kind of new James Bond spy guy.

"I think He'd think of that."

"He doesn't think about anything but grownup drinks."

I caught my breath to hear him say the words out loud. I'd tried to shield him from the worst of it, hoping he was sleeping soundly by the time Joel came home. Obviously, that had been a waste of time like every other freaking thing.

Since I seemed to have brought this on us, I figured I should at least try and make Bert feel okay about it. "He does care, and running away won't help. We have to go. Maybe it'll be fun. I think there will be parrots and stuff, like in that states book we looked at. Maybe there'll be monkeys. Or fish, cool colored fish."

"Maybe an alligator!"

The hope in his eyes made me feel even worse. On the one hand I had no right to stir him up about something I knew nothing about, but on the other didn't he have a right to see some good in something? He was better about that than I was. I almost never did. Joel said I was the youngest cynic He'd ever met. I swear He said it like it was a compliment, and He didn't give many. Maybe He thought it would prepare me for life. Great. So basically it's all downhill from here. There I go again. I tried harder, especially since Bert didn't really get sarcasm anyway.

"Maybe she'll be nice, like Dory says she was, you know, before, since it probably won't be for too long. Maybe she'll be able to take it. We'll be good." I didn't know if I was trying to convince Bert or myself, or if either was working.

His eyes were solemn now. "We'll be good."

I waited until Bert was asleep and prayed it was too early for Joel to come home. I had nothing to lose at this point and plenty to gain, like someone to tell me my life wasn't as bad as I thought it was who I might maybe believe. Mayes would be up for the challenge; she always was. I dialed her grandmother's number and listened to its ring echoing, my pulse pounding in my ears. Her grandmother answered.

"Hello?"

"Hi, Missus Panna. It's An—Lettie. Is Mayes there?"

"Hello, Lettie, dear. How are you? How is your summer?"

Sucky without Mayes. "Fine. Thanks."

"And your family? They're well?"

I hesitated. Where to start? Not. "Yeah."

She gave up the polite adult small talk and sighed. "I'll get Mayes for you. You take care now." I heard her telling Mayes who it was, but before she gave Mayes the phone, she continued. "Keep it short now, Mayes. I know her father won't want a big bill any more that I would." I could almost hear Mayes rolling her eyes.

"Hey, hold on. I'm just going to my room."

I waited.

"What's up? Joel said no calls, right?"

"It was kind of big. I wanted to tell you."

"Tell me what? Now I'm getting worried."

"He's sending us to Florida tomorrow. To see her."

"To see who? No! Holy crap! Your mother?!"

"Yup."

"How did that happen?"

"Me. I did it, I guess, maybe me and Bert, but mostly me."

"You *asked*?"

"No, uh, no. I did something stupid, and this is my payback."

"What did you do? Just tell me. You're killing me here." She can't contain herself though. "Drinking? Did you crash a high school party?" We've talked about doing this, but of course we've never had the nerve or come even close.

"By myself? No. I was at Strangeways and there was this CD, *Best of the 60s*, that I really wanted, and I didn't have the money, and I switched the prices."

"So Joel found it? How did he even know?"

"No, it was worse than that. Much worse. I got caught."

"Oh, Lettie, they called the police? Did you have to go to the police station? What happens now? How can you even be leaving?"

"Whoa, take a breath. Joel talked Greasehead, this totally gross manager bitch, out of reporting me."

"That's good, right? So you have to pay for it, or what?"

"Oh, I've paid all right." The bitterness in my voice even tasted bad. "I guess I'll be paying again tomorrow."

"Is that when you're leaving?"

"Yeah, first thing."

"I still don't get it. What does the CD have to do with your mother?"

"Joel says He's fed up, like maybe I'm a bad apple like her, throw me out with the other rotten one."

"He didn't really say that."

"Yeah, kinda."

"But everyone takes stuff. I'm not saying it's right, but still everyone does. He seems like he's kind of more freaked than he needs to be. Maybe he'll cool off and see that it's just regular teenage stuff... Hey, you ARE coming back, right?" Her voice was scared now like Bert's was earlier.

"Yeah, I'm sure it's just like a break, yeah, like you said, He'll cool off." My voice was so hardy I almost convinced myself. Almost.

"What else did he say?"

"He said He wants us to see what she's like."

"Well, you do want to know, right? We've only talked about it ten thousand times. Here's your chance." She was trying for upbeat now, and I wanted so much to buy it.

I heard a noise outside, and I jumped in the dark. It made my whole body hurt, I mean even worse than it already did. I whispered, "Hey, I gotta go. I think that's Him. I'll let you know where we are. LOLV."

"LOLV, babe."

I hung up as quietly as I could and crept to our room. I lay on the bed in my clothes and tried to breathe slowly. I could hear my heart ticking like an over-wound wind-up car.

After a little while I realized it wasn't Him, but I was too cranked up to call back.

I had the weirdest dream. I dreamed we were there, you know, in Florida, and it was pastel like the magazines. There were huge birds everywhere, and they could talk to you. She couldn't talk though. She just sat and cried. It was like she couldn't see us, even though we were right in front of her. Maybe it's a sign, but of what? This girl Helen I used to be friends with was always talking about signs, but the things I think are signs always turn out to be nothing and I miss all the obvious ones. Helen said she knew when her mother was going to die, she could just tell. She'd seen six crows on the way home from school, and that was supposed to mean death. I see crows all the time, and nothing happens. Or maybe stuff does happen, but I don't think it has anything to do with the crows. Maybe it goes back to when Gertrude left. There must have been signs, right, or at least one? Maybe there were crows that day. Would it be more or less for leaving on purpose than for dying? It's not like I remember her packing my lunch for school and then her not being there when I got home. I don't even know what day of the week it was, whether it even was a school day or whatever. But wouldn't she have had to plan or pack or something? Joel says she just took off, but do people really do that? I mean, did I get off the bus one day and no one was home, and we just went on from there? It couldn't be that though, because then Bert would have been home by himself, and I don't think even she left a three-year-old sitting in the middle of the floor for who knows how many hours. But then again, what do I know?

11 SPLICE

My stomach was in knots from the minute I woke up. I'd never really been anywhere, except the time I went Providence on the bus with Joel to see *Annie* for my birthday. He drank too much in some bar afterward and we hardly made the bus back, but it was a really good play. Anyway, I didn't know whether I wanted Him to be His usual slow-as-molasses self (our aunt used to say that), or whether I'd rather get it over with. As it turned out, it was a little of both. It took us forever to get out of the cottage, first Bert ran back for his Red Sox hat he'd left on the table when he was putting on his shoes, and then Joel realized He didn't have the tickets.

That time we'd made it out to the street in the truck. He'd cursed and swung around and then threw the truck into park so hard I nearly went through the windshield. It didn't do much for the pain in my ass either. No one said anything when He jumped back in, banging His head on the doorframe in the process, or for a long time after we were driving up Route Six. We were crossing some kind of bridge, and not just the one over the Canal, and it was hard to see how everything would be on the other side. We were going to see our mother who we hadn't seen in six years and who we'd heard Him say many times He hoped went straight to Hell when she got done fucking up other people's lives.

Joel said we were going because I had screwed up big time and couldn't be trusted to be in charge (or alone with His pants), but that wasn't the whole truth. He wanted us to see for ourselves what she was like, so we'd see how good we really had it and stop making her out to be some kind of saint in our minds. I don't know why He thought we did that, because we sure never talked to Him about it. Maybe it was something to do with kids always wanting their parents to be together even when they could see they hated each other, like Mayes's parents. Maybe He wanted us to see that that was ridiculous and stupid and not worth thinking about. Maybe He was right, but it was hard to live with anyway.

We had to park in the long-term parking even though He'd only be there a short time because all the short-term parking was full. He argued with the attendant guy, but He got nowhere. The guy was all, I'm going to have to call security, sir, if you don't move along, and so He moved along. It seemed like it took a hundred years for the shuttle bus thing to come; it's always like that when you're waiting. When it came, right away Bert was into everything.

"Look! The seats go sideways!" He sat in one and then slid all the way down to the end without getting up. Good thing there was no one else on the bus. He settled down a little bit when some more people got on at the next stop.

Joel had said Terminal D to the driver when we got on, I'd heard Him, but now He was motioning us to get off at Terminal C. I could see the signs for it, not D, and I felt my face squinch up. Bert did something he hadn't done since he was much littler; he took his pointer finger and traced the lines across my forehead, the "winklies" he called them.

"It's all right, Lettie, this is right. The driver says you have to walk through C to get to D. Cheapo airlines in D probably just didn't finish the job or something," Joel explained.

Now I was alarmed, not just concerned. My face must have showed it.

"Kidding. Everything's gonna be fine. Let's get a move on." He lit a cigarette the second we were off the bus even though the entrance to the terminal was only about twenty feet away.

We shifted foot to foot while He smoked. The airport didn't look like I'd thought it would, modern and shiny like a space-age cartoon. Instead it was grimy and dark, with tall, smeary glass between us and corridors that looked like the mall. There were the same high ceilings and little kiosks selling newspapers and doughnuts and the same beige-gray tiled floors. The airline parts looked like checkout counters at the supermarket except up higher. When He crushed out His cigarette and stooped to pocket the butt, He motioned us inside the automatic doors with a look like we were the ones who'd been smoking.

In the end we were running through the airport with our carryalls bumping against our backs looking for our gate, adrenaline surging as we tried to make the flight. Since we were minors, they'd let Joel through the security checkpoint even though He didn't have a ticket. Bert had wanted to stay and check out the scanner, but I pulled him along. The people being prodded with the little sticks didn't look like they were having a good time, and I didn't want to be one of them. I saw one lady with a stick touch right between another lady's breasts. I didn't have a training bra yet because I hadn't worked up the nerve to ask Joel for the money; God forbid that should lead to some kind of body discussion. I slouched all the time anyway, but I didn't want today to be the day that someone noticed.

"Checking in, sir?" A woman in a blue suit and blue shoes with a little blue tie at her throat stood behind a desk made out of plastic. Her tag said Shavonda. Her head was shaved up one side. Did her name and her head match on purpose?

"Not me, them. The lady on the phone said someone'd sit with 'em, watch out for 'em." He had a hand on each of our shoulders; the weight felt good and warm. He squeezed when He said, "Watch out," just a little.

"Not actually sit with them, no, sir, but they'll be in good hands." She flipped through our booklets of tickets. "I see they have a flight change. We'll make sure they have an escort for that." She spoke into the telephone beside her and requested the presence of someone named Jennifer. When she turned to us, her face brightened into a huge smile that people get when they don't have kids and don't know how to act with them. "So who have we here? Leticia?" I grimaced. "And, and Engelbert?" Bert smiled shyly. "Have you flown with us before?" Three heads shook side to side. "Well, I hope your first trip is a pleasant one." She turned and drew someone forward with the same all-blue deal going. Her hair was oiled back so tightly from her face it pulled at her eyes. "Jennifer, I'd like to introduce…" She glanced again at our papers, "Leticia and Engelbert. This is their first trip with us, and they're flying by themselves with a change in Miami. And who'll be meeting them in Key West?"

Joel stared at her for a minute; Shave waited with her smile plastered on while Bert and me shifted uncomfortably. "Their mother." With these words He took His hands away from our shoulders and pushed them into His pockets, and my spot where His hand had been cooled. I was sorry for that.

"Oh, well, then. That will be lovely, won't it?" Without waiting for a reply, she made the hand-off to Slick. "Jennifer, if you could escort them aboard and help them find their seats. We have these few more patient people behind the children, and then we'll be boarded." Shave flashed the smile at the patient ones, while Slick moved us steadily toward the doorway of a lighted tunnel. It made me think of that old movie with cute little Drew Barrymore, "Don't go into the light…"

"How about a hug for the old man?" Just like that time at Dory and Donnie's, though that was just for one night. His voice caught a bit in His throat, reached for us like a bug's antenna, testing, calling us back.

We hugged Him together, our hands touching behind His back, our bags swinging from their straps.

Joel coughed and let go first. He wiped His mouth though there was nothing there. I knew He wanted a cigarette. "You two have a good time.

Give a call if there's any problem, collect if you need to." He turned away, keeping His head down like He couldn't bear to watch and walking steadily back the way we'd come, back toward everything we were leaving, a clean splice. And then there were only strangers.

I don't know what to expect. I hate that. I bet I never liked surprises. Once a few years ago Joel jumped out to scare me. I cried for like an hour. He kept saying it was a joke and get over it, but I couldn't. Maybe it's because she left. That was a surprise. What kid thinks her mother is going to leave? Sure, kids when they're two and stuff don't like it when their moms leave the room, they think they're gone, but they never really are. But ours was. What's she like? What does she do all day? Does she paint? I'd get bored. When I'm a reporter, that'll never be boring. What will we do down there? Go to the beach I guess. I don't know how long we're staying even.

I dug out the package of tickets and tried to read them. All the letters were capitalized, mostly Xs. There was today's date all in numbers. I looked for other numbers, numbers that weren't ticket numbers or times or flights. There. I stared numbly at the numbers. Maybe if I stared long enough, they'd change. No. They were still the same. I did the math. We were going for six weeks. Unbelievable. I pushed the booklet back into my bag and got out my pen again.

Six weeks. He must really be sick of us. And her. What if we hate her? What if she hates us? What if she leaves again because we're there? No, that's ridiculous. Or is it? She left once, why not again? We'll have to keep an eye on her. Otherwise how will we ever get home? Someone will have to take us to the airport. I doubt her house is right next to it though I think it's a pretty small island from maps I've seen. Joel said there would be palm trees there and these big birds that scoop the fish out of the water with their beaks and flowers as big as Bert's face. He said He'd been there when He was in the Navy. He said He thought we'd like it. It seemed like something about that made Him sad even though He was smiling mostly. Adults smile the most when they're really sad and don't want kids to know it. They must not know that kids know that.

PART TWO: ANYONE'S LIFE BUT MINE
KEY WEST, JULY INTO AUGUST

12 TEMPER

Out onto the Key West tarmac (another new word in my better vocabulary quest), we lugged our bags like tired turtles. The sun was setting in a glowing haze behind a row of palm trees. The heat came across the asphalt at our feet like waves at a beach with black sand. No stairs here, we trudged into the lobby and stopped, blinking. After the bright lights of the other airports, Key West's felt small and dim. It wasn't crowded. And there she was. I would have known her anywhere, like they say in all the books and it sounds so corny.

She was waving. A big man, huge really, had his arm draped around her shoulders, but it reminded me of a leash for a dog somehow. He had on a powder blue zip-up sweatshirt that looked like a kid's on his mammoth body. With his other hand he ran the zipper up and down; the grating sound made a shiver run through me.

Bert, who ran ahead all day once that first fear of the plane had passed, once again drifted to my side and lurked in my shadow. I didn't feel like I could support anyone else right now. I felt weak and lightheaded. Maybe I should have eaten my sandwich. No, then I'd be sick. I felt my stomach heave anyway.

"You two gonna stand there all day? Let's get this train rolling!" the big man crowed. The latest Slick melted away.

Bert and I edged closer, closer, and then like magnets, we were pulled into her orbit. She was smiling and crying now, crouching down. I noticed he still kept a hand on her shoulder even from his towering height. I stared. I looked at Bert, and he was staring too in a scared, awed kind of way. Adults never cried. Plus, she was so beautiful. A long, almost white blonde curtain hung down past her shoulders. She was tan, but there wasn't a single line on her face full of blue eyes and white teeth. Gold bracelets lined her arms; gold earrings ringed her earlobes. A gold collar sat on her collarbones and should have made me think again of a dog but it didn't. It was too glorious, like something an Egyptian pharaoh's wife would wear. We'd studied them in school. The Egyptians had cool stuff, but they were always looking sideways. Not her. She was staring straight at us. She wore a navy bra-strap tank and short shorts, but she didn't look silly in teenager clothes, she looked great. On her feet, long feet at the end of long legs, she wore platform sandals.

"What are you staring at? She looks like you, big surprise. I'm Orlando, your stepfather, I guess. There's a word I never thought I'd use." The guffaw made me flinch, like someone had pinched me in the side, and then he sucked his teeth. I got a chill even though it was like a zillion degrees.

"You're him? You *married* him?" I gasped.

"Didn't he tell you? Typical. I don't know why she bothers. You know she calls you all the time?" He barked this like we'd done something wrong.

I wanted to ask was she the one always hanging up, but I had a feeling I shouldn't.

"Well, let's get out of here, unless you want to hang around the airport all day. True, let's go—"

"Wait." It was the first word she'd said. She stayed where she was, crouched down at eye level with Bert.

"What now? I'm starving."

I could see his temper starting to rise like an actual physical being, a glow from inside like a furnace.

Tentatively she spread her arms and smiled a dazzling smile. Bert and I walked into her arms like we'd never left them. Her smile grew, and the tears kept falling. Us three stayed that way for a long time, or maybe it was only an instant, but it felt like a long time, in a good way. "Leticia, Engelbert, how I've missed you."

Neither of us said anything. It didn't seem like any words were called for. Orlando didn't agree.

"All right, all right, you've had the big reunion. Let's not get all mushy. I'm starving." When he stated this fact again, she came out of her trance and snapped to attention. She held out a hand to each of us, which we took, and we walked out into the sunlight with Orlando striding ahead. In the parking lot he unlocked an ancient blue Volvo wagon. It took him a minute to wrench open the door, and then he reached across to pull up the button on the other side. He walked around and opened that door. With a grunt he turned to our threesome but looked only at her.

"Your chariot, madam." He swept his hand in the direction of the passenger seat and went back around the hood and got in on the driver's side. He drummed his huge hands on the steering wheel.

She was laughing in a nervous kind of way. "Orlando, they have to get in the back." She fiddled with the levers on the side of the passenger seat and it popped forward, almost hitting her in the head. She backed away like the seat might come after her.

I craned my head into the car. Papers, old yellowed newspapers, what looked like a stack of bumper stickers, single shoes, coffee mugs, some still with coffee in them, and more trash filled the backseat. I stood looking at the mess, my back bent into the car like some kind of big bird that Joel had talked about, and Bert stuck his head around my side to see, too. Now I felt like we were playing a bizarre game of Twister.

The drumming stopped. "What's the problem?"

"There's nowhere to sit." Bert picked up a blanket, and drifts of sand settled while clouds of white dust rose. He sounded puzzled more than put out, which I thought was good. I didn't want Bert getting worked up before we even got to their house.

Without a word, which was worse, the silence I mean, Orlando pushed open his door, threw his seat forward, and grabbed armfuls of stuff. He heaved his load out of the car and staggered around to the back. Then he had nowhere to put it all, so he dropped it on the ground. He pulled out a huge ring of keys, selected one, and stuck it in the trunk lock. When it popped, taking the keys for a ride with it, Orlando began throwing the contents of the car into the trunk. When he was done, he reached for the keys like they were within anyone's easy reach and stomped back to the driver's seat. We all still stood outside the car.

"So get in. Unless there's some other problem?" The menace in his voice said get in as much as his words did, like the burr at the back of an attack dog's throat when you walk by its territory. When my seatbelt wouldn't work, wouldn't pull away from its housing like a snail that clings to its shell, I understood. I wished I had a shell. After a few tries, the engine roared, stuttered, and roared again. Orlando backed out of the parking space faster than sane people drove forward down the street.

It was a short drive to their house, a little white house on stilts in a row of them with palm trees and flowering bushes I'd never seen before. The road here was dirt not paved, but it wasn't all rutted like dirt roads on Cape

Cod were, especially in the winter. It was littered with the pods and seeds and flowers of the plants.

"It's like Hansel and Gretel! 'Cept topical!" Bert yelled.

"Tropical, Engelbert. Leticia, why don't you get out Engie's side here, yours sticks a bit." My problem with "my" side had nothing to do with sticking.

"Her name's Annie now."

"What?"

"She got crossed. Now she's Annie."

"Is that some kind of gang thing? You don't look like you have it in you," Orlando growled from the driver's seat. He hadn't gotten out yet and sat glaring into the rearview mirror. I thought about the warning stickers that read, Objects in mirror are larger than they appear. His eyes were huge, like gray storm clouds threatening to swamp the beach.

"No, no gang thing. I got confirmed." My voice sounded like someone else's, someone younger and scared of everything. I hated the sound.

"Oh, that's wonderful, honey. That's just wonderful. Your grandparents will be so pleased. I, um, we don't go to church much ourselves, but we're so happy for you. Aren't we, Orlando?" Gertrude beamed, but Orlando only grunted. "I still don't understand though. What does that have to do with your name?"

"You get a new one since you're all clean and all," Bert chimed in.

"I remember now, you do get a confirmation name. You know, I think mine might be Anne. Did you know that? Is that why you picked it?" Gertrude was breathless; the air in the car was more stifling than ever.

"No, well, I, um, I didn't know that. I didn't pick it. My sponsor did. Sister Evy did. She said I reminded her of Saint Anne. Determined."

"Is that a nice way of saying stubborn?" Orlando demanded. "That would make you just like your mother, that is, before I had my way with her." His chuckle made my heart hurt it was so deep, like the sound of a powerful motor, and I didn't even know what he meant. I just knew I didn't like it.

Her response confirmed this for me. "Big man, we don't need to get into that now." The warning in Gertrude's voice was obvious under its gaiety; it surprised me that she warned him about anything. It seemed kind of risky, like warning a shark that you were going for a swim. "I still think it's nice that we have the same name. And it's great you got confirmed, it really is. But why not use your real name every day? It's so beautiful!"

I stared at her. She looked serious. "You think it's beautiful?" I croaked.

"Of course! That's why I chose it! And unusual. Like Engelbert. I couldn't have my babies having regular old names." The beam was back.

"Well, I feel like an Annie. I don't feel like a Leticia. I want to be regular old, well, not old, but regular like everyone else! That's the whole point!" I could feel the red creeping up my neck to my face as my volume increased.

"Who wants to be regular? Not us!" Gertrude's voice had a singsong lilt now. "You can call yourself whatever you want, but you'll always be Leticia to me. Let's get out of this car. I want you to see your room!"

Orlando was first up the cracked walk, first up the steps into the little house on stilts. It would have looked airy up there, charming maybe like decorating magazines, if it wasn't for the heaps of crap under it. Old tires, rusty wire, bicycle parts, wooden boxes, plant containers, dead plants, and what looked like just plain trash took up most of the space. Orlando yanked open the door and stood in the doorway. He had to hunch, but it looked like he was used to it, maybe liked it. His shoulders filled the space, blocking any view of the interior beyond.

"You coming, or what?" This was for us. "I'm sure I mentioned this, but I'm starving, love-of-my-life."

This was for her. Even my usual litany of nicknames wasn't springing to mind, though there was plenty of fodder. Rude? Puke? I struggled to come up with good ones, but it seemed like they had enough nicknames for each other to turn me off on the whole thing.

Gertrude followed him in while Bert and I leaned over the back seat and tried to haul our bags out of the trunk. "You doing okay?" I peered into Bert's face, my voice sounding like there was nothing okay to be doing.

"He's kinda creepy."

"Yeah. It'll be fine. He said food, right? Let's go get some."

Bright colors and plants jumped at us from all corners of the square living room. A talking bird squawked hello from its cage. That seemed mean, keeping it right next to a window with all the other birds outside flying around free.

Bert ran over to the cage and stuck his finger in. The bird promptly bit it.

"Ow!"

"Give him a little space. His name's Beano. He doesn't like kids." Orlando's laugh agreed.

"I bet he'll warm up to you. Animals love you." I looked at his finger. "No skin broken."

All kinds of noise came from beyond a curtain that separated the living room from the next room, probably the kitchen. While Bert stayed by the cage, I tiptoed over to the curtain and peeked through, hoping maybe I could see what the noise was without the noise seeing me. A square table was covered with dishes, drippy candles stuck in bottles like Italian restaurants on the Cape, and one shoe. All I could see was a vast hand going back and forth; the rest was hidden behind the open refrigerator door. Various bowls came out and banged down, some covered in wrap or napkins, some not. A hail of spoons and forks spilled from somewhere nearby, making me jump. A bulk big enough to be Orlando plunked down in a chair; now I could see one enormous leg but still not his face. Or her. I walked through the curtain, like they always do in horror movies when you're screaming, "Don't!"

"Dig in." The huge foot swung the refrigerator door shut and revealed the rest of the body and the kitchen with the sink and stove, but still no Gertrude. Orlando was doing just that, shoveling food from one container or another straight into his mouth, offering a sickening view of his remaining yellow teeth, dropping plenty on the way. There was only one other chair at the table or anywhere in view. To the left I could see the bathroom now and another doorway, maybe a bedroom, beyond the kitchen. I needed to go something terrible, but the full sight before me made me forget for the time being.

"What is it?"

"Yellow rice. Empanadas. Plantains. Nothing better." The shoveling continued. Gertrude had wandered off somewhere. We stood watching. "Not hungry?" He shrugged. "More for me."

"Do you have any peanut butter?" Bert's voice quavered a bit. I hadn't even heard him come in with the racket.

"Don't know a good thing when you see it? This is it, kid." The deep laugh vibrated through our feet.

I scanned the counter near the sink; a woven, lopsided basket of fruit sat in with more dirty dishes. I walked around the far side of the table trying to stay out of reach of Orlando's long arms and took out two oranges. "Can we have these?" When he grunted, I began peeling one, tossing the other to Bert, and walked back over to where Bert stood. I remembered my sandwich from the airport and felt better.

"Kids, come see. Come see your room." Gertrude's voice came from a height.

I looked around for stairs and found none. I looked back at Orlando. He pointed at the wall behind him. "Not as smart as you make out with them fancy words, huh?" I looked closer. A white ladder hooked to the white wall went up through a hole in the ceiling.

"Cool! Like a tree house!" Bert yelled. All I could think of was trying to get to the bathroom in the middle of the night. Bert was already up the ladder. When I climbed up, a little uneasy at turning my back on him, and put my head through the hole, I felt like Alice after I followed the instructions "drink me" or "eat me," whichever it was that made you big. The only place I could stand up was right in the middle. A window like a porthole gave light in the tiny room. Two beds, one under each eave, looked sized for dolls. In between the beds a table about a foot high held a vase like a thimble with one flower in it. It looked like a pink lantern for mice. What was the flower called? I wanted to find out. It was the first cool thing I'd seen here. Gertrude and Bert were crouched together, looking at the box of a puzzle.

"Naptime!"

Bert and I looked at each other and then at Gertrude. "We don't take naps anymore."

"Oh, well, we do. You can do the puzzle!" Gertrude's bright voice was already heading down the ladder.

I'd caught a glimpse around the corner from the kitchen of a bed way up high off the floor covered with some kind of tent.

"Do you think they have a ladder, too?" I guessed Bert had also seen the sky-high bed.

"I don't know, Bert. Maybe." A variety of grunts followed by soft moans and some high squeaking drifted up through the floor of their room. I looked quickly at Bert. I didn't know much, but I was pretty sure I knew what those sounds were. I didn't want to have to explain them to Bert right now. "Let's go take a walk outside, see the neighborhood."

Bert nodded without saying anything, a sure sign he knew something was up, but he was too off balance to ask what. While we walked, this fire truck painted key lime green roared by with its sirens blaring; I'd have to tell Ralph about it if we ever went home. After that, I started counting the lime hydrants and smiling every time I saw one.

When we got back, Orlando was sitting at the same table eating again. It was like life was in replay mode. I hoped it wasn't stuck permanently. I looked around, trying to be casual.

"She went in to work dinner." So it was restaurant work she did, not just art. "I'm out of here, too. Don't do anything stupid." Orlando laughed and wiped the back of his hand over his mouth. He walked out of the house leaving the wreck of his meal and us behind like beach trash.

"Just like home, huh?" I didn't wait for Bert's answer before I started foraging for something for us to eat, just like home, indeed.

After Bert went to bed, I took a chance and called Mayes. I knew Gertrude's shift would go 'til at least ten, all dinner ones did, and Orlando seemed like a late-night kind of guy. He'd said, "Don't do anything stupid." What could be stupid about calling my best friend to tell her how to reach me?

Happily I got her instead of her grandmother. I didn't need another lecture.

"Hello?"

"It's me."

"I knew it would be. Gran's friends don't call after about five. So, how is it? What's she like?"

"She's... married."

"No! And she didn't even tell her own kids?"

"Clearly not."

"Do you think Joel knows?"

"Who knows what Joel knows. But it's him."

"Him who?" She gasps. "The teeth sucker?"

"Yeah. And he's *huge*. He's always got his hands all over her like she's magnetic. Maybe she is. Everyone checks her out but on the sly since she's with this ape."

"But is she cool? I mean I know you just got there, but have you asked her stuff? Like, you know, about what happened?"

I snorted. "Let's just say I don't think it's going to be like your mom and you at home chatting about stuff and baking cookies. It's like she doesn't even notice we're here if he's in the room."

"Speaking of here, where are you anyway?"

I gave her the address, and then we talked about other stuff like Ralph and this cute counselor guy at her camp and what it was like to go on a plane since I never had. When we finally hung up, it was late, and I just wanted to go to bed. I was too tired to even write.

13 TRIP

I keep thinking about what she said in the car that first day. Not only the name part though that part bugs me, like she still has any right to call me anything, but the part about grandparents. I didn't even know we still had grandparents. Are they still with it and where do they live if they are? I have a little memory of them, of her really, always cooking. He worked outside I think. And how Gertrude mentioned them so casually like we saw them all the time. Then she went back to the name thing because that's what she wanted to talk about. We always talk about what she wants to talk about, not what I want to. I don't know how that works, but it does because I haven't asked her about them and neither has Bert. I don't know if he even got that part. The house isn't too bad, but it's a pit. I don't think anyone's cleaned anything in here in about a hundred years. Our sheets were full of sand that first night. I was afraid to ask if there were any more. They probably wouldn't have been any cleaner anyway from the looks of things. I took them outside and shook them out in the morning. I still have to find out where the laundromat is. And those gross bugs, huge roaches that they call some better name down here, are everywhere. I asked if they're why all the houses are propped up, and Orlando said, no, termites. Great, more bugs, I said before I thought about it. Of course he jumped all over that saying in this prissy voice "Don't tell me Toughie is afraid of a few bugs," and he wiggled his fingers and his eyebrows in this creepy way. I didn't even bother answering.

"Look at you two, always reading." Gertrude came into the living room where we were lying under the ceiling fan. Why she sounded disappointed at the thought of her kids spending the day reading was beyond me. "Would you like to go to the beach? I don't have to be in until four."

Bert jumped up immediately. Beano had been perched on his shoulder and gave a large squawk at being dumped off before he went back to his cage for a snack. Bert dropped his *Hardy Boys* to the floor, and I flinched as the pages crumpled.

"That's a library book. Look what you did." I picked up the book and smoothed the pages.

"Always so serious. It's fine." Gertrude looked at me like she didn't know where I came from and back at Bert. "Get your suit, Engie. We'll go even if Miss Priss isn't interested." Her voice was snotty now, daring me to stay behind.

I felt my eyes fill up and opened them wide so I wouldn't cry. "Why do you have to be so mean? Can't you even try—"

"Don't be dramatic, Leticia. You take everything so seriously. I'd like to go before it's time to come back. Are you in or not?"

I didn't really want to go since it was so hot, but there was no way she was winning this one. If Bert was going, then I was going.

"I'm in. I'll get my suit." I was up and out of the room before Gertrude could say anything else.

Orlando's truck was in the shop. Again. Orlando had gotten a ride that morning because he wasn't sure he'd be back in time for her to go to work. I grabbed up three sort of clean towels, cleaner than any others I could find anyway, and put on my suit in the bathroom. I pulled my big tee shirt back on; I'd keep it on at the beach until I got too hot. That was a laugh; I was already too hot. The suit wasn't getting any bigger either, that was for sure. I could feel it creeping up my ass, and I hadn't even tried to sit down in it in the car yet. Maybe she'd notice and offer to get me a new suit. Wasn't that what mothers were supposed to do? Yeah, right. She'd only have eyes for Bert, like that queer old song, without the Bert.

"This is it? It's so tiny! The beach at home is so much bigger," Bert blurted. I was glad he'd said it not me, because Gertrude wouldn't turn on him the way she always did on me.

"That beach doesn't have such pretty sand, does it?" Gertrude reached down and let a handful of glowing white crystals pour through her fingers. It looked more like sugar than sand. "And look at that water, like someone added turquoise food coloring. There's never any seaweed here either. I couldn't stand that up north, the way it dragged against your legs and got caught in your hair."

"Is that why you left, because of the seaweed?" My heart constricted even though I hadn't been the one to speak.

"No, silly. It was a grown-up thing. Come on, you slow pokes. I can't wait any longer to get in that water. It looks too good!" She dropped her shorts and was off and loping into the water, her pale pink leotard becoming transparent wherever the water hit it. When she came out, everyone would be able to see her hard, dark nipples and the hair in her crotch. Even though it was light when it was dry, the hair on her legs and under her arms was ropy and dark when it was wet, like when she came out of the shower and walked naked to their bedroom.

"Did you really think Gertrude would answer? She hardly answers easy questions like what's for breakfast," I chastised.

"How come you don't call her Mom?"

I stalled for a minute, trying to think why he was asking. I couldn't think of any obvious answer, any obvious change. "I just don't think she feels like a Mom. She's more like that spider I threw in the toilet, the one that exploded with babies, you know, like by accident, and then ran away. Know what I mean?"

Bert looked at the ground. "No, I don't know. Maybe. You're always saying she's the only one we're going to get."

"That doesn't mean I'm happy about it."

"Still."

"Still. Anyway, you call her what you want. I'll call her what I want."

"You think you're so big and grown-up. What'd'you want to be grown-up for anyway? It doesn't look fun."

"You have a point there. But the thing I hate about being a kid is that you need things from grown-ups, like money and stuff. It'd be awesome to always be a kid if the grown-ups did the things they were supposed to do, you know, like going to the grocery store. Somehow ours missed that class."

"Yeah. You do a good job though. Even if sometimes you're annoying. Sorry."

"I know. Not just I know you're sorry, but I know I'm annoying. I just want, oh, I don't know what I want."

"Sure you do."

"Okay, what then, smarty pants?"

"You want to be normal. You say it all the time. But I'm just wondering, what's normal?"

"Normal. You know, when there's a mom and a dad who have regular jobs during the day and some kids and they live in a house and eat regular meals and once a year they go on vacation together somewhere like Disney World. Those kids never have to question if anyone loves them or if there's going to be any dinner or why other kids have stuff like bikes that people don't laugh at. That's what I mean."

"Yeah, that'd be good. Want a cracker?"

"Thanks, but I think I've had it with the crackers. You know what I'd really like?"

"What? A hot fudge sundae?"

"That's what *you'd* like. I'd like a real dinner, you know, chicken or meatballs or something, and vegetables, on a real plate with a fork that matches all the other forks."

"Do I have to eat the vegetables?"

"You don't have to eat anything. You have a better chance of getting what you want anyway."

"Why?"

"Because I bet if you said to Gertrude you wanted a sundae she'd want one too, at least the first few bites. Have you noticed she never finishes anything? But if I said what I wanted, she'd just sing me that little song about how normal is boring."

"Can't we just go swimming?" Bert looked down at his feet.

"Sure." I was a little hurt that Bert wasn't joining in on the complaining. "Let's go."

We had a pretty good time at the beach. We usually did, as long as Orlando wasn't with us, and I didn't ask too many questions. Since we got here though I can't help it, my mouth opens and out comes more stuff she doesn't want to hear. It's like I've been storing it up all these years and now it's boiling over. It doesn't even shut me up when Orlando flicks me if I say stuff he doesn't like (everything!). It's not like it hurts, but it bugs me that he thinks it's fine to do, and like everything else, she says nothing. Like that day we got here when I called Mayes to tell her our address and ended up talking for like an hour, and the bill came it seemed like right after, yikes. Slap upside the head for that, and not a sound from the queen. Bert does better with her than I do. Actually he does better than I do in life; if something's fun, then it's fun, simple as that. Maybe my problem is that nothing seems simple to me. Everything we do is colored by what she did, like a lens over a beautiful picture in the most disgusting color you can think of, for some people that's pea-green or mustard-yellow, for me that's day-glow orange, and I can't see past the lens. It's true that we're on this trip here in this tropical paradise that people must pay big bucks to visit with nothing more taxing to do all day than swim and look for conch shells. I know it sounds great to spend the summer in Key West, but it doesn't feel great, to me anyway. It all feels fake and stupid, like people who go around pretending there isn't a big storm coming when there is. If that makes me a pessimist, always looking at the bad side of things, well at least if I'm already looking at it, it won't sneak up and bite me.

14 FLY

"You kids get your asses in here." His voice gave me nightmares.

Bert and I looked at each other and shrugged. It didn't matter that we didn't know what we'd done wrong. Orlando defined us doing something wrong as breathing on the same planet as him since we messed up his life with Gertrude the Magnificent. He didn't actually call her that, but he acted like it. We shuffled through the kitchen and into the doorway of their bedroom, Bert tucked behind my shoulder, out of range in case a shoe or anything else came flying. This time it was a flyswatter.

Some serious pot smoking had been happening; it was hard to see across the room in the haze, even with the window cracked open. Orlando sat in his underwear in a deck chair by the window, his snowshoe feet propped up on the windowsill. He had a bottle of beer in one hand and some Cuban sandwich thing in the other. He used the sandwich to swat at a fly as it dove for the ham or whatever. A couple others hovered out of range. I'd heard on some nature show that flies poop every time they land. Gross. Orlando missed, but the ham went flying, hitting the floor not far from one of the fly's squashed relatives. It looked kind of far from Orlando's chair for him to have killed it himself. It had probably been there a while. Double gross. The three flies dive-bombed the ham as it hit the floor. I almost laughed. "See these flies? Whole friggin' house is full of 'em. They're driving me crazy. Man's tryin' to enjoy a little lunch break from a hard day's work, and all he gets is aggravation."

Orlando hadn't even left the house, unless we'd missed him when we went to get the mail. There was nothing for us. I'd gotten a letter from Mayes yesterday so I shouldn't be greedy. It was hard to believe he'd actually gone to work unless he'd climbed out the window. I wasn't stupid enough to point this out though. "You two good for nothings take that swatter, there's another one in the kitchen somewhere, and kill every fly you see. I'm such a good guy I'll give you a penny for every fly you get. Got it?" His eyebrows went up.

We nodded.

"I'll be heading to work shortly. There better not be a fly in sight when I get back. He took an enormous bite and continued, chomping. "Now get to the hell out of here. My sandwich is getting cold."

I picked up the rusty flyswatter with two fingers and looked at the head or front or whatever it's called. It had big holes in the mesh. Who knew what it had been used for, maybe cockroaches instead of flies. Bert followed me to the kitchen.

"If anyone used this to hit flies, we should be afraid. Very afraid." I talked in a deep, slow voice and held up the mesh to my eye to look through a hole at Bert. He laughed, which was always good to hear. I fished around on the table and through a few drawers and cupboards and came up with another swatter, actually two stuck together with who knows what. They were freebies from the hardware store. I pried them apart and handed one to Bert. "So, ready to make some money?"

"I only see a couple of flies in here and those three in there. What're we going to do with a nickel?"

"Hey, what's up? This place getting to you? You usually get excited when you find a penny on the sidewalk even when they're all gummy. Don't lose that thrill, Bert, it's keeping me going."

"I'll try. Can you get the ones in there?" He rolled his eyes to the side, in the direction of their bedroom. Bert tried to stay out of Orlando's way even more than I did and flinched pretty much every time he even went by.

"Oh, buddy, sure." I felt even sadder for Bert than I did for myself right then since he was so much younger and smaller.

I hate him. I hate the way he says words with a French accent even though he isn't French and stands over us to show how big he is and the way he laughs at his own jokes, like he's the funniest guy alive. Let me tell you, he isn't. I hate when he says they're going to take a nap, when you know they're doing it. I hate the way she looks at him, all moony-eyed and goofy like some creepy teenager in a movie. Plus, it's the same here as it was at home, her working all the time, him doing God knows what, us on our own. We might as well be at home, especially since there it wouldn't feel like my skin was burning off and the whites of my eyes, too. When I go outside and the light hits my face, I wish I was blind for a second because at least then it wouldn't hurt. At least I don't think it would. It's so hot here I'd like to go naked all the time. Not that I would. Then the sleazeball would get a look. He probably does anyway. I try to stay out of his way as much as I can, certainly out of reach of those arms, but it's hard. They're so long. I open my mouth so often. We've been here an eternity.

I sat in the living room wearing as few clothes as possible. My hair was pinned on top of my head, not because I thought it looked good that way but because it was cooler. The fan above our heads whirled madly, clinking as it canted off to the side. At night I prayed the fan wouldn't give out while we were still here. That was right after I prayed that time would start moving faster than glaciers and that something big and heavy would fall on Orlando while he was at work. Assorted rattles and crinkling sounds came from the kitchen.

"Bert, what're you doing?"

"Looking for something to eat."

"Find anything?"

"Beans."

"That's it?"

"Rice. Old yellow rice, hard as a rock."

"Yeah?"

"Those sicky sweet bitty banana things. Wha'd'ya call 'em?"

"Plantains."

"Those. And some cereal. Grape Nuts. Ugh. I hate Grape Nuts."

"How about eggs? You want me to make you some eggs?"

"There's no eggs."

"Ooh, that's bad. Did she say she was going to the store this morning?"

"If you weren't sleeping, you'd know."

"Not very nice for someone who's looking for help. I'm coming though. There must be something to eat in this dump." I climbed off the sagging couch and pulled up its covering sheet where it had slipped onto the floor. Sand rained down onto the wooden planks and through some of cracks back to the outside. I padded around the corner and into the kitchen. Crumbs littered the counter and the floor below it. Bert and I kept our eyes out for palmetto bugs at all times. The bugs here didn't even wait for dark since the pickings were so constant. Stacks of dishes teetered on the round wooden table, in the sink, and beside the toaster like in a cartoon, but they didn't fall.

I don't know what I thought we'd find. We'd already picked through the mishmash of jars and containers in the refrigerator a million times and found nothing edible, unless you counted some cheese more green than yellow or some cooked pasta that was hard again on the edges like when it came out of the box.

"If there's a stash, it won't be food." If Bert had to write about what he'd learned over his summer vacation, he could always say he'd found out a whole bunch about plants, and he wouldn't mean the kind you eat or put in a vase.

"How about toast? There's gotta be bread and butter. Maybe there's still some peanut butter. It's that gross natural kind, but it's not so bad with butter first."

"Only if you watch the toaster."

I laughed. Our last run-in with the toaster we'd narrowly escaped a visit from the fire department, which might have been funny if we weren't so afraid of Orlando's reaction. We never knew what might spark his rages, excuse the pun.

I picked up the toaster and held it over the sink. I turned it over, its metal doors clanging. Showers of crumbs rained down, most of them burnt. I held the contraption in one hand and used the other to sweep another shower from the counter into the sink. I flipped it back over. When I plunked it down, the silver wings sprung open ready for filling. It reminded me of a bird here called an anhinga that had no oil on its wings so it stood in the sun with them draped open. I got two slices of bread out of the freezer, practically all the food had to go in there so the bugs didn't get it, and placed them in the trays. I slapped the wings shut so now the toaster looked like a nesting bird. Taking a deep breath, I plugged it in.

"Here goes nothing."

We watched the metal coils heat to a glowing red, redder than the flames of the bonfires we had with Joel and everyone out on the Point, like we'd watch television at home. Of course we didn't even have a television here.

"All right, that's set, I'm going to look for the peanut butter."

"But you said—"

"Watch. This'll just take a sec." I rummaged among bottles and jars, many without labels, some without tops, looking for something that might be peanut butter. One sniff in a jar that looked likely made me scrunch up my face. "Definitely not." I rummaged more. "Aha. I think this is it. And look. Butter." I held up the half a stick triumphantly. "Bert! You were supposed to be watching!" Thick snakes of black smoke rose out of the beast. I couldn't even see the bread inside the smoke was so thick. Next would come actual flames, as we knew from experience.

I yanked the cord out of the wall, grabbed a dirty rag that passed as a potholder, and quickly dumped the contents into the sink. What was left of the bread was charcoal. I turned on the water full blast. The pipes moaned and groaned, this house was so pitiful, but then the water gushed. Disaster averted.

"I guess no toast. Want a spoonful of peanut butter? Maybe I can find a few crackers."

I spread my own cracker with as thin a layer of peanut butter as I could. I didn't know how it was possible, but I was really porking up while I was here. It was probably because all we ate were carbs, and those Atkins people have a point: eat starchy food, look starchy. It also made me think of Hansel and Gretel where the witch tries to fatten up the kids so she can eat them. It wasn't like we (or they) had a choice though. It was like those starving kids in India or China that adults were always talking about when you didn't eat something; if all you had was rice, then you had to eat rice, or in this case, crackers. Who'd have thought I'd actually be craving fruits and vegetables (well, okay, not vegetables really, though broccoli wasn't so bad).

We left the flies, all nine of them, in one of his shoes. He wouldn't remember saying he'd pay us, so we might as well get some reward. With any luck he wouldn't even remember telling us to kill them. Huh, luck.

Today was so awesome. I actually found something I like here in this burning inferno. Doesn't that sound good? I took out this book from the library, and I'm working on my vocabulary. When I'm a reporter traveling all over the world, it's going to be a big help. We went to see the sunset, which I thought, Ho hum, it can't be as good as at home anyway, I've seen it a million times, but it was like a circus. Well, more like a circus plus a carnival plus a parade. There were all these people in crazy costumes and people selling stuff (Gertrude bought us some awesome chicken on sticks) and people dancing everywhere. The best was this old guy everyone calls Lizard Man. Bert dragged us up to him from the other side of the plaza. He had this big lizard, it's called an iguana he said, and it sat on his shoulder. It was a she named Dulcie, and she was sweet, just like Lizard Man said it meant, all snuggled against his neck. She was green but not slimy at all. I touched her skin. It felt warm and smooth but not like our skin and not only the green either. It looked like tiny seed beads glowing in the sun. Bert touched it, too. He totally loved her. The sunset was beautiful. I still think it's better at home, but it was cool how when it did set everyone cheered like someone had done something really great. Of course, someone had. But I don't think people were cheering for God. You don't hear about that much, except for in the paper when they're talking about guys you can tell the reporter thinks are nuts. I'm going to be a better reporter than that. This other cool guy I met, Whit, told me how if you stare at the sun exactly when it's going down, all red and on fire, then when it goes you see a green blip. He was standing next to me at the railing overlooking the ocean, and he just started talking to me. I said you're not supposed to look right at the sun or it can mess up your eyes, but he said it was only for a second. I didn't believe him, but it was true. I did it even though I pretended I didn't because I didn't want him to think I was listening too much but I was.

15 CROSS

Like usual we were hanging around looking for something to do. Bert started chasing the little lizards that darted around the trees and the foundation of the house. They were clever; they could change color depending on where they were and blend in.

"Annie, look, I caught one!" Bert yelled. Before I even got there, Bert's yell of triumph changed to freaked out. "He got away! And he left his tail here!" Bert dropped the tail like it was hot. It twitched for a minute in the dirt before it stopped.

"I bet it's like a defense thing. I bet he re-grows it later. Don't worry about it." It'd be cool to be able to just hack off a body part, like your heart, say, and re-grow it later when the danger was past, if it ever was.

I realized with a start that we'd been here way over a week, and I hadn't been to mass. Sister Evy wouldn't be happy with that. Nuns weren't supposed to be sponsors, usually it was someone in your family or a family friend, but what choice did I have? Joel's parents were both dead, though I remembered Grandma E. She used to come to Provincetown and stay at the Hargood House and take us for lunch at Tips for Tops'n. She'd wipe her lips with the napkin after every bite but never smudge her lipstick. At night she drank something called a grasshopper that smelled like mint and was the only drink I ever wanted to try. She wouldn't let me though. She was always buying us shoes. When Joel's much older sister died around the same time, whatever links we had to His family were gone, too. Gertrude's family, well, I hadn't even known if there were more of them, never mind how to get in touch with them. I had thought about asking Dory, I knew she'd grown up Catholic, but she hadn't gone to church in years. That left Sister Evy.

St. Peter's had felt like home to me from the first time I'd walked in the place. I knew I'd been baptized there because I'd found my baptismal certificate when I was looking in some ratty cardboard boxes when we'd moved out of our old house. I'd been looking for photos of her. Most of it was junk, but I was so happy when I found that. It felt like a door had opened that had been closed for too long. I hadn't even known it was closed. St. Peter's with its graying shingles and arched stained glass had reached out to me and taken me in.

Bert and I went looking for a Catholic church in Key West. I could've asked Gertrude, she probably knew even though she didn't go, but I didn't like to show need. And it's not like there was any chance of finding a phone book in her house, never mind a computer. When we found it, it was called St. Mary Star of the Sea, which was kind of promising, but it was pinkish and chalky and made of coral and didn't feel right to me. I crossed myself, knelt, and said a prayer, but I didn't feel like God was there. God lived in the high gray light of St. Peter's where people still talked about sailing ships and fishing boats, even if there weren't many boats left. What did they talk about here, palm trees, how hot it was, what?

A man in a brown robe with a rope tied around his waist and only a little bit of hair in a ring around his head floated up the aisle past us to the altar. He kneeled and bowed his head. He stayed that way a long time, and something about him gave off a holy feeling.

"Can we go now?" Bert always got restless in churches, too quiet.

I shushed him and pointed to the man in brown. "I want to wait 'til he's done."

"Why?"

"I don't know. I just do."

Bert slumped down in the pew and frowned. This was better than a whine session or a screaming session. I took what I could get.

When the man finished, he turned and walked straight toward us. He looked so sure that I almost turned in my seat to see if he knew someone behind us, but I didn't think there was anyone else in the church. Maybe he was leaving. I got a sinking feeling as he approached our pew, sure that he would pass by and head out. I was so wrapped up in the sinking that his voice startled me.

"May I help you with something, my children?"

His voice was so soothing I wanted to give him a list. I was that sure he would be able to help us like he offered. No, he was just being polite, the cynic inside me chided. I started to shake my head when he spoke again.

"I am Brother Augustine." He kept his hands folded in prayer position at his waist; they looked so comfortable there. "I'm so pleased you've come to this lovely church. You are of course welcome to stay as long as you like, but does your family know where you are?"

"How come you have a different suit on than other church guys wear?" Leave it to Bert to break the mood.

Brother Augustine didn't seem to mind though. "I belong to an order called the Franciscans. We are Brothers, not Fathers. We wear these simple, natural robes to remind us of our founder, Saint Francis. He wore one much like it many years ago. He could talk to the animals, even the smallest birds."

"Would you talk to us?" I couldn't believe I'd said that.

"I was right then. You are troubled. Would you tell me your names?"

"I'm Bert. She's Annie. We're no trouble though."

Brother Augustine laughed, a silvery kind of tinkling laugh that made me think of Christmas, the storybook kind. "No, I didn't think you were. Pleased to meet you, Bert," he gravely put out his hand for Bert to shake, and he did, "and Annie." He made a small bow in my direction. "I must ask again, does your family know where you are?"

"Gertrude's at work, and Orlando, he's…" Bert was at a loss to explain to a stranger that Orlando was at the house getting high as usual.

"Are these your parents you speak of?"

"She is. I guess."

"Hmmm. So you are on your own here. Well, let this church be your home away from home any time you need it. I trust if you need additional assistance, you will go to the authorities." Bert's heart darkened at the mention of home. I looked at him hard, trying to reassure him and maybe myself, before I nodded at Brother Augustine. At night when I prayed I sometimes repeated, "We will go home. We have tickets," so many times it sounded like a chant. Brother Augustine registered my nod, found it serious, and continued, "Did you know the church has a long history of sheltering the needy? Isn't it a beautiful church?" His smile looked the way I always pictured Jesus' smile, warm and making you feel like you just ate the best dessert ever. "I am only a visitor myself, but I could show you around if you like."

We both nodded enthusiastically, which would have surprised me with Bert if it been anyone but Brother Augustine. Who wouldn't like wherever he was and agree to whatever he offered? And it didn't seem anything like all the warnings about don't talk to strangers because no stranger ever reminded me so much of Jesus.

Brother Augustine showed us all around, pointing out the stained glass and the Stations of the Cross, but the coolest part was outside. "This grotto is called the Shrine of Our Lady of Lourdes. It was built by a group of nuns in the 1920s. When it was dedicated, one of the nuns, Sister Gabriel, pledged that as long as the grotto stands, Key West would be protected from hurricanes. Whenever a hurricane threatens, islanders come here and light candles to pray by. She has kept her promise."

"That's so cool!"

"Yes, it is." He eyed us and then continued. "A prayer to God can help with many troubles, not only hurricanes. But I suspect you already know this."

"She got crossed."

Brother Augustine looked at me for clarification.

"Confirmed. I got confirmed."

"Marvelous. Then the spirit of God will always be with you." He placed a hand on Bert's head. "And with you, my child. You may stay here as long as you like, but I must return to my duties. I will hope to see you again." He made the sign of the cross over us and left as silently as he had come.

"He was nice. We can come back here another day." This was high praise indeed from Bert. He probably wanted to climb around in the grotto. That probably wouldn't go over so well, but who knew?

"Yeah. We will."

St. Mary's, and especially the grotto, became a common stop on our rounds around town. I almost liked it empty more than I did during mass. It was ours then. We didn't see Brother Augustine again, but somehow it always felt like he was there. Maybe he was an angel and not a real guy at all. I wanted to believe that we could meet an angel, that with all the bad things that had happened that an angel would find us and bless us. It was hard though.

16 CAMP

It was a Monday, and we were crammed in a little wooden boat, a dinghy really, about to row away from the trawler his friend had motored us out in as far as he could. "That's it. Can't get no closer with the coral, scrape up my boat," Phil told him.

"You care more about the paint job than you do about your wife, man." Orlando laughed his bitter laugh.

"You leave Babs out of this. That's a real nice thanks, mate."

"Oh, thank you, Phil. We really appreciate it." She sounded so syrupy and fake next to Orlando's insults, but Phil seemed to think it was genuine enough. "Any time, Gertrude. You and the big man here know that, even if he is an ungrateful bastard." Phil leaned over the side of his boat and spoke next to Bert and me. "You kids be careful out there. I've seen snakes and 'gators and you don't want to know what-all more times than you could shake a stick at. Might want more than a stick." He rubbed his bald skull thoughtfully, like he was considering his best weapon. "Kids, you see a 'gator, you run, run like a snake, back and forth." He illustrated with his hands, moving them serpentine through the air. "Them 'gators can only see straight, their eyes up here." Phil pointed to the top of his bare head. "Remember, like a snake." He paused, and a deep frown creased his dark forehead.

"Don't go scarin' 'em, Phil. They're already afraid of their own shadows." Orlando lurched at us huddled in the prow; we jumped. I wished we didn't, but we did. The boat rocked. "See?" He grinned and hooted in our direction like some kind of maniac. The smell was deadly, or maybe just dead. I'd heard that it was bad spit that gave people bad teeth, but he could still consider brushing occasionally.

"You got enough food and everything?" Phil asked anxiously.

"Yes, Christ, you're worse than my mother was, and that's pretty bad. See you Thursday high tide. Not long after that, True and me'll be millionaires, so you'd better be on time you wanna party with us. Get outta here now, and don't swamp us." Orlando swung the dinghy around and began rowing, his strokes eating up feet of water at a time. Since Orlando won this "goldmine" in a poker game last week, we'd been hearing about nothing else but how he was going to spruce it up and sell it to some "rich sucker." We reached the island in little time, much less time than I personally would have liked. Phil seemed to know what he was doing and to respect the water, something Joel said was the most important thing about getting in a boat. Orlando only seemed to have any regard for himself. He wouldn't have even remembered about Beano if Bert hadn't asked who was going to feed him. Thanks to us this guy Orlando worked with was supposed to, good luck to Beano.

Though there was some sand right at the water line, most of what I could see of the island was alive, tall plants and trees, all interwoven with vines to create a thick wall of green. It was pretty small, like you could walk across it quickly if it wasn't so dense, but I imagined there was plenty of space for animals. Alligators. I hoped they didn't mind us invading their turf, not too much anyway.

"How do we get to the house?"

Orlando barked in his amusement. "House? No house. We're camping, shrimp."

"Oh. But I can't see no empty part."

The bark came again. "There will be."

Orlando beached the boat in the roots of a mangrove tree and ordered us out.

I looked hesitantly at the water, clear enough to see any 'gators that might be coming, but still. "It's deep."

"Oh, for chrissake, it's only up to your ankles. Nothing's gonna bite ya."

Bert looked back and forth from his legs to Orlando's. Fear of alligators had diminished our fear of Orlando. Would that do us in? Only time would tell. "Whose ankles?"

"Just get the hell out. All of you." Gertrude looked hurt, but she didn't say anything. "I've gotta untangle this anchor line."

He sat in the prow and fiddled with the rope while the three of us plunked our feet into the water which hit Bert at mid-leg and me mid-calf and unloaded the bags onto the mangrove's knees. They really did look like knees, with skin like an old man who'd been in the sun without sunscreen his whole life. When we were done, Orlando climbed over the seats and out onto the sandy bottom. The water was well below his knees. He pulled the anchor and its rattling chain off the floor and sunk it in the sand.

"Look at where she is. You're not here Thursday high tide, you stay here." It wasn't the first threat he'd made. I believed every one of them.

"So. Let's get started." He squinted up at the sun, just approaching its height. "We've got a good eight to nine hours before it gets dark. Plan is to bushwhack our way around the island, look for the best spot to cut through to the center, and make a site for the tents and the latrine." He reached into one of the moldy canvas bags he'd brought and pulled out four big knives with curved blades. He slung the bag over his head and behind his back. "Know what these are?"

"Cool! Swords!" Bert was already reaching for one.

I had seen them in the army/navy store in Provincetown. I didn't know anyone actually used them, I thought they were more sort of decorative, or if you were a veteran remembering your days in Nam. "You're giving an eight-year-old a machete. Isn't there some law against that, child labor or something?"

"Now you're a joker, huh? You need to work on your delivery."

"Seriously, he can't use that thing. He'll cut off his leg."

"Yes, I can, I can. See?" Bert grabbed for a machete and then swung wildly to cut down a mass of green growth. I didn't know what it was; all the plants were different down here and grew bigger overnight. I'd seen in the paper that some of the vines in Key West were so strong they pulled down telephone lines.

"No blood, huh? All set then. We'll go this way," he put his leash hand on Gertrude's shoulder, "and you two go that way. We'll meet at that big tree in a couple hours, report our progress." He waved vaguely at the great trees that crowded the central part of the island (like the whole island wasn't covered in trees). "And you better have made some." He put one of the big duffels over his other shoulder.

"You look out for Bert, okay, Leticia?" Gertrude quavered.

"Like I ever do anything else," I muttered. "And don't worry about me or anything. I'm all set for Jungleland here, plenty of preparation."

"Clearly her mouth is her best weapon. Let's go, True. Time's a waitin'," and then they were off. She didn't even look back.

"Wasting, you idiot."

"Annie?"

"Yeah?"

"Is he serious?"

"It looks that way. Let's take some food and water and see what else is here." I began digging through the bags he'd left at the shore. I pulled out a canteen full of water and kept digging. One of the bags was so long and narrow that I had to put my whole head into it to look. After a few minutes, I surfaced with two flattened peanut butter sandwiches that I had made that morning. "Phew. I thought he'd found them."

"And ate them." We shared a laugh now that the danger had passed or was at least on its way in the opposite direction. "How about this?" Bert had been doing a little rooting around himself in another bag. He held up a roll of toilet paper. "No toilet though, right?"

"Right," I agreed grimly. I added the roll to my bag. "Any other finds?"

"This." He held up the tube of sunscreen that I had spent our first few days in Key West trying to convince him to use. After his first bad burn across the backs of his knees and neck, when his skin had been as hot and tight as a freshly boiled lobster, he no longer argued.

"Excellent. Maybe Orlando will frigging fry; serve him right." Orlando burned and badly, all blotchy and scaly. Gertrude seemed immune and kind of darkened and lightened with her mood or some weird thing. With my back to Bert I added a few more items to the bag. "All right, I think that's it. Too much more'll be too heavy. A towel or two would be good though. You have your suit on, right?"

Bert shook his head, head down toward his shoes like he was looking for bugs.

I added a towel to the bag and shook my head in frustration. "Never mind. We're in the middle of freaking nowhere. If you want to go in, you can just go in, what the hell. There's no one to see." No one mentioned alligators or anything else. Right then it seemed like the heat would be our worst enemy. "Okay?"

His head came up. "Okay." Silently he took my hand, and I didn't feel like shaking him off. We started in the opposite direction from Gertrude and Orlando. We didn't look back either.

At first it wasn't bad. The sun was still climbing in the sky and hadn't reached its apex of heat dispensing. Doesn't that sound like a faucet or something? If only it was a shower. Most of the plants along our route were tall, so we got a bit of shade here and there. No unsavory critters made their way across the sand. Crabs scuttled in and out of the roots that crisscrossed the shoreline. The mass of green was impenetrable. I pictured these sentences in my mind to preserve them until I could write them in my book.

We'd been walking awhile, maybe a half hour or so, who knew, when Bert began to whine.

"Are we there yet?"

"If I knew where there was, I might be able to say. It's an adventure, right? You like adventures in books. You're always saying our life is too boring. Well, you can't say that anymore, that's for damn sure. First He ships us off to the other end of the country to see a woman we barely know, and now she ditches us on an island in the middle of the ocean. Jesus. Pretty exciting, right?"

"I think I liked boring better."

"Me, too. Want to go swimming?"

"Yeah!" His face clouded. "I can really go in in nothing?"

"I'd put some sunscreen on if I were you, but yeah." I panned my arm like a person indicating the crowd. "You see anyone who gives a rat's ass?"

Bert laughed. "Birds. I see some birds."

"So give 'em a show!"

I shed my tee and shorts and battered Keds, revealing my ever-tighter suit beneath. I tugged at the crotch. Bert stripped down and wiggled his toes in the sand. He giggled some more. "I should put the sunscreen… there?"

"Here," I squeezed a dollop into his hand. "A few swipes'll be enough. We're not going to swim all day; we'll have to find some shade soon." I grimaced, remembering. "Oh, yeah, and we have to get going with the machetes." I rolled my eyes.

"I can do it." Bert's face was so earnest I almost laughed.

"I don't even know if I can do it. Who knows what these plants are? Let's hope we don't get poison ivy or whatever else there is out here. Hopefully nothing worse."

"I'm going in. Last one in's—" For a change I beat him, but there was a price. "Cheater! Cheater!" rang down the beach.

For my punishment Bert started a splash fight, getting water up my nose. I dove then surfaced spluttering. "The water's great, huh?" I laughed a real, full laugh for the first time that day, and then I looked at Bert's face. His eyes widened, so wide the skin of his face looked tight, or maybe that was sunburn already. His heart glowed and seemed to pulse. His voice was reverent. "Annie. Annie. Behind you. Is that…?"

I stole a glance over my shoulder, and time stopped. My gaze telescoped until all I could see were the eyes, two yellow and black cat's eye marbles resting on top of the water. Neither blinked. They were wedged in a bumpy log, a log at least seven feet long. The log shimmied, sending ripples through the water until they bumped against the mangroves and ricocheted. My breath froze in my chest despite the hundred-degree heat.

After what seemed like hours when no one and nothing moved, I turned, slowly, so slowly, to face the alligator. My eyes never leaving his, hers?, I began to back up, one step at a time. What had Phil said? Like a snake. I stepped side to side, side to side, backwards, one step at a time toward the shore trying to upset the water as little as possible. My two eyes stayed glued on the opposing eyes, neither set of them blinking.

When the water got shallow, I risked half a glance behind me, searching for Bert. I found his form, shadowy in my peripheral vision but there in the shallows, and went back to my duel with those eyes. If I focused on the eyes, the rest of it didn't seem so huge. Suddenly the water began to churn, and the whole animal revealed itself, not a log at all but a beast careening through the water with awesome speed.

"Run! Run in zigzags! Run for the trees!" Bert and I burst out of the water, droplets flying every which way, and made for the scrub at the back of the narrow beach. Branches and brambles tore at our skin, but we kept going. My ears strained to hear pursuit of the scaly, scary variety, but it was hard to tell since we were making so much noise ourselves.

"That tree! Crocky can't climb, can he?" Bert reached a big tree hung with Spanish moss and looked like a wet squirrel that'd lost his tail as his white bottom flashed up the tree. I followed, breathing heavily, dragging our bag behind me. I didn't even know I'd picked it up on my way by.

A rustle in the underbrush might have been the toothed monster giving up and sliding back to the water, or maybe it was a turtle or a rat. Who gave a damn? I looked at Bert, and he looked back at me for a long while without saying anything. Then, like always, it was hunger that got us.

"You got the sandwiches in there?" I handed him one without saying a word. I couldn't find any yet that made any sense.

We're in the middle of the ocean on some godforsaken dirt clod they own (I always wanted to use that word) that he's decided to clear a trail through. Easier said than done, it turns out. Not only are there no bathrooms, there's barely any food. What there is, he'll eat, I'm sure. We could have been killed today, and who would have known or cared? Not Gertrude, oh no, that would be asking too much. She walked off without even a "Do you have enough water?" What kind of a mother is that? The only kind we have, clearly, but what use is she? I wish we'd never come down here. I wish she'd stayed out of our lives. I know I used to want her to come back at least to visit or to say she missed us or something, but this is worse. We're here, and she doesn't even care. She only cares about Orlando. And he is worse than the worst. He totally hates us. I think we remind him that she had a life before she met him, and he wants none of that. He wants her all to himself. Well, he can have her. They can have each other. If we ever get off this stinking island, which by the way is ugly and totally not like any tropical island I've ever heard of, no pretty birds or anything, I don't care if I never see either one of them again.

We stayed up in that tree the rest of the time, whatever time it was. It wasn't bad as trees go. The bark was pretty smooth, and there was enough moss hanging down to give us some shade. We found out later that Spanish moss gives you chiggers, but right then we didn't care if it was deadly poisonous as long as it shielded us. The biggest branches, like the one where we were sitting, went out mostly horizontal from the trunk before they curved upward.

"Annie?"

"Yeah?"

"You think we're gonna be stuck here the rest of our lives?"

"Even she wouldn't do that. Eventually they'll come looking for us." I tried to say this with conviction, I so did.

Really, what I felt like doing was crying, "Mommy, Mommy, Mommy!" at the top of my lungs, but I didn't. As usual, there was no point. We'd come all the way down here, and I kept thinking she'd change or pick us over him or SOMETHING, but we got nothing. I should be used it by now, but it kept sneaking up on me.

"We got any more food?"

"Here, have a granola bar."

"Is that all?"

"I think you know the answer to that. After that it's nuts and berries, or whatever those poor bastards stranded on desert islands are always eating in books."

"I don't like berries. Except for strawberries. You see any of those?"

I gave him a look. "Yeah, well, I don't see any nuts either. Like I said, she'll come looking." I rooted around in the bag, making a show of finding something I knew was there. "Hey! Look what I found! Wanna play?"

We played cards, game after game of Crazy Eights and Gin Rummy. We couldn't play Spit, Bert's favorite, because the cards would fall out of the tree for sure, and I for one wasn't going down to get them.

"Would you look at that, two monkeys, and one of 'em the rare bare-assed monkey. You two been up there the whole time we been working like dogs?" Orlando looked up at us in disbelief.

I looked down with disbelief of my own, disbelief that he was as cruel as he showed himself to be over and over again each and every day.

"Now, Orlando, be nice. Come on down, kiddos, and see the site we've got started. We'll get water going, and we'll have beans and rice ready before you know it."

I couldn't believe I was actually glad to hear the words beans and rice in the same sentence. I looked at Bert, and he looked just as glad. For a boy who wouldn't eat a black bean when he arrived, he couldn't get out of the tree fast enough.

"So, what have you two sluggards been doing all this time?" Orlando clearly wasn't going to give this a rest. "I hope you haven't lost the machetes in all your fun and games."

"Yeah, getting chased by an alligator the size of a car is fun, really fun." I tried to inject as much sarcasm as possible into my voice to cover up the fear.

Gertrude sucked in her breath. "Oh, honey, are you all right? Engie? You all right?"

"Thanks for your concern, *Mom*," I felt like I had to highlight her lack of participation in our all-rightness, "but we did what Phil said. We made it to this tree. Obviously."

"Sure it wasn't a little ol' lizard, like your pal at sunset has?" Orlando widened his eyes like he was calling a spade a spade.

I decided that remark wasn't even worthy of an answer. I turned to Gertrude. I tried to hold my voice steady. "Where's the so-called site? We're starving."

Bert and I followed them through the brush to a rough clearing near the center of the island, like he'd said back at the boat. That seemed like a whole other day that we'd been on the boat with Phil, but really the sun was only just starting to turn the sky pink.

"Red skies at night, sailor's delight!" crowed Orlando, for probably the millionth time since we'd met him. If I never heard that expression again, it was too soon for me.

We set up two little tents and brought the rest of the bags from the mangrove tree. Ah, all the comforts of home, if you didn't count having to relocate the tents twice to escape the killer red ants. When we did see a snake, it was almost a letdown after the size and menace of the alligator, just a brown ribbon that slid away into the endless plant life that seemed to grow when you turned your back. We stayed on the island clearing and burning brush until Phil picked us up three days later, and I was never so glad to see another human being in my life. The guy who paid anything for this piece of hell was a sucker indeed.

17 PRONE

"I need caller seven to tell me the name of the song with no name by a group known nationally that went to number one for three weeks in 1972. Caller seven, and you'll win a nice prize."

I was up reading; it was after two in the morning. I'd found that if I stayed up late, then I could sleep in and miss seeing Orlando in the morning entirely. Mostly Gertrude worked in the afternoons or evenings, so sometimes she could do stuff with us before she went. When she couldn't, or when we were too hot to stand another minute and lying prone under the fan wasn't enough, we went to the library. Books let me go anywhere, anytime, and anywhere but here was where I wanted to be. I was reading my way through Agatha Christie; Bert stuck with *The Hardy Boys*. We'd had to forge Gertrude's name to get a library card since we didn't live here, but it wasn't hard. It was all spikes and loops, and it was on all her sculptures. I'd looked around the house to see if she had a card before we bothered with forgery, but all she seemed to read were trashy romance novels, and she got those at the used book place for a dollar apiece.

I reached for the phone. I knew the number by heart; the guy said it between every song. I knew the answer, too; this guy liked to give clues that you had to think about, that you couldn't look up in a flash, even if I had any looking-up resources. He liked word games. Known nationally. That was the clue.

"You're caller seven. What do you think it is, the name of the song with no name by a group known nationally that went to number one for three weeks in 1972?"

"'A Horse with No Name.' By America."

"You are correct! Who do we have here?"

"Lett—no, Annie."

"Well, Lett—no, Annie, where do you live?"

"Not here."

"My, my, aren't we the cryptic one. So, Lett—no, Annie from Not Here, you head on down to Sloppy Joe's Bar tomorrow before two and you can pick up your prize. What's the best station in the Keys?"

I went blank with the thrill of winning something. "W…KYZ?"

"Good thing you didn't have to answer that right to win. This is Mighty Mouth at Key103, your station to win. Night-y, night, Lett—no, Annie."

In the morning I asked first thing, even though it meant I had to talk while Orlando was still there. "Can I go downtown this morning?"

"Why, look at that. She can talk."

I glared at him and addressed my question directly to Gertrude. "Can I?"

"I guess so, if you take your brother. What do you want to do?"

"I have to get something."

"You don't have any money, unless I am missing some." Orlando arched his eyebrows at me, pursing his lips at the same time.

"I don't need any money. I won it."

"Won what? How? You been fooling around with some gambling thing or something?" If I wasn't mistaken, there was a bit of envy in his voice.

My eyes said you wish. "It was a contest. On the radio. I won."

"Wow, honey, that's great. What did you win?" The things it took for her to call me honey, it was amazing.

I looked down. This would surely earn me ridicule; I just wasn't sure what kind. "I don't know. They didn't say."

"That's strange. I hope it's appropriate for a child." That was a laugh; my whole life was inappropriate for a child. "Where do you have to go to pick it up, whatever it is?"

"Sloppy Joe's Bar, he said."

That laugh boomed out; I cringed. I gritted my teeth. "You'd better go down there with her, True. It's probably hooch, and she is a minor, even if she does have a major mouth. Wouldn't want her getting her hands on what's coming to me!"

When we got there, the place was getting ready to open for business. A few sad sacks waited in the street for first dibs like they did outside the bars back home. I always vowed I'd picture those guys, never mind Him, if I was ever tempted to try a drink, they looked so pathetic. A woman who looked like her double shift had gone over from last night into this morning eyed us as we approached. Her features were sunk in her face, and her hair pillowed out on one side but not the other. Her once-white apron had a slash of red down it, maybe ketchup, maybe blood. "Whachu want? Them kids cain't hardly come in here. We ain't even open yet. We don't need no trouble here."

"Good morning to you, too, miss. My daughter here," Gertrude glanced at me like she'd found me under some rock and was surprised I wasn't a salamander, "she won a prize. From the radio station. They told her to come here this morning to pick it up."

"She a night owl, or what?" Puffy exhaled like she was smoking and propped her battered mop on one side of the doorframe. "Wait here." She came back with a long, flat box. "Enjoy." She handed it to Gertrude and returned to her weary work sloshing gray water over gray floors.

"What is it?" In my haste I tried to grab it from Gertrude, who snatched her hand back like we were playing slap. "Sorry. I just want to see."

Gertrude handed over the box. It was pretty light in my hand, and the flimsy cardboard was closed with a single piece of tape. In a flash I clutched three abnormally big, thick cassettes in one hand and the box in the other. Joel had cassettes, Billie Holliday and Miles Davis, in His truck at home. Last year, after I dropped the portable CD player Dory and Donnie had given me for my birthday so now it only played out of one speaker, I had asked Joel if we could get a CD player instead of a cassette player when He got a new truck.

"You know something I don't?" He'd eyed me speculatively, like He was looking for where I kept my hope for better things in the future so He could do me the favor of smashing it now. "Unless you do, we're not getting a new truck anytime soon, and I don't give a good goddamn about any CD player."

I could see that these cassettes wouldn't fit in His player or anyone else's I'd ever used. "What the heck are these?"

Gertrude began to laugh. It wasn't a nice noise.

"What? What's so funny?" My voice cracked on "funny."

"They're eight-track tapes. I haven't seen those in years. I don't know anyone who even has a player for them anymore." Gertrude shook her head in disbelief while she read the labels aloud. "KC & the Sunshine Band. The Captain & Tennille. Tony Orlando & Dawn. Lettie, Lettie, you just weren't meant to be a winner."

I felt so stupid, getting all excited about winning something. And then she had to make it worse, of course, by pointing out how stupid I was. Aren't parents supposed to be proud of their kids, even when all they're doing is walking down the street without falling down? I'm always seeing these parents applauding their kids riding their bikes or catching fish or whatever. All we ever get is a slap upside the head or, on a good day, ignored. I'm going to do so much better when I'm a mom. What the hell am I saying? First of all, I can't even get a date. Second of all, people who are as screwed up as our family obviously is shouldn't even have kids. There should be some kind of test or something, maybe a license. That doesn't seem to have really helped with drivers, but at least it would be something.

18 EDGE

I don't get what all the fuss is about. Sex is everywhere, in magazines, on TV, in music, in their room, God knows. You'd have to be deaf to miss it. My body is the only thing I have to myself. A hug is all right, I guess, as long as I only use one arm. I don't like being touched much. I guess that makes me weird, like everything else. Every other teenager in the world is dying to get into someone's pants. Me, I just want a normal life, not to get all hot and bothered. I like that expression. I saw that in a magazine, too.

After standing beside the front door for what felt like an hour, listening for any sound from the tiny room I shared with Bert or from their room, hearing nothing but the ceiling fan doing its crazy dance, I decided to risk it. Bert had gone to bed at his usual time, around nine o'clock, and Orlando always dragged Gertrude off to bed for her "beauty sleep" when she wasn't working. Beano was quiet under the cover of his cage. I edged open the door enough to fit my body through and pulled it back shut just as quietly. There, I was outside. The air didn't feel as heavy out here, and it was alive with the sound of tropical buzzing. It smelled good, almost as good as at home where the sidewalk cracks burst with alyssum and even the privet hedges had flowers, little tiny white ones that smelled better than all the loud, flashy ones combined.

I wanted to look up the plant that smelled the best down here the next time we went to the library. It had flowers that were the same color and size as peeled bananas but with a lily stuck on the end. They only opened at night. That was cool, and smart. I had learned some of the flowers here, the ones Gertrude knew, like the little lanterns called bougainvillea, and hibiscus, the ones with the middles that looked like penises. The night bugs she called cicadas. They sounded like crickets on tropical drugs, like the flowers down here were all bigger and brighter and showier, and the birds, too. The pelicans were my favorites with their greedy bills always open, skimming for food like lemon-colored bulldozers. Bert called them pterodactyls with bent beaks. I'd never understood the little boy/dinosaur fascination, but Bert knew all their names, the flying ones, the running ones, and the swimming ones. That was it, I'd walk down to the water, maybe see some birds, whatever tropical night birds were. Were there tropical owls? I hadn't seen any.

I started walking. No one was around. These walks were my new thrill. I hardly ever saw anyone, and that was fine with me. Gertrude said a lot of people in the neighborhood either worked nights, like she waited tables wearing a brown halter pantsuit that showed almost all her skin, or else did construction and were out early.

"The night owls are working, and the early birds are snoozing. What does that make me?" How come people say you're crazy if you talk out loud to yourself, I mean, when you're not on the phone? It's not like everyone doesn't have a little conversation going in their heads all the time; it can't just be me. I'm not that original.

I knew my way around now without having to pay too much attention. I wandered up one little street and down another, kicking the nuts from some tropical tree with the toe of my sneaker and smelling the exotic smells of the night-blooming flowers. It was hard to believe that most of these plants would be blooming in the winter like they were now, that winter wouldn't come here with its cold, bright fist to smash all that was living and make merely walking a chore. I'd have to write that down. Not that I would ever come back here in the winter to see for myself, I wouldn't, but it was still hard to believe. Maybe it kind of made up for how hot it was in the summer during the day. Bert and I both lived for that late afternoon hour when it nearly always rained a little, even a few minutes helped, but this was better. The breeze was the perfect temperature, not too hot, not chilly, just about the movement. The leaves of the trees stirred above and around me, and then I could see the water, turquoise even in the dark.

I didn't know the name of the street I was on, and the sign was stuck in a flowering tree that probably no one would ever get around to trimming. Stuff grew so fast here, what was the point?

I heard him before I saw him—Whit, the cute guy from sunset who always had something to say. I knew who he was now, the son of Gertrude's friend Wayland. All her friends were beautiful and really tall like some models' club, but Wayland was the only other one who had kids. She also had some daughters, two of them I'd met, so beautiful, too, that I couldn't stand them, even to look at them. I had slouched into a corner of their porch and stayed there until it was time to go. Their names came from some Southern thing about naming your kids with last names or streets or anything that didn't sound like a first name so everyone would know how special they were. Those two were Willoughby and Wallace.

There was another one, Wishart, I'd never met since she was a model (of course) up in New York. When I saw pictures at their house that time, I realized I'd even seen her in a magazine once. You'd have to be pretty spectacularly beautiful to go through life with names like those; luckily for them, they were. Gertrude told Wayland she must be Southern at heart since she hadn't wanted to name her babies any plain names, our loss. The husband's name was John or something like that. The name thing seemed to fall squarely in the mother's court, which Bert and I could obviously vouch for, and I didn't hear much about him.

Whit hadn't been home the day we went over there, but he was in the family pictures that were everywhere around Wayland's house. Whit was cute enough, but not like a magazine, so I could at least say hello without tripping all over myself. His name wasn't really Whit, it was Whitlock for some old guy back a few generations, maybe the one who'd made the boatloads of money they had. He didn't seem stuck up though. We always ended up in the same spot at sunset, looking out at the sun edging toward the horizon, waiting for the green blip. We didn't talk much, but that was okay with me.

He was out on a dock with some of his buddies, three of them, laughing and drinking beer, it looked like. They wore the standard conch uniform, tank tops, denim shorts, and flip-flops. Conch meant local down here, like townie at home. One guy had a baseball cap, its brim flipped toward the back. I thought about walking away before anyone saw me. Too late. That one saw me and tipped his chin up at Whit. Guys here had the same no-words language that guys had at home.

Whit turned and peered into the darkness. I couldn't tell if the one streetlight made it harder or easier to see who it was. "Hey. Annie, right?" I liked that he called me Annie even though Gertrude had said Leticia when she introduced me to his family like she always did, not knowing or probably caring that we'd already kind of met on our own, but she had to be in charge of everything about her friends. Of course I'd been stupid enough after that to mention that I already knew Whit, and now Wayland and Gertrude made little kiss-y noises when they talked about us, like there was an "us." I nodded.

"No sidekick tonight?"

I shook my head and willed myself to say something. Nothing came.

"Hey, cat got your tongue or what? You want a beer?"

I shook my head again but walked closer. The three guys took that as their cue to head out the opposite way I'd come. "Later, man." "See ya." An arm raised back over the head in mock salute came from the third.

I found my voice. "Hi. I was taking a walk."

"So I see. Looking for something special?"

"No. Just walking."

"Shouldn't you be in bed about now?" Whit raised an eyebrow, the double meaning of his talk all over his face. It was like the leer that Orlando used with Gertrude, only cuter, much cuter. The magazines said sex was all teenage boys thought about, except maybe sports and pizza.

The magazines also said guys like innocent girls. I decided to take his crack literally instead of trying to come up with some sexy comeback since I had no practice at that. "Everyone else at—back there—is sleeping. I'm not tired."

"Want a seat?" Whit gestured at a pair of lounge chairs making a V pointing out toward the water.

"Whose are they?" What kind of stupid question was that?

"Who cares? They're probably sleeping, like at your house and mine. We're not gonna hurt 'em any, just warm 'em up a little." Whit laughed and swung a muscled leg over one chair, its webbing glowing white beneath his tan skin. When he laughed, a long chunk of bleached hair fell across his eyes. He tossed it back in a practiced way. He patted the other chair like he was gesturing for a nervous dog to come.

I bit my lip and then made up my mind. I walked with a determined step and plunked myself down in the second chair so hard it tipped a little toward his. The leg thunked loudly when it hit the decking again. Even since I'd grown so tall, I couldn't sit right, couldn't stand right, couldn't walk right. It felt like someone had stolen my old skin and left me new, badly fitting skin, too tight in some places, too loose in others.

"Easy there, easy. No need to alert the Marines."

I laughed a small laugh.

"That's better, eh? Take a load off. What have you been up to today, Miss Annie I'm Not Tired?"

"Nothing really. It's too hot. How can you stand it here?"

"Me? I've never lived anywhere else. I wanna cool off, I just take a jump in the big pond." Whit indicated the water in front of us with his hand. It reminded me of waiters displaying the buffet in restaurants. "You like to swim?"

"Yeah, but I like it at home better. It's not even refreshing here; you feel the same when you come out as when you went in, just wetter."

"Wetter's good." Whit leaned closer and kissed me, quick, so quick I wasn't quite sure it had really happened. It was dry and kind of papery. Since the only boy I'd ever kissed was probably Ralph in the sandbox about a hundred years ago, I wasn't sure what it was supposed to feel like. I didn't want to think about Ralph. When I didn't draw back, he kissed me again. We did this for a while. It was okay. His lips pushed against mine, nudging mine open so his tongue could get in. Now it was wetter. And hotter. I didn't know what to do with my hands, so I left them at my sides. Then his arms pinned me in place when he hugged me. My eyes were closed, but I heard him twisting around, getting closer with his body, scraping the chair against the dock. He ran his hands up and down my arms, and I shivered. It seemed like he liked that.

I let him push me backward and then lie on top of me on the lounge chair. My feet were still on the dock from when I'd sat down, so I was kind of twisted. It didn't seem like I could move without making a big fuss. The kissing part wasn't too bad at first, I kind of liked it, but then he started wrenching my lips around until they felt chapped and sore. I don't know how they could when my face felt wet, but they did. His tongue went down my throat until I could hardly breathe. I pushed up against his chest with my hands and he backed off a little. His hands skimmed my flat, braless chest and kept moving. They ran up between my legs as he crouched like some kind of huge grasshopper. The hands reached for my belt, and I grabbed his wrists. Whit whined like Bert did when I told him enough dessert.

"Jack me off, then. That's fair," he gasped.

I didn't know what he was talking about, but when he moved my hand to his hard, hot crotch, it was clear quickly enough. The word hard-on seemed a lot more accurate about what he felt like than the real word erection that sounded like a building site. He unzipped his pants, inserted my shaking hand, and rubbed up and down, up and down, his hand guiding mine, faster and faster against my hand until it ached. Then, as suddenly as he'd begun, he was finished. Whit slumped against me like a ton of wet sand when Bert buried me alive. My hand felt like it did when Bert and I picked up clamshells the seagulls had dropped from on high, oozy and warm. I guessed it would dry stiff and white like that too. I had to get out of there. I struggled out the same way I'd come, to my right, and was on my feet.

"I gotta go." I was off running before Whit could grab me. I took one quick look back before I turned a corner to see if I'd left my skin behind. I wiped my hands on my shorts. I felt like I'd turned into someone else, someone cheap and sleazy, and he had, too. Whit was lying back in the lounge chair, looking out at the water or maybe dozing off. I grasped my elbows with my hands and hugged myself, trying to shake off the feeling of being such a loser.

When I see Whit again, I'll look him in the eye like nothing happened, blip, hey, that's his name now, Blip! Maybe I should've let Blip do what he wanted, gotten it over with. Having sex is just another step toward being an adult, and I've made most of the others. Then I can choose to have no one touch me ever again if I want. Being a kid hasn't been any great shakes in that department, other than the occasional good hug, and I sure could have done without the hitting.

19 FOOL

All my clothes are ugly. Or too small. Or something. Gertrude has clothes that look like she found them in the trash, like all the stuff she uses to make her sculptures, but somehow she looks all right when she's dressed. Plenty of guys check her out when we go anywhere, though not when Orlando's with us, her very own guard dog. She wears shorter shorts than some of the kids here, but I have to admit she has the legs for it. Too bad I didn't inherit those; my thighs are like hams and about that color too, sunburned. Then she makes sculptures in her so-called good clothes, and they look even worse from paint and glue and burn holes. There's this little girl in their neighborhood that has sores all over, and Gertrude says we should stay away because she's dirty. How does she define dirty exactly with dirt and crumbs and butts everywhere? The only person who lugs laundry down the street is me, and the shower is an orange dribble. Even Bert complains about the shower, not having to go in it like usual but "being rusty" when he comes out. Mayes would just die. She takes showers like twice a day. I'd call her and tell her more about this hellhole we called The Rock, like they called Alcatraz, even than in my letters, but Orlando of the giant hands has made it crystal clear no more long distance calls, too expensive. I'd do it in the middle of the night anyway, maybe we'd be gone before the bill came again, but Mayes wouldn't be able to come to the phone then unless it was an emergency. I could say it was an emergency, an I'm sure as hell dying here emergency. It's hard to explain that in a postcard, especially since everything looks so nice in the postcards that they give out for free in the hotel lobbies.

"Let's go down to Duvall. I want you to meet someone."

"Who?" I was hesitant because Gertrude was always wanting us to meet someone, and the someone was always weird, like the guy whose only name was Blue and had about a hundred ferrets. He talked to them like people, except he barely noticed people, and they were mean, like trying to bite you mean. He noticed Gertrude though; everyone did. Plus, whenever we met someone, then she just talked to them and ignored us. People all over town knew her name and called out and waved. Usually they said you must be her kids, she's always talking about you. I kept my head down and wondered what she talked about since she didn't know anything about us. Then that would be the last time Gertrude or her friend would take any notice of us.

"You'll see." Gertrude got her bag and walked out to the bikes.

"We're riding?" Bert wailed.

"Orlando has the truck picking up supplies. You know the car's not running. It's a beautiful day. Come on, Bertski." Gertrude always called Bert some nickname or other when she wanted something; she didn't call me anything but Leticia, not even Lettie usually.

Bert and I trudged around the house to the bikes, a pathetic collection of wheels, seats, and handlebars scrounged from what had to be a bunch of other bikes. Bert could hardly reach the pedals on any of them, and I couldn't get used to coaster brakes and was forever rolling through intersections, Bert yelling look out to all comers.

Bert and I mounted unsteadily and wobbled to the street. Gertrude was already off up the street, her hair flying behind her and giant sunglasses covering her eyes. We pedaled fast to catch up, Bert standing since he hadn't had time to get up on the seat.

When we got into town, Gertrude found a bike rack midway down the street. She never locked anything, cars or bikes or houses. It was a good thing too since she lost the car keys about once a day anyway. Bert and I pulled up, me slowing with my feet. Bert looked around and honed in on the ice cream place.

"Can we go?" He smiled his biggest smile.

Gertrude smiled, too, something I was sure she wouldn't have done at me. "Maybe after. I want you to meet my friend."

Who could the mysterious friend be, and how could it be such a good friend if we were just meeting them for the first time when we'd been down here forever it seemed like?

"Where? In there?" Bert pointed hopefully to the department store. He'd shown me a set of sand buckets and shovels he wanted. I had looked at the price and told him there was no way. The set was too big and clunky for me to get out of there with my usual alternative to paying for things.

"No. That's tourist junk. She works in the greatest place. Leticia, you're going to just love it. She's been up north the last few weeks, but now she's back." Gertrude said up north like it was a bad disease. She turned in down a winding path made out of stones. At the end of the path was a little gray and white cottage with curtains in the windows. Bert and I looked at each other. We'd passed this place when we went around town on days it wasn't too hot, days I defined as ones I could consider coming out from under the fan.

"It looks like a house, not somewhere anyone would work."

"Maybe she sells furniture, but why would Gertrude think I'd love that?" I answered my own question. "Who knows what she thinks about anything."

We followed Gertrude up the path and in the front door. Bells tinkled, so maybe it was a store then. Inside it looked like a house though. Pillows swarmed the armchairs, tablecloths and napkins were heaped but kind of arranged on a table, and clothes on silky hangers hung from open doors of cupboards and coat racks. It looked like a magazine shoot for what you could do with a cute seaside cottage. A woman with all her hair piled on top of her head and skewered with sticks was cleaning a glass case.

"Samantha?"

The woman looked up and her dreamy, soft face glowed. If there were angels on earth, they looked like this woman. "Gertrude! I was hoping you'd come by today. And look, you've brought them!" She breathed this last sentence like we were awesome.

"Yep! Engelbert and Leticia, I'd like you to meet Samantha." Gertrude waved us forward. "Come on, she won't bite. I bet after five minutes you love her as much as everyone in town does."

We edged in, glancing around as we came. Everything was so sparkly. A row of crystals hung in the windows and threw rainbows dancing here and there. A basket of fool's gold sat on the corner of a table and twinkled. A bowl of agate marbles, itty bitty ones like peas and ones as big as walnuts, sat next to a wooden maze. Bert slowed.

"Careful, Bert."

Samantha's laughter sounded like her door chime. "That's all right. You go ahead, that maze has your name on it." Bert grinned and reached for a marble. Samantha came forward; it was like she floated. "Now, Leticia, if you're like me when I was your age, you have a nickname instead of the mouthful of syllables your mother saddled you with." She held out her hand, a silver ring on each finger. I glanced at Gertrude. Samantha didn't seem to notice the pouty look Gertrude had.

I shook her hand loosely. Hers was warm and soft, and I didn't want to let go. "Annie. I like Annie."

Samantha looked from me to Gertrude and back. "What do you think, if you call me Sammi, I'll call you Annie. You can be Leticia when you're older if you want, you say the word. That's what friends do, they respect each other's wishes. And you and I are going to be good friends. I can feel it. Deal?"

"Deal." I took my hand back and put both hands in the pockets of my shorts. When my stomach rolled over the top of the shorts, I took my hands back out and pulled my tee shirt down.

"So how's your visit been? What do you think of our little island?"

"It's pretty nice. Kind of hot though."

"Oh, you get used to it." Sammi laughed. "I came here from the Midwest. We got feet, feet! of snow there. When I first came here, I missed home like anything. But I got to like it so much, now when I go back to visit, I'm always freezing there, even without snow."

"You like it better here now?" I picked at the hem of my shirt where it was unraveling.

"I do." She looked at me appraisingly. "You know, I think one of the reasons you're so hot is those clothes! Three of you could fit in that tee shirt. Let me take a look and see what I have. I love a new guinea pig!" She buzzed around the store, stopping here and there like she was collecting pollen. Usually I thought it was corny when someone spoke with exclamation points, like who could really be that excited about life, but Sammi seemed for real. That bit about the guinea pig bothered me though.

I turned to Gertrude, hoping against hope that she wouldn't sucker punch me, but I had no one else to ask. I wanted to like Sammi. "What does she mean, guinea pig? Does she think I'm fat?"

"Fat? No! She meant guinea pig for trying things on, haven't you ever heard that, like a test?" Gertrude asked. "But Sammi's right, hiding under that huge shirt isn't the answer. Women should show off their bodies." She looked at Sammi for confirmation as she circled back our way.

"That is so right. Women are always making that mistake, buying bigger to hide the parts they don't like. I say there are no bad parts, only bad clothes. Let's get you out of that tent and into some of these!" She held up an armload of multi-colored clothes and pointed. "Right in there."

Even the curtains were beautiful with spangles that glimmered when Sammi's arm swept them aside. Clearly she liked shiny. Then again, she wore all white with not a sparkle on her. Maybe she thought tourists liked shiny. She'd be right.

"Let's start with these," Sammi handed me an assortment of tee shirts, a little skirt, and some overall shorts. I obediently went in, and Sammi let the curtains fall.

I had pulled my shirt over my head and was undoing my belt when Gertrude called, "We're going to get a little snack. Bert's restless. See you in a while." Her breezy voice headed toward the door.

"You two take your time. We have plenty to keep us busy!" Sammi cried with a whoop. I didn't know people really whooped. Is that a word?

"'Bye, Annie." Bert sounded eager to leave, even without the promise of food. He wasn't a big shopper. I liked to look until I remembered that I couldn't buy anything, then the shopping trip soured. I wasn't sure where this one was going, but Sammi's enthusiasm made me game to find out.

While I was changing, the bells rang. Sammi went to help the new customer. "You hang tight there, girl, she's been in before. I'll have her in and out before you know it."

I peeked out to watch. A woman with linebacker shoulders was saying she'd come for those shoes she'd put on hold. Sammi dangled these tiny pink sandals from straps thinner than licorice whips. The woman grunted when she reached for them. Her legs below her enormous shorts drooped in folds around her knees and ankles like a giant tortoise in a cartoon and looked about as fast. I could hardly see her feet. I glanced at Sammi, and she shot me a look that clear as day said don't mess up this sale. I smirked and waited where I was.

"I thank you, and you come again now."

"Thank you, I will." Tortoise had a deep, booming voice that went with her big, booming self.

When the door had closed behind the giant tortoise, oops tourist, Sammi exhaled. "That'll pay the rent! Now I know what you are thinking, but doesn't everyone deserve to feel beautiful? She did have tiny feet, a size five, under all that, that self," she frowned that she couldn't think of a better word, "So I guess she likes to focus on them. She might even have a disease or something, we can't say for sure."

"Sure we can, the disease of sticking too much food in her mouth," I declared.

"It's easy to judge others when we are perfect ourselves, is it not, miss?" Sammi arched her eyebrows at me, and I felt bad that she thought I was stuck up. I wasn't really, it's just that I felt bad about myself so much of the time that it was a relief to focus on someone else's faults. I couldn't explain that to Sammi though, I didn't know her that well. "You ready? Show yourself!" Sammi demanded.

I came out looking at the ground. I had on a green and white striped tee shirt with a scoop neck and khaki shorts cut smaller than any I'd ever worn. She was a good guesser on size even though I didn't like what the tags said. Twelve. When had that happened?

"Ooo, cute. What do you think?"

"I don't know."

"How can you not know? Those are you, girl. Put on something else, and give me those." Somehow there was no resisting that voice, kind but firm at the same time.

I paraded through in outfit after outfit and began to really enjoy myself. I didn't even look in the mirror after a while; I just tried to imagine I looked as good as Sammi said I did. Once I caught myself strutting a little in a white strapless bathing suit with black tuxedo trim.

"That is spectacular! I knew it would be. I know what it needs though," Sammi raced around the store, poking here and there, and came back with a pair of shoes and a hat, "and it needs these!" She thrust the new items at me.

I held the shoes like they might melt away in my hands. They were clear plastic with what the magazines called a kitten heel, who knows why since I didn't think high heels were called cats. It was cheesy, but when I slipped my feet into them, I felt like Cinderella. I'd never tell anyone that. Now the hat was a different story. It was a little black pillbox with an elastic strap that went beneath the chin. Who wore these? Bellhops like in that Eloise book. I looked at it hesitantly.

"For me, put it on for me, please!" Sammi pleaded, her hands clasped at her chin like in prayer.

"Just for a second. It's going to look silly," I murmured. I took a quick peek at the door to make sure no one was coming, then I perched the hat on my head with one hand and snapped the string beneath my chin.

"Wait! Wait right there!" Sammi ran for the counter and dashed around behind it. She sunk from view and then came back up, camera in hand.

"Oh, no—"

"Oh, yes, you could be an ad you look so darling. Look right here, sugar." Snap. "This is a great idea. Let's do some more. Put those short-alls back on with the tank, but keep the shoes. The shoes are it."

I could have stayed there all day, trying on clothes and listening to Sammi talk. Her voice was soothing and made it sound like everything was more fun than I could ever imagine. I even forgot about being hot with the big fans whirring up on the ceiling and the magnolia trees shading the little house. Maybe I had fallen into a fairy tale. If so, when would the clock strike midnight? It always did, and for sure in my life.

The bells above the door tinkled, and they might as well have rung a death knell. "Samantha? Leticia? Where is everyone?"

"We're over here." Sammi waved a hand from the dressing area. I dropped the curtain and pulled off the latest shirt and skirt. "No, wait, show them how cute you look!"

"Too late. Just me," I came out in my own shorts and big shirt and reached up to loop the curtain back the way it was. I crouched and began putting clothes back on hangers. I knew better than to keep Gertrude waiting.

"You're quick! Hold on though, Miss Neat, what are we getting here?" Sammi waved an arm at the heaps of clothes on the chair and the floor.

I kept my head down, letting Gertrude answer and dreading it. I held my breath and prayed anyway.

"Oh, Samantha, you know we don't have the money for this. I told you. I thought it'd be fun for her, and you said this was your slowest day."

"I know, I know, but she looked so cute! She even smiled a few times. Let me think," Sammi began pulling clothes from the piles. "This one here's on sale, and this one, it's nothing, nothing I tell you, and she has to have these." She pushed the short-alls at Gertrude. "Those are my treat. I'm buying her those. You've been working a lot lately; I know you have. You get her these," She held out the khaki shorts and two shirts, the striped tee I had on first and the tank with the lace trim that I loved the most. There was no room for argument in her voice.

"I don't know…" Gertrude began.

I prayed harder, even though you're supposed to pray to be a better person, not to get stuff.

"I know," Sammi snatched back the clothes and sped to the counter. "I'll check the sale prices and ring them up."

"She was really nice, spending all this time with me, and she's your friend, right? Can't you just buy them?" I wheedled. I hated the sound of my voice.

"Easy for you to say, young lady. I don't see you paying for them or anything else. Money doesn't grow on trees, you know."

I lost it. "That makes you sound like you're a hundred, you know," I mimicked back her tone perfectly. "It's not like you've ever bought me anything. Why did you bring me here anyway, if you weren't going to get anything?"

"I thought you'd enjoy meeting my friend," Gertrude spoke through her nose when she was angry. "I thought you could have a fun time together. And don't talk to me about not buying you anything. I've paid in more ways than you can ever imagine."

"Paid for what? What are you talking about? You never talk about anything real. Why'd you leave anyway? Were we too expensive? Or were you just too selfish to be a mom?"

Gertrude dragged in her breath like she was trying to breathe through a snorkel. "Who's talking about selfish? You're the reason I couldn't have Bert. Your father wouldn't let me take him. He said you wanted to stay together. How do you think that made me feel?"

"I was seven. You are blaming a seven-year-old for your problems? You're the one who left. You're the one who's supposed to be a grown-up. I guess that's still not happening, huh?" I didn't wait for a response. "I hate you! I wish you'd just stayed out of our lives! We were better off!" I swiped at my eyes, furious with myself that I'd cried because of her. I bolted for the door, and when I had it open and one foot out, I made myself stop to call out, "Thanks anyway, Sammi. It was great to meet you." I needed her to be my friend since she'd stood up to Gertrude. And I needed something else, too. "Are you coming, Bert?"

Bert looked back and forth a few times like a spectator watching a tennis game. He ran to my side and took my hand. I breathed. I hadn't realized I was holding my breath. We went out the door together, and

Gertrude did nothing to stop us.

Gertrude was all smiles when we got back, tired from walking around the rest of the afternoon in the heat. "Do you want some iced tea? I just made it." Iced tea was the only thing she could make without burning it. She waved her hand at the pitcher, the glasses, and the sugar bowl. She even had a cut-up lemon ready, a budding Martha Stewart.

I looked at her wearily. Bert did his back-and-forth bit again. What choice did we have really? It's not like we had anywhere to go. "Sure."

Bert smiled and held out his hand for a glass.

The tea was icy cold but bitter. I dumped in one, two, three spoons of sugar and stirred. When I drank the sugar gritted in my teeth, like biting your nails without the blood. Perfect.

She is too much. I can't believe she blamed me for everything. That is so typical. Who blames a seven-year-old for the mess of her life? Did I really say I wanted to stay with Joel? I wish I could talk to Dory, but since I can't use the phone, that's going to be tough. I swear Orlando would wake out of a druggie sleep if I even picked up the receiver. Orlando has perfect hearing for the things he wants, but he's totally deaf about everything else. Like the other day when I said we needed milk for cereal, and two minutes later he was yelling that there was no milk for his precious coffee. The Bustelo. With that phony accent, like he's so hip on foreign culture. I don't know how the guy made it out of fifth grade with his vocabulary; maybe he didn't. How does he do the math for his building projects the way he cooks his brain? People are always calling complaining about him not showing up for days on end once he has the advance, but new people are always calling, too. He must have some charm I can't see. Didn't he ever see that ad with the egg, the one about drugs and your brain? Yup, fried. Or maybe scrambled. Luckily I know he didn't build this dump, or I'd be worrying about it falling down, like I need a new thing to worry about. She's no better, pretending she's only smoking clove cigarettes when any idiot knows it's pot. Does she think I'm that stupid? Even Bert knows what pot smells like by now. Not to mention what a hypocrite she is, raving like a lunatic whenever she has wine, which is often, when she said drinking was why she had to leave or at least that's what Joel said. She's like this kid at school who took Advil and then was screaming and yelling and tearing off his clothes like they burned since he's allergic.

20 BLOCK

You never know with her whether she's going to hold things against you forever or whether she's already forgotten it as soon as it's out of your mouth. Maybe that's her plan, to throw us off so we won't go after her on the tough stuff. That's the first thing I've ever even gotten her to say about back then, that I picked to stay with Joel. Usually I ask stuff and she answers back talking about something completely else. I know she hears me though because she does this thing with her shoulders, pulls them up against her ears for a second like she's cold, and then they're down and she's moving on. I'd like to be able to do that, block out whatever I don't want to hear. Like with Joel, it's always, I'm waiting for an answer, young lady, like He ever answers me. Then it's always some preachy thing like Wait 'til you're older and find out for yourself. Maybe that's how they got together, each of them talking but only hearing themselves.

I hunched my shoulders when I entered the kitchen like I could make myself smaller or invisible or something. Orlando and his friend were sitting at the kitchen table, and Orlando's legs were stretched across the floor in front of the refrigerator, my goal. Billy was skinny where Orlando was wide and pale where Orlando was sunburned. It was hard to imagine Billy working outside; he looked more like a night creature, slick and white like a slug oozing its way across the path searching for its next drink. It was only two o'clock, but they were done for the day. Later, when they saw Gertrude, she'd hear about how hard they'd worked today, how hot it had been out in the sun. They were passing a crooked joint back and forth, their squinty eyes red and dry. A beam of light through the window above the sink cut through the dust in the air and illuminated the slow smoke as it drifted toward the ceiling. I tried not to breathe, and I didn't look at either of them as I went around the backside of the table.

"She's a hottie. Whyn't you bring her around the job?"

"She's a little young for you, Billy. Plus she's got a mouth on her."

"I like 'em with a good mouth, you know, for—"

"I am STANDING right here, you lunkheads."

"See what I mean about the mouth?"

"Oh, that kind a mouth. I don' like that kind so much. I like the kind—"

"Shut up, Billy."

I retrieved the half-empty container of iced tea and two kind-of clean glasses and left the kitchen without further comment. Beano squawked hello as I went by, but I didn't even look his way. I felt bad he was in here by himself, but I was too scared of Orlando to risk bringing him outside. Sure, Beano loved Bert, all animals did, but Beano might love freedom more. So now we had a drink at least, but we were stuck outside.

I got us started on hanging out in town. I didn't give my real reason, but it became obvious pretty quickly. "We need some exercise. We'll go into town and walk around for a while. It'll be good for us. I bet it's more exercise in the heat, your heart working and everything."

Bert didn't mind. He had tons of energy and nothing to do.

"Let's see if we can go in every store in town. Maybe we'll see some cool stuff."

"But we don't have any money, Annie."

"It doesn't matter. We'll just look. We'll make our Christmas lists. You know, for Santa."

Bert looked at me to see if I was serious and decided I was. "Okay."

I mostly took little things like I had in Provincetown, a pencil with stars on it, a tube of mascara. I practiced the casual stroll around the store, the close inspection of something far from what I planned to take, the check around for cameras or security guys. Stores that had those we headed back out right away. Bert didn't say anything after the first time.

"Annie, what about what happened in the music store? They don't check or anything like that, do they?"

"You mean do they know what happened all those miles away? I don't think so, big guy."

"Why are you doing it? Some of the stuff you don't even want, I know it."

"I just feel like it. I like the thrill. You got any better ideas of what to do?"

"Maybe we could make some friends, you know, look around some more—"

"Have you noticed any kids really? I haven't. It doesn't seem like a real family kind of place here, you know? Maybe only selfish people live here. That's it. I'm trying to fit in."

His puzzled face wobbled, looking for the joke and not finding it. He played it as straight as he saw it. "I still wish you wouldn't. I know you're not really selfish. You do lots of nice things for me. Even for Him." Bert's eyes clouded. "What do you think He's doing now?"

"Probably drinking." I continued hurriedly when I saw his face crumpling up like a used napkin. "You mean, do I think He misses us? Who the hell knows?" I did miss Him, I missed a lot of things about our life that I thought was crap before we came down here, but damned if I was going to tell Bert that. Like most things about feelings, what good did it do you to tell anyone? I'd feel worse if Bert started blubbering.

"You think that makes you sound so grown-up, swearing and everything. You're not though. We're just kids."

"I feel like I was never a kid." I looked hard at Bert. "You haven't had the best childhood either, though I've tried to do most of the work." Five years between us most of the year (Bert loved the few months after his birthday when it was only four), but sometimes it felt like twenty. "I wish you could have had better. Want a pencil?"

I took bigger risks when Bert wasn't with me. I brought heaps of shirts and shorts and skirts into dressing rooms and put them on under my baggy clothes. I made friends with salesclerks who were bored in the long, slow summer and then robbed them blind when they turned their backs. I nicked scarves and hairclips off counters while they rustled underneath for register tapes or pens. I stole a pair of gold silk pants that were as thin as tissue paper and a green shimmery sweater that slid off one shoulder and gave up the fantasy that anyone would ever believe I'd bought these things.

I don't know how I'll get all the stuff home. I hide it in grocery bags under the bed and never even look at it. It's like I'm collecting more and more to see what will happen, but nothing does. Isn't that what everyone says about teenagers, they're acting out to get attention? Not me. I'm acting out because, well, what the hell? It's hard to imagine my life getting any worse, and actually it's thrilling every time I get away with it, like it's soothing every time I rip a piece of skin off my cuticle and then lick away the blood and the sting. It's funny though, taking all this stuff doesn't remind me of taking the CD in Provincetown and what happened after that. I don't know why I'm not afraid of getting caught. There are signs everywhere about shoplifters. I just feel so invisible that I can't imagine anyone even noticing me.

21 SEPARATE

Time moves so slowly here that I think it's going backwards, like in those teen movies about school where the clock ticks in reverse and everyone gawks.

Jimmy Buffet drawled out of the speakers, like he did everywhere we went, "son of a son of a sailor" that he was. "He should be the national bird of Florida, with that "Parrothead" thing. Why don't they ever play anything else?" I complained.

"Oh, you're no fun," Gertrude threw back. "Jimmy's the best, now that Jerry's gone."

"Right, more drunk party songs, that's what the world needs."

"Better than those depressed whiners you listen to all the time. Neil Young can't even carry a tune he's so down," Orlando scoffed. "Lighten up a little, Leticia. It's all right to have a good time." He began to sing along with Jimmy, scuffing his flip-flop back and forth against the wooden floor in time. It was so big it looked more like a surfboard than a shoe.

I winced. I looked around. Diamond Lil's. It was flashy all right, but more like CZ. Pink CZ. We'd been waiting a while, but now the hostess or whatever was coming our way, sashaying to the music. It was hard to imagine that she was this enthusiastic all the time, but maybe she was related to Sammi.

"Howdy, folks. Welcome to Diamond Lil's. Ya'll been here before?"

Orlando spoke up with his voice booming over her squeak. "We have," the usual leash arm hung over Gertrude, "they're new." He hitched a thumb at Bert and me, like he meant to insult us somehow. Me, I liked it every way that we were separate from them, every single way.

"Ah, virgins, my lucky day! Well, Ah'm gonna seat you with an ol' pro, she'll show you a good time. This way." We followed her wiggling ass to a table in the center of the floor, one of the few empty ones. "Ya'll's server'll be right along. Enjoy."

Just like the hostess said she would, our server came right over. Her boobs in her uniform stuck out straight and pointy like ice cream cones. One of them, Lefty, wore a pin written in curly-q letters that said her name was Sal. She was taller than Orlando with her hair, also pink. Sal had a heavy drawl, so heavy it sounded like bad TV, and she smelled like she'd been out back smoking then covered it over with perfume and bubble gum. Her teeth were huge like pasted-on Chiclets. Grownups were so obvious about trying to look younger.

"Well howdy-doo. Ah'm Sal, like the tag says," a finger jabbed her breast, but it didn't move, "and I'll be ya'll's server ta-day. What kin Ah git you from the bar?" Her laugh brayed like a donkey and traveled. Other diners looked around like where was the farm.

Orlando ordered, of course. "We'll have a couple of longnecks, nice and cool, and whatever they want, Shirleys or Bobs, like that." He winked at Sal like they were old friends.

"Ha! Bobs! Ah love that! Ah'm gonna use that my-self!" Sal's face split wide with her grin. It looked real. Maybe it was. She turned to Bert. "Honey, you want a Shirley Temple? Or else we got root beer, real good root beer, and Coke and that stuff, too. What it's gonna be, sweet boy? Is thayt a heart bu-tween your eyes? That is just the cutest thang I ever seen." She looked closer at Bert's face.

Bert beamed. I was surprised. Maybe Sal reminded him of Martini Tina. "Can I have root beer? Please?"

"Sure, sugar, you kin have any little ol' thang your heart desires, either of 'em." Sal sent a wave of laughter around the restaurant, bouncing against the mirrors. "You, too, sweetie-pie?" She looked at me; everyone at the table did. Maybe it had been a little while since she asked.

"Uh, no, iced tea," I gulped.

"Cat got your tongue? What do we say when we want something?" Orlando growled like some kind of beast on show for Sal.

"Please... please."

"Why, sure, I'll be right back with those. Y'all take a gander at the men-you," she said it like two different words, "and Ah'll be back in a flash. Y'all be good while Ah'm gone; I wouldn't wanna miss nothin'!"

"She's a riot! I think she remembers you, Orlando, from last time. I'll have to watch out; she's got her eye on you!" Gertrude did her little kitten face, which worked every time. I wanted to throw up.

"Now, cupcake, you know it's like you're the only woman in the room wherever I go. It's me who has to keep an eye out. All men are pigs—I should know!" His laugh boomed out again, and my skin crawled.

I kicked Bert under the table while the two of them made kiss-y faces at each other and whimpered. Why did people call each other food products? Like cupcake wasn't bad enough, a million calorie hunk of dough, sweet. There's Sugar, Honey, Sweetie Pie. Bert isn't the only one who is obsessed. But back to them. They are so queer. "Pop-Tart."

"Pretzel."

"Twinkie."

"Devil Dog."

"Scone."

"Scone? What the heck is a scone?"

I shushed him though we were both clearly dying to laugh. "We should look at the menu. What kind of thing do you want, Bert, chicken?"

Orlando jerked his eyes away from Gertrude's. "None of that namby-pamby crap. We're all having meat, big meat!"

"Do I hear an order, big man? Steak, is that what you're talkin'?" Sal had snuck back to the table without us noticing. Who knew someone so loud could sneak?

"Better. Cheeseburgers. Cheeseburgers in paradise!"

"The works?"

"The works!"

"But, Orlando, we don't—"

"Could you not be such a fucking spoil sport? For once?" His glare told me he was going to take my head off if I didn't. "The works!"

"All right, man wants his beef, man'll get his beef before y'all know it." Sal swung her hips away from the table while she snapped her gum. It sounded like those crackers guys throw in the street on Fourth of July.

Orlando's eyes returned to Gertrude's face like they were magnetized there.

"So what'd we get?" Bert whispered.

I quickly scanned the menu and groaned.

"What?" Bert's voice sounded a little hysterical.

"It's all right. I'll scrape everything off. You'll see."

"But what is it?"

"If I tell you, you won't eat it."

"I will. I promise. I just want to know."

I narrowed my eyes at him. I struck the first blow. "You asked for it. Cole slaw."

Bert stayed strong. "Is that all?"

"Pickles."

Still he didn't buckle. "Yeah? More?"

"Mushrooms. Onions."

"Raw?" His voice rose.

"Shh. Yes, raw. I told you, I'll take everything off. The cheese and the ketchup will hide the taste."

"What kind of cheese?" Only a squeak came out now.

"Um…"

"Tell me." I'd never heard anyone on death row, but I was pretty sure their voice would sound like Bert's.

"Swiss." We gave that the moment of silence that it deserved.

"Do you think he picked everything I don't like on purpose?"

"Who knows, Bert, who the hell knows?"

Sal had plates balanced up and down her arms like they weighed nothing. When she put them down, they barely fit on the table. Fries spilled off the sides and onto the tablecloth. I leaned closer and sniffed. Spicy pepper, it figured.

"Anything else I kin get y'all? More drinks, all around? Free refills for the kiddies." Her smile shone with new sticky pink lipstick.

Orlando had already wrapped his mitt-sized hands around the ginormous burger and mashed what looked like half of it in his mouth. He grunted.

Sal didn't even look disgusted. "O-kay, then, y'all enjoy. Save some room for dee-zert."

I glanced at Orlando to check whether he was watching, too busy stuffing his face. Starting with what was in front of me, I took hold of the burger the size of a cow's head and began to scrape; big blops of sauce and vegetables rained onto the plate. A ring of shiny purple onion bounced off the slippery tablecloth and rolled across the floor. Let someone else clean up something for a change. When the meat was bare, I ladled on ketchup and swapped it for Bert's. I tried a fry, and my eyes teared up. My throat was on fire. I chugged from my water glass.

"The fries're pretty hot so you keep your water handy. Eat. I know you're hungry."

I denuded my own burger—what a word—and took a bite. A fat drop of ketchup oozed out the side of the bun and fell onto my shirt. Perfect. I tried to chew without breathing to block the raw onion taste. I looked at Bert. He was eating itty bitty bites like some kind of sparrow. When I looked at Gertrude, she was doing even worse than we were. She hardly ate anything when other people were watching anyway. Her second beer was empty, and she was playing with her pickle. When Orlando asked her how her food was, she picked up her burger and nodded eagerly. When he looked away, she put it down.

I thought we were going to make it through a meal without someone freaking out, but then Orlando noticed what I'd done to our food. Bert had even taken off half of his bun because otherwise it was too tall to fit in his mouth. "What the hell is wrong with you two? It looks like giant birds took a crap on your plates."

"What does it matter, *Monsieur Lion*?" She pronounced it lee-oh.

"Enjoy your meal. There's no need to get all upset." When she got going with the nicknames in French, I knew we were all walking a fine line. Gertrude wasn't taking our side or anything. It was more like she didn't want him to check out her plate next.

"What matters is that Paradise Ain't Free, you know, like I put on those bumper stickers. We're gonna make a mint on those, but still, I'm not throwing it all out the window on these two little Commies who won't even eat a good old, All-American burger."

"Like you're so American. You don't even pay taxes."

Bert looked at me like I had finally lost my mind, egging Orlando on when we were already twigs in a hurricane about to be snapped with the next gust.

"What would you know about that, Miss High and Mighty? You been rifling my drawers, I swear—" He raised his hand in my direction.

"It's not tough to figure out. You make everyone pay you in cash. That's a big clue. People do it all the time on the Cape, too. I don't know what the government has ever done for me, but don't go dissing me when you are so much worse."

"Right, always the bad guy. I try to take you out for a nice dinner, people are dying to get into this place, and all you do is bitch and moan."

"Maybe if you'd let us order for ourselves, we'd be eating something."

"This is their specialty, known far and wide! You are so uptight. Why don't you live a little? Be more like True here?" Orlando put his arm (in the gnarly blue sweatshirt of course) around Gertrude and pulled her close. She started whispering in his ear, probably trying to calm him down or who knows, maybe trying to distract him from her own full plate. He didn't say anything when a busboy came to clear and asked if we wanted anything wrapped up to take home. He waved his hand over the table like a movie star waving away the riff-raff.

When Sal came back blabbering about their five million dessert specials, Orlando cut her off and barked, "Just the check."

She gawked at him, but it must have been obvious that the fun was over. "All right-y then. Too full, huh? I'll be right back with that."

They make me sick. Do they think they're cute? It's disgusting the way they paw at each other in public. It's bad enough Bert and I should hear it at their house. I'm hoping Bert doesn't know what they're doing. One time he asked me what all the noise was during "naptime," and I said someone must be having a bad dream. What am I supposed to say? They're screwing around like the dogs you see in the bushes? It's enough to make me never want to have sex, it's so disgusting sounding. The thought of him touching her makes me want to puke. I try to keep as far away from him as possible so he doesn't get any ideas. He's like some kind of sicko circus clown with those teeth and those huge hands and feet and that hair, flyaway blond toupee hair, and that laugh.

The laugh is the worst. No, I take it back. The fake accent is the worst. And she eats it up, all of it, like he's the best thing she's ever seen, and everyone should want to get their hands on him. That's her genius though: when she gets insecure she always turns it around so he starts talking about how great she is.

22 SAIL

"Get your suits on. Today is your lucky day. The master is going to teach you a thing or two, even though you think you know everything." Orlando leered and beetled his eyebrows across his forehead. I didn't know if he was going to beat us or sell us to passing gypsies, but I went to do what he said. I decided not to get into all things no one had taught me; who had time? Some days it just seemed easier than arguing.

Bert looked surprised when I didn't say anything, but I just tilted my head at the ladder for him to go ahead of me. Then I remembered our suits were in the yard drying. "I'll get the suits and throw yours up to you. See if there are any dry towels up there."

I went out front and got Bert's suit off the railing. It felt pretty dry. The lining had snagged on something, but Bert probably wouldn't care. I looked around for mine. I was sure I'd left it on the railing, too, when we'd come back from the Pier House. Sneaking in there was the best fun we'd had since we came to The Rock, as we called Key West, and it was really easy since Sammi got us those pink towels. You had your pink towel, you were in. The water was great and actually cooled you off with a diving board and everything. They had these water aerobics classes for guests that I thought sounded like a blast and might do something for my flab, but that was probably pushing it since it was hard to define us as guests.

I walked down the steps and squatted. I turned my head to see if it had blown under the house. Nothing. I heard a scuffling sound down the alley and looked toward it. Two dogs whose ribcages were showing were fighting over something colored, meat maybe, no, too stretchy, ugh, my bathing suit. As much as I hated that thing, I wasn't happy to see it caught between two sets of fangs. What had gotten them started on it? Then I remembered the ice cream bars we'd had after our swim. Being a klepto had its advantages, but I must have dripped. It was surprising I hadn't thought of it before, but now I realized I'd have to steal me a new bathing suit. God knows I needed one. I'd come up with something for where I got it, Sammi maybe. She wouldn't rat me out. It wasn't like I'd steal from her. Trouble was I needed a suit now. Maybe I'd go in in my clothes. Who cared how I looked anyway? All right, I did. I trudged back inside with Bert's bathing suit. I threw Bert's suit up to him and then stood in the hall thinking whether I had any other options.

"You ready? You got your suit on?" Gertrude's voice startled me out of my reverie where I had been contemplating what my new suit should look like. Right. I hadn't yet had the nerve to wear anything I'd stolen.

"No. I can't find it."

"It can't have gone far; you were swimming this morning, right?" Somehow her tone implied that we were the luckiest children on earth swimming more than once a day. I begged to differ but held my tongue.

"It's out in the yard being ripped in half by two dogs. Is that what you'd call far?"

"I know that suit is not your favorite, but there is no need to be snide and go making up stories, young lady. If you can bring your snooty self to ask nicely, you could wear one of mine for today."

I could think of nothing worse than wearing her idea of a bathing suit, that is, until I thought of wearing nothing at all, which is what I had. I debated if it was worth telling her to look out the window for herself but decided that with the way my luck went, the dogs would be gone by then anyway. "That'd be good. Thanks."

She sniffed sharply. "I'll bring you one. Then let's hurry. Orlando doesn't like to be kept waiting." In case I didn't know that already.

She'd had the grace or forethought or sheer dumb luck to bring me a dark colored leotard so at least all my private parts wouldn't be on display. I didn't know what she had against real bathing suits, but she didn't have a single one. I'd checked when I'd rummaged their drawers. I thought Bert was going to wet himself while I did it. Not me though. The thrill was deep and wide in me, coursing up and down my veins while I looked and laughed at what I found, rolling papers and fruit flavored rubbers and pills of different colors and sizes like M&Ms and Skittles but not. They had more toys than we did, and we were supposed to be the kids. Typical.

We didn't go to the beach where we usually went, that postage stamp that belonged to the town surrounded by the spreads of the rich-y riches. Instead we went toward the bridge that we'd taken to Diamond Lil's and pulled into a shell parking lot right beside it.

"What are we doing here?" I asked.

"I see your patience is as good as ever, Leticia. Perhaps Her Majesty wouldn't mind getting her ass out of the car and giving me a hand."

Orlando's face was inches from mine, so much for personal space, and his bulk completely filled in the cutout between the seats. I could smell pot and onions on his breath. Maybe I should call him His Highness. He probably wouldn't even get it.

I got out. All around the lot people were toting big surfboards and armfuls of bright, shiny cloth. I looked at the harbor and didn't see any big waves, but what did I know. Then I got it. Further out people were sailing on the boards, standing up and holding on. I realized I'd seen people do it in the Provincetown harbor, but I'd thought they were in little boats like Sunfish or something like that. They looked like bright birds, swooping and flashing among the waves, going so fast it reminded me of cartoons where boats sail into the sunset in an instant, flash, and they were over the horizon. I wanted to be like those birds more than I'd ever wanted anything, and that included when I'd wanted Joel to quit drinking and when I'd wanted her to come back to us. I figured this wish was just as unlikely as the rest.

I walked closer to the water and stood watching two guys put the pieces together with my arms crossed over my chest. One with a crew cut and a totally flat stomach looked up, saw me, and looked back down. That was encouraging.

I heard movement behind me and turned to see Orlando, Gertrude, and Bert coming my way with their arms full. Orlando and Gertrude each had one of the surfboards; Orlando also had the sail rigging in his broad arms, while Bert staggered along with another one and two wooden sword-like pieces. When they got close, Orlando laid down his gear more carefully than I think he would have a baby. I was surprised to see him slot the pieces together like he'd done it thousands of times. I couldn't picture him making the moves the surfers out there were making, swoops and turns and even jumps when they hit a swell full on, but maybe I was wrong. I was even more surprised when I noticed Gertrude was the same, practiced and sure. She was telling Bert what she was doing as she went along.

She held up the wooden sword by its handle. "This is the rudder, Engie, it helps you steer like it does in a boat. It goes in this hole here on the board, but you can't put it in until you are in deep enough water. If it gets wedged in the sand on the bottom, it could snap." She shivered at the thought of this, maybe because of a sudden chill or maybe the thought of how mad Orlando would be if that happened.

"What're they called?" I hoped she'd answer rather than Orlando; for once I got my wish. Hopefully I hadn't used up my quota on something so stupid.

"Windsurfers. Haven't you seen them in Provincetown?"

"Yeah, but I thought they were boats. I didn't know you rode on them."

"It's kind of like a boat except you can't sit down. Well, you can give someone a ride, but that's not really sitting down either."

"Did you rent these?" I didn't see anywhere that could have happened, and plus they'd come down to the beach pretty fast.

"Oh, no. These are ours. We keep them here; everyone does." She pointed to a rack kind of like a bike rack but with bigger slots at the back of the parking lot.

"Is it hard?" I tried to sound nonchalant.

"It's a little tricky at first, but then you get it. Orlando's a great teacher." She looked at him adoringly, and I thought we'd lost them for the duration. It'd be hours before they resurfaced from the murk of each other's eyes. But I was wrong about that, too. "You want to try?"

"Yeah. Yeah, I do. Can you show me how?" I held my breath, praying she would agree but knowing in my heart she wouldn't.

"Oh, no, I'm only learning myself. I told you, Orlando's a great teacher. Let's get down to the water. You'll see." She moved with her board assembly down toward the water where Orlando was waiting in his tiny red suit. "I can't wait for you to learn. You're going to love it, just love it. It's the best feeling."

I dragged my feet through the sand, torn between wanting to learn and dreading the lesson.

Maybe she'd be impressed if it turned out I was good at it. That would be something. The things that usually impressed grownups, like being smart and getting good grades, actually seemed like turn-offs to her. That was me though, and weren't you supposed to love everything, or almost everything, about your kid? Then again, weren't you supposed to love everything about your parents until they embarrassed the hell out of you? Somehow we'd skipped that step, too. What step were we on, exactly?

"You going to do it?" Bert eyed me quizzically.

"How hard can it be, right? If he can do it." We both knew who I meant. Still, it wasn't like I was much of an athlete, not like Bert who was the pride of Little League. I could run all right, for a long time anyway, if you didn't need me to go too fast. I had puny arms though. How strong did you have to be to hold the sail thing up?

His voice boomed out as I reached the water's edge. I cringed and thought about Washboard Guy, like he cared. "You coming or what? The tide's gonna be out at the rate you're moving. Jump on in here. It's better if you're all wet to start so you're not thinking about that when you're up on the board."

I shucked my tee shirt and waded in. The water was a little cooler here than it was in town, and plus it was getting kind of cloudy. It would probably rain before I got a chance to learn. That would figure. I walked out until the water was to my waist and then ducked under. When I came up, Orlando was right beside me. I took a step away.

"I'm going to show you the same way I showed True. She's a natural. Look at her." He pointed off to his left, and I looked where he pointed but didn't see her. "Not in here, out there."

I looked again and remembered the colors of the sail, orange and pink. I couldn't believe my eyes; she was way out, going faster than I could have believed possible. Her arms stretched wide across the sail, and one leg was on either side of the mast part. What was that on the back of the board? The rudder? A towel? "Is that Bert? She's so deep! He shouldn't be out that deep!"

"I told you, she's a natural. He's having the ride of his life. Better than Disney World. Now you want to learn how to do this or what?"

"Yeah, I guess."

"Leticia, are you ever enthused about anything? You're gonna have a long, boring life if you don't get in there and live it. Now, I'm going to climb up here and tell you step by step what I'm doing, and then you're going to try. Got it?"

I mumbled agreement, my eyes still on Bert.

"You can't learn if you don't watch. I know you're good at school, but this ain't no book. This is a direct flight to Heaven, the only one I'm ever going on," his laugh rumbled out of him and across the water. He climbed up on the board and got to his feet. Maybe it helped to have such huge feet to anchor him. He leaned over and picked up a rope.

"See my feet? They're pretty even on either side of the mast. I've got my balance here," he seesawed back and forth to make his point, "and I'm pointed into the wind." He gestured with one hand while he pushed down the rudder with his foot and used his hips to rotate the board a bit. "Once you have your balance, you pull up the sail with the rope hand over hand. When you're learning, stop right here and get your balance again." His hands were at the top of the rope, and the sail hung limp and dripping out of the water.

"Here's the only tricky part, and I'm about to tell you the trick to beat it. You always want to reach left over right to get the boom, then out with your right as far as you can." He did it, smoothly reaching over his right with his left to grab the boom thing and pull it in toward his chest. Then he held it there while he reached his right arm out as far as it would go. The muscles in his shoulders rippled and bulged. The whole thing started to move as the wind caught the sail.

He immediately dropped the sail back into the water and jumped backward off the board. I took several steps back at the same time. Holding one hand on the board, he turned to me and smiled that smile I hated, the one where you could see all his teeth like they were getting ready to eat me. "Come closer. I can hardly see you way over there." Didn't the Big Bad Wolf say something like that to Little Red Riding Hood?

I was in big trouble. "No, that's okay, you do it."

"Don't tell me Leticia Who Fought the Lizard is scared of something? Think you can't do it? Come on. I told Truc I'd show you, and I will." He patted the board with one hand and looked impatient.

What the heck. It didn't look like there'd be any reason for him to touch me. What was the worst thing that could happen? I'd make a fool of myself, and that would be that. It's not like I hadn't done that a million times in my life. I'd lasted such a short time in the bent-arm hang during gym for the physical fitness tests that the clock hadn't even started running before I dropped, but I'd held my head up (while slouching, of course) and walked away. The thought of trying something like this in front of Orlando was another matter though. I couldn't bear the thought of him laughing at me. At least when he called me stuck-up (why do they always call shy kids stuck up?) or brainiac, I'd heard those before. But I thought so little of him, I hated the idea that he was better than me at something. It didn't matter that I bet I could beat him at every board game I'd ever played. This was his game. That did it. I walked toward the windsurfer.

"Okay, so climb up there. Easy, it's different in the water than it is on land."

I got myself up there and then stayed hunched over on my knees as the board pitched and turned toward Orlando.

"Steady, steady." He put one huge hand on the back of the board, and I was glad. It stopped moving. "Now stand up."

If he'd said do a cartwheel, it wouldn't have seemed any more impossible to me. Unsteadily I began getting to my feet.

"Take the rope with you."

I reached for the rope from my squatting position and tumbled forward into the water. It took me five more tries to stand up with the rope.

"Okay. You made it. Took awhile, but you made it. Now pull the sail up like I showed you, hand over hand." I pulled, and nothing happened. The sail didn't move out of the water even one little inch. I pulled again, and I felt myself fall backward into the water, the board scooting out from under me. When I stood up, a fish, a long thin gray fish with a pointy face that looked suspiciously like a barracuda, bumped my leg. Perfect. Now I looked like an idiot and I was going to lose a limb.

I climbed back up on the board without looking at him. He was saying something about using my arms, but I couldn't hear him through the pounding in my head. I got to my feet with the rope and did the exact same thing, probably twenty times.

His voice cut through my fog. "Use those arms. You're being too pussy about it. Aren't you like True at all? She can fly on this thing. Pull it up then reach like I told you, left over right. Pull—"

I yanked as hard as I could and sent myself over backward, this time with the sail rig on top of me. The boom cracked me on the shoulder on the way down. I pushed out from under the fabric, which made me kind of panicky about not getting air, and stood massaging my shoulder and frowning, trying hard not to cry.

"Ah, Christ, now she'll be sulking about that. It never stops."

I realized he wasn't talking to me, but to Gertrude and Bert. Perfect, they'd witnessed the disaster, too, along with everyone else on the beach. I trudged away, and when I looked back, the three of them were riding, Orlando's thick arms around Gertrude's on the boom and Bert on his stomach like a drowned puppy, but a smiling one. The site of my failure, the other board, pointed tauntingly in my direction. I felt like the boom had hit me in the gut instead of the shoulder.

It's official. I am totally uncoordinated. And now I've humiliated myself in front of Orlando, something I swore I would never do, and all because I couldn't stand the idea of stupid him being better than me at something. Oh yeah, and I wanted to impress Gertrude, let's not forget that. Now it feels like even Bert is against me, riding off with the two of them. I'm sure I'll be hearing about this the rest of the summer. Sure, I could blame it on Orlando, because I'm sure he's a sucky teacher like he sucks at everything else, but really I know where the blame goes. I'll stick to sports with my feet on the ground. Anything else is just stupid. Oh, I guess there's bike riding, but if I haven't gotten the hang of that since I've been riding forever, that would be pretty lame. It's not like I think I'm going to win any races, but at least I don't fall off. Fifty times. Ugh.

23 PICTURE

I found this picture of Gertrude and Bert in one of her drawers, under the underwear, all the way in the back. There was just the one. Her paintings and ones by her friends hung all around the house, but no photos. I don't know how I missed it in my earlier scavenger hunts. It must have been taken in our old house on Bradford Street where we all lived because Bert's so little. He looks like he's about two maybe. And squatting there looking at that picture, I could suddenly remember the whole scene.

I'd been at school, and I came in the back door with my pink backpack. It had My Little Pony on it. Man, did I love that thing. I was singing some song that my teacher had taught us and generally loving that "I'm six, I'm so big" feeling. I knew better than to call out when I came in since she might be painting and not want to be interrupted. She'd told Angel the bus driver to just let me off so long as the car was in the yard. I walked through the house and heard murmuring coming from their bedroom, hers and Joel's, Daddy's I used to say then. The door was open and I starting to walk through but stopped as suddenly as if I'd walked into a closed door.

Gertrude, well, Mommy and Bert were in their bed. They were still in their pajamas. The sun was pouring in through the window at the side of the bed, pouring through the crystals hung on fishing line and throwing crazy rainbows all over them and all over the room. She was pointing to something, a rainbow maybe, and Bert was following her finger with his eyes like she had the keys to the kingdom. The two of them were so enveloped in the light that they looked like they would float away on a cloud and go live with the angels, like maybe they were already angels. I didn't want to be left behind.

I started to talk, I don't know what I said, but I swear this happened. Right when my first words came out, a cloud passed over the sun in the window, and everything went dark. They both turned and looked at me like I'd just ruined the best day of their lives or maybe even their whole lives.

That's all I remembered, but it was so clear, that feeling of being shut out, that it was like someone froze my heart, just took it and yanked it out and put it in the freezer. I had that feeling again right now.

I don't know who took the picture, maybe Joel. Maybe He'd come in and witnessed the same scene but had a little different reaction to it. He wanted to capture it. He had, but then He'd backed away and left them to themselves, maybe even turned around and left the house, since He wasn't there when I got home. He hadn't felt right interrupting either, or that scene wouldn't have been still playing for me to see. It was way too intense to have been interrupted and then restarted. I don't know why I was so sure about that, but I was. Joel wasn't much of a picture taker. Maybe He'd been burned, too, just the way I was feeling standing here looking at the evidence.

Bert had gone to the bathroom to pee. It always made him nervous when I dug around, and nerves meant pee. He sidled up behind me where I crouched and put his chin over my shoulder so he could see better.

"What's that?"

"As I'm sure you can see perfectly well, it's a photo of you when you were a baby. And her."

"Mommy? That was her?"

"Uh, yeah, unless you have another egg donor I don't know about."

"Why are you being so mean to me? I'm not the one who's going to pound you if they come back and find you in here."

"You're in here, too, ever thought of that? And no one's getting pounded. At least not so far. Let's get out of here." I left the picture on her pillow.

"Is that where you found it?"

"Shut up, you little pain in my ass."

Needless to say, Bert and I weren't really speaking the rest of the afternoon. He went outside to hunt lizards, and I dove into *Carrie*, a beat-up book I'd found under the couch. I wasn't a real horror fan, but it was great to read about someone's life that sucked more than mine. At least no one was dumping buckets of blood on my head. Yet.

"How did this get on my pillow?"

"How should I know? You aren't exactly Susie Homemaker. More like Susie Homewrecker."

Bert came in then to see what all the fun was, but he didn't rat me out.

"I heard that, young lady. I don't appreciate your sorry attempts at humor."

"Seems like you don't appreciate me much altogether. Did you save any pictures from when I was little? Did you even take any?"

"I took very little with me. I wanted a fresh start."

"But you took Bert's picture."

"Do you hear yourself, Leticia? You sound like a five-year-old child."

"Do you hear yourself? You sound like the meanest woman on earth."

"Oh, I assure you, much meaner exists."

"Is this when we talk about how good I have it compared to kids with one arm? I just wondered if you ever loved me at all. Because—"

Orlando chose this moment to walk in the front door. "What's she whinin' about now? Forget it, I don't want to know. My day's been shit as it is. I need a drink."

No one talked after Orlando went through to the kitchen. It was like a tornado had passed, you know, with the eye, and when it had gone, we all scattered. Gertrude followed him to the kitchen, natch. Bert headed back outside, and I sat down again with my book. Maybe Carrie's life still sucked more than mine. It was worth a try.

Maybe Dory was right, and I didn't want to know what our lives had been like before she left.

24 LEFT

"Can you believe it? Disneyland! I always wanted to go to Disneyland!" Bert was hopping in place he was so excited.

"Disney World. Disneyland is in California. Aren't you curious about *them*?"

"Who? Mickey and Minnie? Yeah, and Goofy—"

"Our grandparents, you idiot. We haven't seen them in years, in more years than we knew them for, I'm pretty sure."

"I guess, but how can I get excited about people I don't know? Mickey and Minnie, everyone knows them."

"The ads are clearly working. All right, what about the RV? Are you excited about that?"

"Yeah, Artie's dad has one of those. I don't see how we're all gonna ride though."

"Not an ATV, an RV. It stands for recreational vehicle, you know, those camper things that drive? People bring them to the campground in Provincetown. I know you've seen them. They'd hardly fit down Commercial Street."

"Those? We're going in one of those? Cool!"

"I guess. The good thing is Orlando'll have to be driving, he probably won't let her, so he won't be able to bug us. Hey, look, he's back."

Bert ran to the front door and didn't stop until he was at the door of the RV. This he wrenched open with a bang and dashed inside. "Awesome! Come see, Annie! There's a table and a bed and everything!"

I stood looking at the RV from the doorway. A huge decal plastered the side of it, shouting TravelAmericanStyle.com in a whoosh of waterfall and green fields. Great, we were going in a moving advertisement. It had been around, too, judging by the number of dings and scratches up and

145

down the sides. I looked back at the decal; something was wrong. The "L" was missing in style. Wasn't a sty some creepy thing people got in their eyes? Perfect. I sighed and went in behind Bert. I peered around, not saying anything.

"Isn't this the best?" Bert was busy opening the cupboards and the little refrigerator. "Oh, I guess it doesn't come with food."

"What do you think, Miss Judgmental?" Orlando had to stoop a little to stand beneath the low ceiling. He sounded like the big bear shouting who's been sleeping in my bed to Goldilocks.

"Well, you know, where do we sleep?" I looked at my feet to avoid Orlando's face, too close to mine as usual.

"So smart and you didn't figure that out? Hey, Bert, scoot over and I'll show your know-it-all sister a little something." He fiddled around with some levers or something I couldn't see, and when he stood to one side, the table had turned into a bed.

"Cool! How'd you do that?"

"That's for me to know and you to find out."

"I'll figure it out, Bert. It can't be that hard, if he can do it. We'll figure it out, right, Bert?" The middle part, mumbled under my breath, probably only registered in my own ears. I wasn't in a fighting mood. Maybe Orlando was wearing me down.

"You bet!"

"Go get 'em, tiger. I got bigger fish to fry. We're outta here early tomorrow morning. Leticia, unlike Mr. Up-and-at-'em here, you aren't so good at getting your bod out of bed in the a.m. Why not take this chance to get some beauty rest?" Orlando laughed nastily. "That means no night-owl radio shows, no late night walks, yeah, I know all about you. I mean it. Be ready." Orlando edged his way out of the camper, a bear trapped in a metal can, and was gone.

"Isn't this the coolest?" Bert jumped up on the bed.

"It might be the coolest, but I don't know if it's the sturdiest. Don't break it before we even start. Get off, and I'll see if I can change it back."

Bert gamely slid off and stood aside.

I leaned down and saw that there was a perfectly clear diagram posted on the wall that explained the sliding mechanism. A few quick, easy maneuvers and the table reappeared. "Here, Bert, here's how it works."

After we left, I realized that now Joel didn't even know where we were or how to find us. The thought made my throat tight, like we were riding off into the sunset never to return. Maybe we were, or maybe we already had when we boarded that airplane.

Mostly we drove, only stopping when Orlando needed to sleep. Gertrude said she couldn't drive such a beast; she said it with a little girly flip of her hair while Orlando goggled. I knew we'd be hearing plenty of disgusting noises when we stopped.

It took us two days of driving after the excitement of the first day, days of looking out the window at the palm trees going by then the scrub pines sitting by the side of the road like hitchhikers and the birds flying over. Bert and I both loved the bridge between Marathon and Little Duck Keys, once the longest in the world we heard from other people hanging over the railing waiting for the traffic to start moving again. In the middle it was hard to see either end, only miles of turquoise sea in either direction. A group of dolphins danced by, playing in the swells and waving their fins.

The RV only went about thirty miles an hour, and that was if there wasn't a hill. On a hill it huffed and whined like Joel's truck when it rained. Luckily Florida didn't have many hills. Orlando didn't like highways, who knows why, probably the cops were after him on *America's Most Wanted*, so once we were on the mainland, we took only back roads, the smaller the better, he announced. Whenever I was sure we'd already been down a stretch of road, Gertrude assured us that this wasn't true. Since Gertrude was the navigator and constantly turned the map (old and ripped and missing some roads if they were in the folds) this way and then that, I wasn't so sure. Bert and I counted birds. We played cards. We read. Sometimes we just sat side-by-side looking.

One of our favorite distractions was a series of hand-painted road signs that announced all the goodies you could get at someplace called Michael Johnson's: honey, pecans, oranges, maps, cheap tee shirts, free juice samples, shark's teeth, 75% off Florida attraction tickets, shells, hats, a thirteen-foot alligator (the sign didn't say if it was alive or stuffed), souvenir 'gator heads (no mention of whether you had to detach this yourself), and on and on. When we finally saw Michael Johnson's (and didn't stop, of course, though we begged), we couldn't imagine how all that stuff fit inside that one little squat building that was mostly roof.

"Do you think He misses us?"

I didn't have to ask who. "Sure, of course He does."

"Really?"

"Really. I think so, yeah."

"What are you going to do when we get home? What's the first thing?"

"Go to Mayes's house. No, Dory's. Mayes's. Oh, I can't decide. What about you?"

"I'm gonna see Bobby. And Mousie."

"Yeah. I know I bust on you about him, but I'm sorry you couldn't bring him. You know there wasn't room."

"It's okay. Mousie doesn't like to get dirty anyway." I raised my eyebrows in surprise; I hadn't thought Bert noticed things like dirt. "Anyway, he knows we're coming back."

"That's right, we are." I hoped Bert felt surer of that than I did.

I don't know why I worry about this. It isn't like I think Orlando and Gertrude would want to keep us, me anyway, but somehow the longer we're gone, the more impossible it seems that we will ever go home. I'm starting to feel a little like Dorothy without the dog or the magic shoes. And if I ever had any doubts, which I did, I don't doubt anymore that our cottage is home.

We sat at the table looking out the window. Three strings of barbed wire ran along each side of the road on rusted metal poles. Watching for a long time was kind of hypnotic, the way they swooped down from one pole and up to the next.

"Annie."

"Yeah."

"You looking at the wires?"

"Yeah."

"It's making me kind of sick, you know, looking at them just going and going."

"So stop looking, stupid."

"What else can I do?"

"Orlando will be mad if you get sick. Want to play cards?"

"Yeah, I guess, but what do you think those wires are to keep in? I don't see any animals."

I had no idea, and what did it matter anyway? "Maybe buffalo. You've heard of buffalo farmers, right? Or maybe dragons. Dragon farmers then."

"Dragons! There's no such thing!" Bert blurted and then paused, reconsidering. He got like that about things he'd been really into when he was littler and was trying to act all big about now. He still liked stories though, at least usually. I guess he decided now was one of those times because he practically started in on one himself. "No, they couldn't be for that, 'cause dragons can fly. They'd be flying right out of those fields, up into the sky, breathing fire and everything."

"Maybe they clip their wings, you know, like they do with parakeets."

"Yeah? Then how come I don't see any?"

"They're invisible." I nodded my head quickly to make my point. "Yup, invisible."

"And what are they raising invisible dragons for? How do they even know how many they have?"

"For the government. All the top-secret projects are for the government. You know that, don't you? Everybody does. The generals, they're going to make an army of them, and then they're going to take over the world. They have these special glasses that only they can see the dragons with. The farmers just put out the food three times a day. They don't know exactly how many there are. It's for their own protection actually. That way, if some reporter comes around asking questions, the farmers can say they don't know anything. They're only following orders. See, the generals can harness the dragons and fly on them instead of driving cars. Or RVs. So whoever has the dragons is going to be in charge of everything."

"You mean like the President?"

"Better than the President. Head of everything. And if you try to get in their way, they have the dragon cook you with his flames. Oh, now that I've told you, you're at risk. You'd better watch out—"

"Annie, not really though, right?" Bert's eyes were wide; his heart was glowing.

I could tell he wasn't really up for a whole outrageous story. Maybe too much about his life felt outrageous right then to want more, even in a story. He had a point. "No, not really. Maybe it's buffalo."

"There was a buffalo burger on the Diamond Lil's menu."

"There was. Maybe you can order that the next time we go there, in another life. Ha."

When the RV pulled into a parking lot during the day, Bert and I immediately looked out the window.

"A hotel! Are we staying here?"

Gertrude's voice came from the front cab. She hardly ever talked to us while we were moving; she talked to Orlando. ""No, silly Engie, we have the RV. This is where Mommy and Daddy are staying with Troy and his friend."

"Whose Mommy and Daddy? And who's Troy?"

She ignored the first part of the question. "Who's Troy? My brother, of course! Don't tell me you don't remember Troy? You two spent so much time with him when you were little, you and all those dogs."

"What dogs?"

"Don't say that to Grandpa. Those dogs are his life."

"What—"

"Get your shoes on now. We'll go and say hello."

I froze. I'd spent most of the three days thinking about our grandparents, talking to Bert a little when he didn't get frustrated, but now that the time had come, it was scary.

Bert and I got our shoes on, and I pushed around my hair with my hands. I needed a shower. Who knew I'd actually miss the shower at their house?

25 SCREAM

When I climbed down from the RV, I stood blinking in the sun. It was still early; the sun sat low in the sky, warning that it hadn't really gotten started for the day. I hoped we didn't look as bad as the RV did. The RV's windows were streaked with dust and dead bugs and bird poop; Bert's fogging them up to write on them with his fingers hadn't helped. He and I had had some epic rounds of hangman that way when we ran out of paper. His best word, the first time he had ever stumped me with a real word, was kayak. I'd been cocky with only five letters, rattling off e and a and then s, t, and r, and found myself hung. I hadn't even known Bert knew what a kayak was, never mind how to spell it. It turned out there'd been one in the parking lot of the last rest stop when I'd gone to the bathroom, and he'd asked Gertrude what it was and how to spell it.

"Come on, they're in room 7." Gertrude herded us toward the motel, but Orlando lagged. I looked back; he was looking in his wallet. That was always bad news.

We went up to the door with the reflective seven, and Gertrude knocked. Bert and I stood behind her looking at our shoes. I bit my cuticles.

"Stop that, you'll make them bleed." Gertrude had those mother eyes in the back of her head even though she'd as much as quit being our mother by leaving. It was so unfair.

I put my hands in my pockets.

The door opened. A small blonde woman with a shy smile and a perm stood in the doorway. She wore mint polyester slacks and a polo shirt buttoned to the neck. I thought she must be hot since I was, and I only had on a tank top and shorts. "Hello, dear!" She hugged Gertrude, who had to lean over to hug back. "And here they are, so big!"

Before I knew it, she was hugging us. I couldn't have explained it out loud, but I didn't feel hot anymore or nervous or dirty or anything bad. I just felt loved. She felt exactly the way I was sure a grandmother should feel, even if she didn't feel like mine.

"Now where's Grandpa? I know he can't wait to see you." She called back into the motel room, "Grandpa! They're here! Come on out and say hello."

A barrel-chested man loomed up in the doorway behind her with his yellow sport shirt tight over his muscles and his pants pressed. I could see comb marks in his hair. "Hey, you kids! Come on over here and give me a hug." There was no resisting the command in his voice, but it was warm underneath. When we were in his arms, he went on, "So what's happening? Are we going to the Kingdom or what? We'd better get moving. That Mickey doesn't wait around, you know."

Bert laughed, big-eyed. "You know Mickey?"

"Oh, Mickey and I go way back."

"You've met him?"

"Me? Five, six times, right, babe?"

"Oh, I'm sure you're right."

"Where's Troy? And Steven? They can't still be sleeping, can they? I told them to order a wake-up call. Go check on 'em, will you, babe?"

"Oh, yes, yes. I'll do that right now."

She was back in a minute with two boys who towered over her and everyone except Orlando. Their shoulders and chests filled all the space behind her head. They wore matching State Champion football jerseys. Neither of them said anything. "Now, Troy, you know Leticia and Engelbert. You haven't seen them in a while. And this is Troy's friend Steven. He came down with us from up north. He was a real help with the dogs on the trip."

"What dogs?"

"What dogs?" The man called Grandpa bellowed. I didn't know what to call them, even in my mind. Maybe I should call them TMCG and TWCG, not very catchy though. "These dogs, of course!" He waved an arm at a huge green pickup with a full cap backed up to their motel room. The hatch opened in two sections, and the top half was cracked open. A pair of brown and white snouts nosed at the crack. "We never go anywhere without a couple of 'em!"

Bert ran over to the truck and threw up the glass. The two noses snapped his way and in a flash two tongues covered his face. In a blur one head flashed white and other patched black then white. Bert's giggling bounced all over the parking lot, bumping into cars and returning to us standing in the doorway.

"That's some welcome, huh? Wanna take 'em for a quick walk before we head out?"

"Yeah! Yeah!" Bert was hopping up and down.

The man called Grandpa, no other name mentioned, walked to the truck in two strides and barked, "Down now." The dogs didn't argue with that voice either. He reached in and took two thick woven leashes from a hook and snapped one on each of the dogs' collars. He didn't open the door; when he said so the dogs leaped over it like horses jumping a hurdle on TV. They were shaking and prancing with joy now that they were out of the truck. "Here now, Leticia, you take Speck, and Bert, you take Snowball." He handed us each a leash. Like they were in charge, and who am I kidding, they were, the dogs took off toward the trees at the edge of the parking lot. I held on desperately, jogging and then running to keep up. When they got to the grass, the dogs stopped running and started sniffing and pawing at leaves and mangled pinecones instead.

"Aren't they pretty? I wonder what kind they are."

"They kind of have flags instead of tails."

"Look at this one, what's his name? He's standing funny."

"That's pointing. That's his job. Good boy." I whirled around to find that TMCG had come up behind us. He was pretty sneaky for such a loud man. I liked him though. I decided I could call him Grandpa, at least in my head. He snapped, and Snowball started moving again. "They're English setters. See their fur, how it hangs down like that? That's called feathers. I raise 'em."

"For eating?" The terror in Bert's voice was obvious.

"Eh? No! For field trials. I ride my horse, and they run alongside, and they point like that, see the foot up and the nose? Now look up in that tree. See the bird?" He pointed a finger, and there was a fat brownish bird, not moving either, maybe hoping it was camouflaged. "They find them every time. Get good scores, these two. Good girl, Speck." He snapped his fingers and turned back to us. "Well, they about done with their business?" I looked at Bert, who clearly didn't have a clue either, and then looked at Grandpa blankly. He waved an arm in a sweep, taking in the trees and the sky and everything around. "They use the outdoor toilet?" I nodded solemnly, hoping that was a good thing. Was I supposed to scoop something? "Well, what are we doing here then? Can't keep Mickey waiting. Should have been there already, the lines are something terrible, but you know your mother. Couldn't be on time for her own wedding."

I had no answer for that, so I said nothing. Bert looked at his shoes until Snowball yanked on his leash. Then we headed for the truck.

"We'll take one car. No sense paying that parking twice. You two want to ride in back with the pups? Your folks here can come up front with us," Grandpa was already opening the back, assuming that the answer from one and all would be yes. Troy and Steven took the humps of the tire wells; that left Bert and me the floor. Once Speck and Snowball came and lay down with us, neither of us minded. Troy made one attempt at conversation before the truck bed fell silent.

It wasn't much of a ride to Disney World; the famous pink castle came in view within ten minutes. Grandpa circled the lot in search of a space once he'd paid the admission for everyone. Orlando must have bugged at the prices posted by the booth; for once we agreed on something. Bert and I were looking out the puppy-kiss-covered windows, gawking like idiots. People milled everywhere, on the sidewalks and in the street. Women carried babies and pushed strollers. Men had children on their shoulders and by the hands. Packs of kids milled around their families' legs. Many of them were sunburned. Most of them wore clothes that said Disney. Winnie-the-Pooh looked like the favorite with the mothers.

I tried to keep an eye on Bert, but there was so much to see. My eyes were attracted everywhere at once, and Bert kept wandering off. Troy and Steven walked side by side in front of us, and the crowds parted before them like waves in front of a boat's prow. They looked less than impressed whenever I got a glimpse of their faces.

"All right, we're in. What's first?" Grandpa looked at Bert and me.

"What do they have?" Bert was practically hyperventilating.

Troy and Steven laughed. I felt like even more of a bumpkin, if that's possible.

"You don't know? Oh, that's right, this is your first time. Let's take a look at the map here, and you can pick something. Grandma, show 'em where we are on the map." He flapped the map at her while he eyed the crowds surging past.

She led us to a nearby bench and spread the map across her lap. We sat on either side of her like we'd done it a thousand times. Maybe we had. "Okay, dears, see the admission booth at this gate? We're right here. So we could go here," Grandma pointed on the map to a group of rides decorated with teacups and giant toads.

"Not there! That's baby stuff!" I tilted my head back. Even upside down Troy and Steven looked like mountains looming above the bench. "Let's go here." Troy's huge finger stabbed at the map and sunk it in her lap like a torpedoed boat.

"Okay. That's good. Let's go there." I spoke quickly, trying to satisfy the giants above us. I knew something about that. Plus, what did it matter? Probably everything here was fun. We'd never been on any rides but the ones that came for the carnival on Route Six every year, and I was pretty sure the worst ride here would be better than the best ride there.

And it was. Everything was fun. I kept thinking something would happen to spoil it, but nothing did. We went on rides all morning until it was time for lunch.

I felt a little queasy at the idea of food, but it seemed like I was the only one, me and Orlando, I should say. He was looking a little green around the gills after the last trip on some rollercoaster. They all had names, but who could keep track? I sure as heck wasn't going to align myself with him about anything, so lunch it would be. Troy and Steven were in line for hotdogs and fries. They were arguing about which size soda to get, pointing at the different combos. Bert and I got in line behind them.

"Not you, little man. I've got your lunch right here." Orlando reached into a stained olive green bag that made my heart sink. I looked at Bert, and sure enough, his face looked like I felt. Orlando handed us each crushed foil-wrapped packages. I could smell the tuna before I touched it.

"Are you sure it's all right, with the sun and—" Gertrude ventured.

His scowl closed her mouth for her. "One for you, my dear."

As soon as I could, I threw my sandwich in the trash and motioned for Bert to do the same. We'd been hungry before; it wouldn't kill us. While we watched, Troy and Steven ate half a picnic table full of food and then called for more rides.

Space Mountain was the most awesome thing ever. I think the line was even longer than the sign said, but I really didn't care. I'd do it again a thousand times if they'd let me. It's a good thing it didn't cost extra or we wouldn't have been able to go at all. But the ride was awesome, totally worth it. When it started, it was completely dark. I couldn't even see my hand. But I wasn't scared. I couldn't see anyone, and no one could see me. No one was looking at me, or not looking at me. It was just the dark and me. There was screaming in my head, or maybe I was screaming out loud, but I didn't care. It felt clean and good. I could let go, and nothing happened. I wasn't responsible for anything or anyone. I was just flying through the dark. I think real flying has to be like that. It felt like it went on and on and like it was over in a second at the same time.

Orlando hadn't argued about going out to dinner, so I figured Grandpa must be paying. We pulled into the parking lot of an Italian restaurant. Gertrude said it was the only kind of food he liked. Steven had gamely tried to suggest Chinese food, but Grandpa had put that thought down quicker than the one glimpse we'd had of Mickey Mouse. "What do you want to go there for? Can't even write the menu in English, all 'moo' and 'goo.'" He gave a backward wave of his hand like he was tossing that idea right over his shoulder.

"You get what you want here," he pointed to the kids' meals that clearly said ten and under. I didn't think anyone would argue with him. No one had so far. When the server came back with the drinks, including his supersized iced tea, she looked only at him. You could see her hipbones through the tight fabric of the uniform skirt. Her tag said Candy, but it didn't look like she ever ate any. Grandpa ordered for everyone and himself last. "Here's what I want. I want: two meatballs, big ones now, not those dinky ones, and sauce, and cheese over the top. And—"

I couldn't believe it when Candy interrupted Grandpa. "Do you want ziti or spaghetti with that, sir?"

Bert's mouth opened wide then snapped shut with a pop. Troy and Steven were unfazed as usual.

"Now listen here. I want the meatballs like I said. Two big ones. You got that? And garlic bread. You bring that right away for the table, see? And don't forget the butter." He folded his menu and handed it to her. Everyone else followed his lead.

When Candy brought the garlic bread, she set the baskets down in front of him. He looked at her for a second like he was waiting for something. "Where's the butter?"

"It's on the bread, sir. See? They put it on before they bake it—"

"I know that, missy. I still want butter. Bring that along now."

Candy started to say something then maybe thought better of it. Her breath was coming quick and short. She turned away and went for the butter. When she came back, she set it down in front of him, and I thought I saw her hand shake. "Anything else I can get you, sir?"

"Well, our food, of course, but that's probably not ready yet. You bring that right out when it is though. I don't want any cold meatballs that have been sitting under one of those heat light things. Right out of the oven."

Her sigh was audible. "Yes, sir." She walked away from the table as fast as she could and still be walking. They probably had a no running rule.

26 WEAR

The sign for River Country was one of those fake old wooden ones with the carving that looked burnt on. It swung back and forth in the breeze and creaked. Maybe they had a fan that blew it if there wasn't any wind. They had everything else here. The opposite of the water rides in the park yesterday, here the signs said no shoes allowed, bathing suits required. No cut-offs. No street wear, whatever that was.

Grandpa wore plaid trunks. Grandma wore a yellow one-piece with a wide skirt. Troy and Steven wore matching Sperry trunks and went straight to the line for the biggest diving board. Gertrude wore her pale pink Danskin that would be nearly see-through as soon as she went in. I cringed just thinking about it. Orlando wore a Speedo so small it was almost invisible. It was *rouge*, of course. His belly hung over the waist. I had caught Grandpa shaking his head when Orlando took off his shorts. He gave me a little grin. I grinned back and ducked away. I was torn between the friendliness of our grins and the fact that I'd been nabbed even looking in Orlando's direction. I tried to keep my head down in all my dealings with Orlando so I wouldn't have to see those teeth. Luckily, Orlando hadn't been the one to notice. Orlando took Gertrude's hand and pulled her toward the pool. I looked away, not wanting to see her leotard disappear and her everything else appear.

The pool was so big I couldn't see to the other side with all the splashing and the mist rising from the water. They probably made that. Why would it be misty? It was already so hot, even though the park had just opened. Grandpa had been serious about the getting going this morning, not listening to Orlando's grumbling about *café*. When I saw the line to get in, I could see why he'd been in such a hurry. Orlando had grumbled some more about what's the difference, a pool's a pool, but even he had been impressed, I could tell. He stood there shaking his head from side to side, his big jaw hanging open and unshaven like some zoo animal. Swings and ropes and slides with water snaking down them and diving boards so much higher than the slides at our town playgrounds were everywhere and every color.

Troy and Steven had shucked their clothes, that really was the word for it, first down one arm and the other and then down one leg and the other, and "ta da," two fresh ears of corn ready to roast. They had already been roasting plenty this summer; I could tell because their tans were deep and solid, not peeling like Bert's and mine. The only thing was their tans ended at their sleeve lines and their necks, but I guess that made sense since they looked like such jocks.   And like jocks at school, they high-fived each other all the time. There were signs everywhere that said "No Running" and "No Horseplay," but I didn't see too many kids paying attention. What was horseplay anyway? I mean, I knew it meant playing rough, but why was that called horseplay? I hadn't seen many horses in my life, but I hadn't seen them yucking it up either.

"You going in, kiddo?" Grandpa had come up behind me, but he didn't sound like he was accusing me of anything, like I was wasting his money (and it was his money, I'd seen him pay) but more like he was curious.

I glanced around for Bert out of habit, and I saw him waving madly from the top of a high rope ladder. His grin was so wide it reminded me of when you first cut into a ripe watermelon and it cracks all the way across. I waved back. "Yeah, I'm getting ready."

"You want to sit here for a minute while you get ready? Grandma forgot her bathing cap in the changing room, so I'm going to wait for her. Can't have her going in without her bathing cap; might mess up those nice curls." He winked at me but it was sweet, not creepy. It was so cute, the things he said about her. I didn't know there really were people who'd been married a million years and were still so nice to each other. I didn't know old people could be romantic, not just dried-up adults.

He dragged a webbed chair over next to his and patted the seat. I usually thought it was gross to sit right where someone just had their hand, but not today. Sometimes stupid stuff bothered me, sometimes it didn't. It kind of depended on what other stuff there was to bother me. I sat.

"You having a good time? You seem a little quiet." Again, I liked it that he was only noticing, not accusing me of something like Orlando always was. "You and your mom getting along all right?" I made my scoffing sound, blowing air out my nose hard, but he didn't seem to notice. "You know, she loves you so much, both of you. It's really tough for her that she doesn't see you more."

I couldn't believe what I was hearing, and I couldn't keep my mouth shut either, even though he'd been so nice up to now. The first part of what he said was hard enough to take, sounding like nothing more than a flat-out lie even if he believed it, but the second part had me sputtering. Love that word. "Tough for her? It's her fault. She's the one that left!"

"Well, she did, yes, but your Grandma and me, we think she meant to go back for you. She didn't have any money, always too proud to ask though we would have done what we could, and we thought she meant to get set up somewhere first. It didn't work out that way though. Your dad wanted you to stay with him, and that judge agreed to it. It nearly killed her."

I snorted. "She looks fine to me."

"Looks can be deceiving, like they say. You look fine, too, but I bet inside you're not. What do you say about that?"

I wasn't going to get into that, thank you very much. "Do you know Joel?

"Sure, I know him."

"Did you get along with Him?"

"Well, now, he's a hard man, keeping my daughter's children from her, but I guess he thinks he's doing right by you."

"You think she would have done better? Ha." I looked at him sideways, but he didn't seem to be taking my remarks too badly. I was surprised at myself, but he was easy to talk to. Maybe it was because we weren't facing each other, we were facing the pool, and there was all the noise so definitely no one was listening. Plus, I hadn't seen him in a thousand years and probably wouldn't for a thousand more, so what did it matter? The thought of that made me sad though.

"She's a good girl, always has been, though not much of a sticker. Always floating from one thing to another. I think she's finding her way though. If she'd come back to the church, I think that would help, be an anchor for her." Now he did swivel to look at me, his face glowing with enthusiasm. "Hey, she tells me you got confirmed! That's a piece of great news. Grandma was so happy to hear that. She should be coming along any minute now. Why don't you stick a toe in that pool? I think you'll be glad you did." I thought he was done talking, and I was a little sorry. I was surprised. I almost never wanted a grownup to keep talking except for Dory and maybe Donnie. He did have one more thing to say. "Give her a chance. You've got a tough shell on you, and she doesn't think she has the right to try and crack it. Grandma and me think it'd do you both a world of good if she did." He smiled at me, and then, like he sensed her coming up behind him, he said, "Here's my girl now. Why don't you two bathing beauties get yourselves in that water? I'm going in." His plaid trunks laced up the front like you saw in some old movies, but they suited him.

"Hello, Grandpa. Hi, dear." Grandma was tucking her hair into a white bathing cap with a pink flower on the side. It even had a strap that snapped under her chin. Her bathing suit, too, had an old-fashioned feeling to it with thick shoulder bands and a reinforced chest that looked like it wouldn't move if a tidal wave came and the skirt that swung a little when she walked. He held out his arm, and she took it. He held out his other arm to me, but I shook my head. They waved briefly and then made their slow way to a kind of quiet spot, if there was such a thing. She had good legs; I had to give her that. I looked from one to the other of them, and suddenly I could picture them when they'd been young, before they had kids, and how much they had loved each other, and how beautiful they'd been, and how much they still did and still were.

When we left the next morning, I had a lump in my throat the size of a grapefruit. I didn't think I'd felt this bad leaving Joel at the airport, though it was close. Grandpa and Grandma were their usual cheery selves, and Troy and Steven were their usual silent. They were off to Epcot and were impatient to get going.

"Sure you folks can't take another day? Gonna be some good stuff there, I'll tell you." Grandpa herded the dogs back in the truck with a quick motion of his hand. There was no hesitation on their parts when he was in charge. That was true no matter who it was. I held my breath and hoped that he would insist; I knew Bert was doing the same. He had left the top open, so Bert and I walked over to pet the dogs. I think we both had the idea that Speck and Snowball might be a comfort right about now.

"We have to get this tin can back on time or they charge us all kinds of fees. Plus, you know, we gotta get home. Not much space to spread out in there." When Orlando leered at Gertrude, my stomach clenched. Didn't he think about that this was her father?

Grandpa didn't respond to that at all. It was like he saw the world in a certain way, his way, and that was all there was to it. I was going to practice that.

"Bye, Daddy," Gertrude hugged Grandpa and then turned to her mother. They jockeyed a little, trying to hug but a little awkward about it. Gertrude and Grandma both mostly paid attention to Grandpa, not to each other. He was pretty magnetic, even more so than what I'd thought about her on her bike, guys' eyes following her. Bert and I weren't much better than the little iron filings in those magnet games when he was around.

"So long, kid. You take care of this bunch, okay? We'll see you soon." I liked how it sounded like a statement of fact, not just a polite thing to say. He walked over to hug us. Speck had her head under my armpit while I stroked as far as I could reach on her back. Grandma followed in Grandpa's wake. "You be good now." Bert and I hugged them as long as we could, but you couldn't keep him still. "All right, let's get going. The lines are going to be long enough to give us all sunstroke." Grandpa started around the truck, and everyone else snapped to attention. Bert and I waved until they were out of sight. After there was no chance they would hear me, I yelled, "Bye, Grandpa! Bye, Grandma!"

Who knew that saying goodbye to someone you might as well have just met could wreck you? Grandma and Grandpa seemed so regular and loving, and Troy is the classic jock, seems pretty normal, so it makes me wonder, what the hell is wrong with Gertrude? I've thought a lot about what Grandpa said about me having a tough shell, and the only conclusion I come to is, Thank God! How else would I have survived? Maybe someday I could go to a therapist and dump all this crap, but for now, I was keeping my feelings safe and sound, inside (and in this book). Gertrude sure as hell hasn't given me any signs that it might be worth the risk to ditch the shell; in fact, I'd say her every word screams, "Keep it on! You're going to need it!"

27 LIE

Now that we were back, I started taking stuff from Gertrude, just to see if she'd notice. She never does, though, no matter what I take, jewelry, or money I find around, or whatever. If I slit my wrists she might notice, but it seems like a big risk to take since I'm not actually interested in killing myself. Sure, my life isn't perfect by a long shot, but I'm not ready to "cash in my chips," either. I heard one of Orlando's lowlife friends say that. I like how it sounds. But it wasn't even my stealing that set things off.

The dog catcher had come to haul off the two mangy, nasty dogs that always hung around in the street looking for someone to bite, who cared about that, but when he put them in the truck, I saw this cute white dog in there, a little terrier. Bert and I had the crazy idea that maybe we could adopt him and bring him home with us. Gertrude had said no about the dog, of course, like she said no about anything she thought there was even a chance Orlando wouldn't like. For a minute I thought maybe we had her when I said that they were going to kill him if we didn't take him, but then she just laughed that off. This had been risky, because I might have had to hear about it from Bert later, about how long I thought they kept dogs and how I knew they killed them, if Gertrude had decided to use it against me. I'd have had to backpedal and say they have them take long, long naps, that I'd only said that to try and get Gertrude to let us have him. He might even have laughed about that, with all the naps Gertrude and Orlando took. We were always joking about that. But it all went differently.

"They wouldn't really do that. It's their job to take care of animals they pick up. You always see those pictures in the paper of ones you can adopt."

"You can tell yourself that. You're good at that, telling yourself what you want to hear."

"What's that supposed to mean, Leticia? That sounds like you are accusing me of lying."

"Why would I accuse when it's the truth? You lie about things all the time."

"I can't imagine why you would say that, unless you are simply trying to hurt me. It seems to me that you do that quite a bit."

"Oh, really? Now we're going to make this about me and how bad I am? That's one of your other big strategies. Maybe we could talk again about how it's my fault you don't bother to see your own children."

"Your father made that very difficult. If he hadn't gone to court and told them, told them…"

"Told them what? The truth? Are we back to the truth again?" I hated the sound of my voice, full of unshed tears and rage. She really brought out the best in me. My eyes were stinging, and I clenched and unclenched my sweaty hands at my sides.

"Your father is no saint, Leticia. Don't kid yourself. Joel had no right to tell them the things he did about Orlando and everything. He did it to hurt me. If you build him up that way, you are bound to get hurt and hurt badly, the way I did."

"Here we go. Get out the violins."

"I don't have to listen to this. I'm tired. I had a long, difficult shift. I am going to bed now." Her voice sounded like she had a fur ball in her throat. I was shocked.

Maybe I'd gotten to her for a change. Could that be possible? I tried and tried, and she'd just shrug me off like you'd bat away an annoying bug. Would an apology of some kind be too much to wish for? I shouldn't get my hopes up.

I was used to my late-night schedule now, and I wouldn't be tired for another hour or so. I snapped on the headphones, crappy sounding but better than nothing, and cranked up the radio volume. I flipped channels, looking for one that wasn't playing a commercial. I'd just gotten Jackson Browne singing "Doctor My Eyes" when someone plucked the headphones off my head, snagging one of my earrings on the way and nearly pulling it out of my head.

"Ow!" I whipped around to see who had done it (though I had a bad feeling, one that told me someone large was no longer sleeping), holding my injury with one hand. "You almost took my ear off! What's your problem?" Pain and surprise and it being the middle of the night made me reckless.

Orlando growled ominously. "My problem is you, Leticia."

"What?"

"The usual. You causing True pain. I can't have that."

There went my hopes for an apology, or any progress at all. "That's a laugh. What about her causing me pain?"

"You have some nerve, you know that? You think you can say whatever pops into your fat head, and she just takes it and takes it. Like at lunch. You can't go around saying shit like that, unless you don't like eating. That doesn't seem to be your problem though, huh, tubby?"

"Nice. Calling a kid names."

"You're all grown up, right? Isn't that what you're always saying?"

"Like I had any choice. If we had normal parents, Bert and I could BE kids."

"Normal, normal, normal. I am so sick of that fucking word coming out of your mouth like you're entitled to something. Who the fuck do you think ever had a normal childhood? Your life's better than working your fingers off in some Chink factory, huh? Or how about my life? My father beat the shit out of me every day until I was too big and hit him back. Then he moved on down the line. Way of the world. Tough."

"So that's why you're such a nice guy, always threatening Bert and me, high on drugs, wishing we'd never been born so you could have her all to yourself? Well, you're welcome to her. When we came down here, we were hoping we'd actually find a mother, but no. We just find more crap. And that part at lunch about your cooking? That was the truth. It sucks. Not as bad as she sucks at being a mother, since she's so bad she doesn't even have the right to call herself that, but bad."

I hadn't seen Gertrude standing there. I heard her take in her breath like she was swallowing an icicle though. Her face blanched and looked really, really old, like she'd aged since she went into the bedroom and came back out, like the Wicked Queen in *Snow White* when her mirror breaks and she finally knows the truth.

Orlando lurched in her direction, maybe to prop her up, and then he changed his mind. He yanked me out of my chair by the collar of my shirt and spat in my ear, "That's it. That's fucking it. We don't need this shit. Get in the fuckin' truck. I'll be right there. If you're not there, I'll beat your fat ass when I get a-hold of it."

I had no doubt he meant every word. I went out the door, turning back with the handle in my hand to look at Gertrude. Orlando was standing above her where she was slumped in a chair. He petted the side of her face and talked low and soothingly to her. I hadn't even known he had a soothing voice. She didn't seem to hear him, and she didn't look at me in the doorway either. My heart was racing a million miles a minute. She didn't tell him no. She didn't do anything. She just sat there. I let the door bang and walked out to the truck. I felt like my heart was going to explode if it didn't slow down. If I had one of those extra hearts that Bert has, it would be pulsing now. What was he going to do with me, throw me off the nearest bridge? I didn't really want to think about it, and I certainly wasn't going to ask any questions. My mouth had gotten me in this fix; it seemed unlikely it would get me out of it.

When Orlando came out, he slammed his way into the driver's side, the rage pouring off him like water off a windshield in the rain. He rammed the truck into drive, and we were on our way to wherever it was he'd decided to dump me. I tried to guess to entertain myself (or to keep myself from freaking out), but I gave up after we drove away from all the obvious water access points.

When we got to our final destination, even I was impressed, that is, when I wasn't completely sick to my stomach. The airport looked a little different in the middle of the night than it had when we'd arrived during the day, but not much. There weren't as many cars in the parking lot, but the whole complex was blazing with lights like they were expecting big crowds any minute.

"You're kidding, right? Our tickets aren't for another week." My voice shook, and that made me feel even sicker.

"If you haven't noticed, I am not in a kidding mood. Of course, when I am kidding, you miss most of the jokes, since you have your head stuck up your ass."

I was going to have to tough this out. I was not going to cry or even yell in front of this loser. "So you're trying to scare me? I've wanted to go home since the day we got here, maybe the day before. All the scary stuff is here."

"Your wish came true then. Be clear that wasn't my goal though. My goal is simple: get you the hell away from True because you're making her fucking insane."

I made my voice as cold and steady as I possibly could. "I hardly think I can take credit for that. She was obviously many cards short of a full deck long, long ago. Why else would she ditch her kids for a creep like you?"

"You think you know everything, don't you, Leticia? Yeah, yeah, I know, you're 'Annie' now, like I give a crap. That's what she named you; that's good enough for me. Seems like nothing's good enough for you, but that's your problem. And you know what? Your precious father drove her away; that's a little different than I stole her away. I just rescued her from the bumps in the road. You could even say I was a hero, because she was sure worth saving, but of course you wouldn't see it that way. She was dying there with your father, just dying. And she's cried more about losing the two of you shitheads than you could ever deserve, that's for sure. You come down here all full of yourself and beat on her, and I've had it. You're out of here."

"And what are you going to tell Bert?" My throat closed up a little, thinking of him waking up and finding out everything was different, again.

"I'll tell him the truth. I'm not a liar, Leticia. I'll tell him you and True had another huge fight, and you went home."

"Without him. Yeah, he'll believe that."

"I don't much care what he believes. He'll be fine. He's not a firecracker like you, always setting something blazing. He seems pretty good with True when you aren't around. They would have been really tight I think if that friggin' judge hadn't listened to your father about not splitting you up. Made perfect sense to me, one for each parent like you split up the bucks and the gear when everything goes south."

My outrage almost overwhelmed my vow to stay calm. "Kids are people, too, you know. You can't do whatever you want with them just because they're yours. It would have been terrible for Bert and me to grow up without each other."

"You have no idea how it would have been. That's why it's called the future, 'the great unknown.' Your life has gone one way, but it could have gone a million others. Big deal. And you know, like you say I can't do whatever I want, you should take your own advice. You can't say whatever you want and not have to pay up. You opened your trap one too many times, so here you are." He reached across me and jerked open the door of the truck. I flinched as his arm went by, and I prayed he hadn't noticed. They say big animals can smell fear in their prey, so he probably had.

"You're not coming in? What if they won't let me on? Did you even call?" My voice was panicky, and I hated that.

"No, I didn't call. You're on your own. They don't let you on; you can camp out here until next week. I don't give a shit." He fished in his pocket and pulled out my ticket and a ripped ten-dollar bill. "I'm sure there's a vending machine."

There didn't seem to be much point sitting there in the truck. God knew how I'd avoided sitting around anywhere with him since I'd gotten here, and certainly nothing had changed for the better. I sniffed hard, got out, and walked toward the terminal without looking back. I could hear the truck peeling out before I even made the doors.

The airline people were really nice. They said they didn't have a flight going to Boston until seven a.m., but they could get me on it. One of them gave me an airline blanket and pillow and steered me to a bench. The other one gave me a candy bar. That made me cry; it was so kind.

"Don't go anywhere now." Yeah, like I had anywhere to go. "I'll try and round up your father at the numbers you gave me; I'll bring you the phone when I've got him. Then you can try and sleep. It will all seem better when the sun comes up."

28 LOAD

I can't believe she didn't say anything. She just sat there. She didn't even come to the airport. I don't care, I really don't. I only care that Bert is still there. I'm writing on a napkin. This is so lame.

I crumpled up the napkin and heaved it as hard as I could. I waited for the airline guy to come back.

"Jesus H. Christ, I'd like to give her a piece of my mind, or better yet, a kick up the ass. You all right? They said they're looking out for you. The son of a bitch just handed you your ticket and dumped you there?"

"It's not so bad. I've got my own bench." I tried to laugh, but my stomach heaved. I swallowed and tried again. "What about Bert? Will he think I just left him?"

"Now, Let, you know better than that. Of course he won't. I didn't talk to him yet, seeing as it's the middle of the night, but I will. I will. Want to tell me what the hell happened down there?"

It registered that we were having an actual conversation. "She's such a loser. I told her. I told her she was the worst mother who ever lived, that she had no right to call herself anyone's mother."

"Bet that went over well. She always did have a certain view of herself, better than everyone else. If only I'd seen that a long time ago, back before I got hooked. What brought this on?"

And it was continuing. "Her usual crap. She was talking about 'this family' this and 'this family' that, 'cause Bert and I were complaining about the food during lunch. Some lunch. If I see another black bean, I'm gonna scream."

"Don't tell me she's doin' that veggie shit now, too? Is that what got you? Christ knows it would get me."

169

"No, they eat meat, this weird pork thing mostly, which I detest. It wasn't that."

"Then what was it?"

"It was him."

"Bert? You two always—"

"Not Bert. He was asleep. Him. Orlando..."

"He touch you?" I was quiet for so long He yelled, "Lettie? Annie? You there?"

"I'm here. No, it wasn't that." This didn't seem like the time to get into the slaps upside the head, and I didn't know if it ever would be. "She said, 'Orly here... Orly works hard all morning, and then he makes a nice lunch for this family' and I just, I lost it." I wondered if He liked hearing the 'family' thing any better than I had when it was coming from her mouth and was obviously such a load of you-know-what.

"What happened then?"

"Then she started crying, blubbering about how I'd always hated her, I'd never given her a chance, I'd always picked you. She said I picked you." I sniffed hard, but it did nothing to unclog my nose. "Is that true?"

"God help me, that is so Gertrude. It's always about fuckin' her. No, you did not pick me. You didn't pick anything. You were seven fucking years old. She wanted to take you both, and I said over my dead fucking body, you whore. She said she wanted Bert then, Engie she called him, Christ. Does she still do that? Fuckin' kid's gonna have a complex. I must have been whipped somethin' awful to agree to that name. I said he'd be stayin' here with me, permanently, same as you. The judge saw to that, smart man, thank God."

I'd never heard Him thank God for anything. Somehow that set me off even more. I cried harder now, my sobs filling my head like steel wool until I couldn't see or breathe. Joel waited until my crying subsided, like a storm passing, and then stilled. It was like He was listening to my breathing, like people do with little babies when they're sleeping. I didn't mind.

"I'll see you at the airport. You try and get some sleep. They said they'd wake you to get on the plane."

Later I hardly remembered my trek through the East Coast airports that finished back at Logan. My gate let out in front of the same Dunkin' Donuts kiosk, which made me feel like I was in a time warp. Maybe it wasn't the same but it looked like it; that's what my life felt like, a life that looked like it was the same but wasn't. Joel was standing there at the end of the row of seats. Somehow He'd convinced them that waiting out past security would be too far. I was glad. I didn't say anything, and He didn't either, but I ran up to Him and hugged Him hard, with both arms.

PART THREE: LIFE, HERE I COME
PROVINCETOWN, LATE AUGUST INTO OCTOBER

29 GARNISH

I'd slept most of the way home from the airport, so I had missed the first glimpse of the Monument that Bert and me and most townies probably used as the landmark for when we were home. It hadn't been enough sleep though, and my mouth tasted like I'd been eating something nasty, maybe sand mixed with fish bait. My head hung to one side, and I couldn't seem to straighten it.

Joel shut off the truck with a rattle, rattle, thump. He came around to my side and opened the door. I almost fell out, but His hand rested against my shoulder and held me steady. Around His cigarette came the words, "Well, here we are, home sweet home and all that. You want me to get your stuff? Oh, right, you don't have any. Come on then, you'll feel better the next time you wake up."

When He took away His hand, I stumbled out of the truck and walked in front of Him up the steps of the cottage. I opened the door and stepped inside, looking around like I'd been away for months instead of weeks. My eyes stopped when I ran into them, two redheads who weren't there when I left.

"Oh, you're a little early. I was planning to be all done by the time you got here." The taller one had a mop in her hand; the shorter one's tongue was hanging out of her mouth. They had the same feathers around their faces, the same long thin bodies, and the same way of startling at a new noise, in this case me.

Joel came up behind me. "This here's Karen. She's the new salad girl over to the Surf Club. She offered to come clean this sty when she heard you were coming back. Guess she figured I'd done a shit job. Oh, and this is her dog, Nancy. You'll never see one without the other."

I looked the pair of them up and down like guys do when they're checking out girls. Karen had on a knit halter-top—purple and black and pink—and baggy khaki shorts, with hiking boots and socks. Her hair wasn't really red, just highlights, and Nancy's was more orange really. Nancy had on a knit collar that matched Karen's shirt, purple and black stripes. "Hi, Leticia. Oh, right, Joel says you're Annie now. That's cool. Nancy's name used to be Jezebel when I got her from the pound. Some names should be retired from the pool, huh? Good choice, Annie. Nice and simple. Here I am running on, and you probably want to head right to bed. It's all made up, nice and clean, and I'll see you again, maybe down at the Surf Club?" Karen stuck out her hand, and I shook it dazedly. "I saw you looking at my top. It's crochet. I can teach you if you want. It's a cinch."

I nodded. "Yeah, that'd be good." Nancy nudged my leg with her nose, and I pet her head.

"We'll find a time then, when you're feeling better." Karen smiled, and it didn't look fake. She whistled for Nancy, who gave my hand a final lick. "You've made a friend. Good. Well, I'm off."

"Thanks, Karen. We appreciate it. Like I said when you offered, you didn't have to do it, but we appreciate it." He nodded for emphasis then a frown crossed His brow. "I didn't see a car when I pulled in. How'd you get here?"

Karen shook her head in exasperation, like can you believe this guy? "Joel, Joel, I don't even have a car. You ought to know that. My bike's on the side there. And don't mention it, it was my pleasure, especially getting to meet the lovely Annie. See you at work." They let themselves out.

I'd been standing up for about as long as I could take. "I'm gonna go lie down." I started to walk toward my room, our room, but it hurt to think about Bert so far away. "You gonna call Bert today, tell him I'm sorry I couldn't say goodbye?"

"You could call yourself, if you want."

"No way. I might get her. Or him." I shuddered.

"Want to talk about it some more, maybe not now, later?"

So it wasn't just some fluke, some twilight zone thing, that Joel was actually talking to me, checking up on me, wanting to know what I thought. The band around my heart loosened a little.

"I think I'm talked out. They're not worth the time. But maybe we could talk about some other stuff." I kept my head down and away.

"Alright. And I'll give Bert a call first thing when I get into work, after the meeting." I didn't ask what meeting; I was hoping it wasn't with Al to put a few back. "You left all your stuff there, right?" I nodded. "He can bring it with him on Saturday. I'm taking the day off so we can go and meet him at the airport, maybe get some chowder downtown before we head back." Joel looked at me, narrowing His eyes as He did, like He was trying to see inside me and check if I still had all my parts. "I've got to get going, I don't want to be late, but I'll be back for supper. I'll bring something. You get some sleep, don't worry about nothin'."

"I'll try. And tell him to say hi to Beano for me."

"Who in the hell is Beano? Oh, you can tell me later. If you want. I'll see you. Annie. It's gonna be all right." He ruffled my hair like He usually did to Bert's, and I still felt kind of like a puppy but good anyhow.

I slept until late in the afternoon. The sun was thinking about going down, hanging at that midpoint between high noon and dark. I took a shower and pulled open my drawers for something to wear. There wasn't much to choose from. I thought about all the clothes and stuff I'd left jammed under the bed in Florida. I didn't think I'd be seeing any of it again, and I didn't know if I wanted to. It wasn't like I was going to wear it. My stomach lurched when I remembered that I'd left my bluebooks. I sat down on the bed with a thump and tried to decide how I felt about it. The journal had started as a school project, but then it had gotten personal. I sure as hell didn't want Gertrude and Orlando reading it, the assholes. Maybe Bert would think of it. I'd have to consider whether it would be worth the risk of calling. I knew who would help me decide. I got dressed and turned to make the bed. There was a lump down by the foot once I jerked up the sheets and the bedspread. When I reached down to grab it, a stray sock maybe, I found a pair of panties that weren't mine. They were clean and pale pink with a little bow in the front and two sizes smaller than mine, like a garnish most people leave on the plate. I'd think about them more later, but right now I needed to see Mayes.

30 BUCKLE

I left Him a note on the scarred little table by the door, in case he came back early. A heap of mail sat in a woven basket in the middle of it. That had to be a Karen addition. I picked up the pile and shuffled through it, bills, ads, a postcard from Bert and me, and a brochure for AA with a meeting schedule at the church. Hmm, he had said 'meeting,' right? I went to get my bike. It was only a short ride to Mayes's, but if felt weird to be back on my old bike. It didn't help that I was so out of shape. Summer would be over before I knew it, with back to school and no money for cool shoes all over again. At least Mayes and I could start up our bike rides; most days after school that we didn't have something going on we rode the loop, cycling over the rollercoaster of Bradford Street, around the hairpin at the breakwater, up Commercial with its game of dodge and weave better than any obstacle course, around the old gas station that announced "Welcome to Provincetown," and back home. We owned the streets of our town the same way we owned our yards, back when we had our own yard, that is.

In the fall we'd be doing it after high school. We'd finally made it, the big time. Maybe we'd think the race was little kid stuff, and we'd be too cool for it. I didn't think so though; so far we'd taken it way more seriously than the Tour de France thing, whoever cared about that. We kept a little tally of who won inside the door of Mayes's closet, and we were pretty much even. I had longer legs, but Mayes was focused, like she was when she was drawing. Her knees didn't know one thing about buckling, not in any situation. Mayes was the best artist I'd ever seen. She could draw things and make them look so alive you thought they'd walk right off the page. Even the popular kids would come over to see her drawing if she was in the cafeteria or something.

Mayes's house was a typical Cape, two windows up and two down, then dormered on the roof for two more that were her and her brother's rooms since the renovation. I envied her that house like you wouldn't believe because she'd known it since she was born. Sure, it had been her grandmother's house, but she still knew it inside and out. The house had weathered gray shingles and white trim, and Mayes's mom had planted hydrangeas all across the front because she'd heard that Cape soil would make the flowers blue, and blue was her favorite color. It's hard to find blue flowers, real blue ones not purple, except maybe bachelor's buttons, but Mayes's mom called those weeds. Mayes's mom is really particular about things. It drove Mayes crazy, but not me. I wished someone in my family was particular about something, instead of every day being about getting by until the next one. I stood outside the white door for a minute thinking of knocking but then shaking my head and pushing my way inside.

"Hey!" Mayes was painting in the living room, but she jumped up and ran over when she saw me. I leaned over and hugged her.

Mayes and I were opposites in most ways looks-wise. She looked like her grandmother, short and dark and "built for delivering babies." I felt like my hair looked better than usual when I was with Mayes, and I didn't slouch as badly and wasn't so conscious of my size. But mostly I felt happy and didn't think about my looks at all because I was with my best friend.

"Let! I was going to call you, but I thought you might be sleeping. I heard what happened, you know, with your mom and everything."

I breathed a sigh of relief. That was one of the best things about small towns (or worst depending on what mood you were in): everyone heard everything about everyone. To me today it was great. I wouldn't have to start from scratch, which sounded tiring even after all the sleep I'd had. I did want to know who'd said what to who and how accurate they were. "Yeah, it was a bummer all around, I'd say. Not the best day, night, whatever. Who'd you hear it from?"

"Missus Fava, you know, next door, who used to baby-sit for you? She was out walking Reggie when Martini Tina was opening up. You know Martini Tina, she's always ready to talk, so with this, she was raring to go. Then Missus Fava couldn't get over here fast enough. She was like some kind of manic woodpecker when she was knocking. From the looks of him, she practically wore little Reggie's legs off, pulling him down the sidewalk. He drank like a half-gallon of water."

"He doesn't have much leg to spare, poor guy." Reggie was a dachshund with legs so short his belly scraped the ground, and not just because Missus Fava fed him as much as she used to feed her dead husband. She brought him into restaurants in her oversized purse. "So, what'd she say?"

"The way Missus Fava told it, little angelic you, she still calls you Little

Leticia, had to walk fifty miles in the snow uphill to the airport."

"Carrying an elephant on my back."

"Oh, yeah. And you had a broken leg."

"Not two?"

"Even she thought that would be a bit much."

"What'd she say, really?"

"Why do you want to know? You're gonna tell me everything anyway."

"Yeah, but I just want to know what people are saying, you know, for when I have to see people and stuff. Like whether everyone knows what I did." I looked down at my hands so I wouldn't have to see her face right then.

"It was stupid, but we've all done stupid crap. What kid do you know who hasn't taken stuff? You just got caught. So what if people know? I think you got punished enough, don't you? You don't need to beat yourself up." Mayes eyed me like she was looking for scars or bruises or something. Of course, I had some good ones, but I'd told her about them in my letters, most of them anyway. "You really don't look so good."

"Thanks."

"No, I mean, you look like you are too wrecked to even cry. Do you feel sick?" When I shook my head no, she continued. "What then?"

I didn't answer. I didn't have the words for all the things I was wrecked about.

"Come on, 'fess up, my little Leticia. This is me. We tell each other everything. And no, I'm not going for the Annie thing. We're Mayes and Leticia. We have been since grade school, after you stopped hanging out with mopey Helen all the time and decided to have some fun, and I'm not giving that up. Mayes and Annie doesn't sound right. Plus, I can't be the only one with the weird name. At least you weren't named for some dead baseball player because your father wanted a boy. Baseball. Me. What a laugh. But enough about that. What is up?"

"I'm just beat. I slept all day, and I'm still beat. It's like the whole trip down there kind of wore me out."

"It wasn't like you thought it would be all sugar and light, was it? I mean, all these years you wanted to have your mom back in your life and you finally do, so what happened?"

"I told you when I wrote. It all went to hell, when it wasn't hell already. I thought everything would be different."

"Different how? Like she'd say she was sorry and cry and want to move back here, marry your dad again? You've been watching too much TV if you really thought that."

"I know, but I thought maybe I'd be able to tell that at least she loved us, loved me anyway. She loves Bert like she did before."

She let that sit. Who could blame her? "Bert's still down there, huh.

Have you talked to him?"

I shook my head. "I don't want them to answer. It'll be another week almost."

"Was it really awful, the whole thing, or only the airport?"

"The airport was pretty grim, even though the airline people tried to be nice. You could tell they thought there must be something pretty whacked that I just got ditched there." I thought for a minute, thought about the sunset and the times we did things just with her and meeting Sammi, and shook my head. "The rest, well, some was, and some wasn't. HE'S awful."

"Your dad? What did he do?"

"Oh, no, not Him. He was great. Sorry. I meant Orlando."

"The teeth sucker? He just dumped you at the airport? And she didn't even say anything or run after the truck or whatever? I can't believe that."

"Me either. It was like some kind of bad movie. All last night I kept thinking she'd show up and say how sorry she was and how she'd thrown him out and how she loved me so much. I'm so frigging stupid."

Mayes had her arm around me and led me to the couch.

"It's not stupid to want your mother to love you. It's going to be all right now though. You're back home with all the people who really do love you. You sit here while I get us some soda. And some tissues." Mayes always provided snacks in a crisis. It was one of the many great things about her.

I sniffled and called after her, "You don't have any iced tea, do you? I kind of got hooked while I was down there?"

"Yeah, sure, my mom drinks that. Less sugar anyway." We'd see about that.

When she came back with the tea, the tissues, and a tin of homemade cookies, I pulled myself together and only needed one tissue for a good, long blow.

I reached for a cookie and took two. "How was the last week of camp?"

"Ugh. Don't even ask. As if sports from morning 'til night weren't bad enough, would you believe this horror called color wars? Team lanyard making was supposed to count as the art part. Gavin was in heaven. I couldn't wait to get my hands on some real paints." Mayes arched one eyebrow at me. I'd always wished I could do that. It looked like a movie star thing. "I will say I'm going to beat the pants off you in our next bike race." She looked me up and down, not missing a thing about my increased weight, my thighs that spread across the cushion, the little double chin I had going. "In your letters, I thought you said you were starving."

"Yeah, well, it was feast or famine. Who knew you could bulk up on rice? I found out everything was cooked in pig fat. That could be it." I grimaced at the very thought of beans and rice. "Plus, Sammi, you know the super nice one of Gertrude's friends, she was always buying us ice cream cones, these huge double scoop things or shakes, from the place near her store whenever she saw us. I think she took pity on us, orphans that we are."

"Hardly. You know, you should look on the bright side. At least you don't have to listen to your parents screaming their brains out at each other. I'll tell you, it's no picnic having your folks stay together when you know they hate each other. I mean, my mom's got a point, it's gonna be pretty weird to see this lady walking down the street with her baby carriage knowing it's my half-whatever-she's-having, but my dad's not a bad guy. I think if they tried they could work it out. Who doesn't know that guys think with their you-know-whats? As far as I can tell, my mom and dad haven't had sex in this decade, so maybe he got a little restless."

Leave it to Mayes to snap me out of my whine session by talking about sex. Neither of us had any real experience, but we could talk about it all day long.

"You might have a point there, though it's a little weird thinking about anyone's parents having sex, ever. Us, now, that's another matter. Anyone happen with Cute Counselor Guy?" I tried raising an eyebrow at her but failed miserably. I'd written Mayes a million letters from The Rock (I'd escaped!) and tried to keep her up to date on the mess that was my life. My letter about my late-night run-in with Blip had gotten me a phone call, but of course I couldn't talk. The only phone, and with a cord no less, was in the living room, and the living room was suddenly a bus station as soon as I said hello.

I'd written to Joel a few times (He didn't write back), to Dory and Donnie (who weren't much on the writing either), and even to my old friend Helen who I'd pretty much ditched years back since I didn't want to be part of the we-only-have-fathers club which she was the president, only member, and biggest cheerleader of. Her father Paul wore his grief at all times like a sword at his side, razor sharp and ready to spear anyone who had the nerve to wish him a nice day. It got to be a little much since we were kids trying to have a life, though he clearly wished he didn't still. Helen wrote back, but it was pretty much same old, same old. She'd scolded, "At least you have a mother; you should try harder." That was so not what I wanted to hear. I almost wrote back to Helen that she was the lucky one that her mother was dead, that there was no chance of having a relationship with her so she could forget about it, but I chickened out. Mayes was the best letter writer though. She had penmanship to die for, and she remembered everything.

Mayes laughed, shaking her head at the same time. "Ivan? Ha. Nice try, but we're not getting sidetracked so I don't get the dirt on Blip."

"There's nothing else to tell, I swear. I'm just going to become a nun and skip the whole thing. It'll all be a lot easier."

"You can't become a nun because he wasn't Prince Charming. So it was a one-time thing and not so romantic, so what? It was an experience. And you did say you liked it at the beginning."

"I know, I know, it's just that the whole sex thing confuses me. One minute I think I'm going to die if I don't get a boyfriend, and the next I don't want anything to do with anyone. I just want to keep my body to myself, thank you very much. Hey, speaking of bodies, guess what I found in my sheets?"

"Something gross? Did something grow or something while you were gone?"

"You could say that. But it's not what you think. I found underwear. Pink underwear. Underwear a few sizes too small to be mine, not to mention too cute."

"Whose? Not… No way, you think your dad got lucky while you were gone? With some skinny chick?" Then she thought of something else. "In *your* bed?"

"No, I think they just got left behind somewhere, and when she did the laundry, they got stuck in my sheets. She came over to clean and all, and she's not that skinny, just skinnier than me. I met her, I think. She was there when I got back, the new salad girl at the Surf Club."

Now comprehension grew on her face. She *had* heard something. "Your dad, getting lucky."

"Let's not keep saying that. It's grossing me out."

"That's okay, you know. You think only you think like that or about all that other stuff you were saying, your body and everything? I bet even Camilla and Justine do. It's all the hormones running around our bodies, making us crazy. You know what we need?"

I groaned. "I'm too tired. Don't say it."

"Yup. On your feet, soldier. How are you ever going to get that date with Ralph if you keep sitting here eating all my cookies?"

We rode the loop, me huffing and puffing the whole way, and I found out what Mayes was really after. Turned out she had the hots for this guy who delivered ice to all the restaurants in town. And he was cute, but I didn't notice him giving her the time of day even though we swerved in front of his truck a few times. We didn't see Ralph, but Mayes was right anyway. It felt good to get up off my ass. The sunset was going to be beautiful, and I wasn't going to let Blip—or Orlando and his stupid sayings—ruin it.

31 FAST

I walked and rode a lot that week, not dawdling (or shoplifting), thinking about everything that had happened and about starting high school in the fall. Sometimes Mayes came with, and sometimes I went by myself. I wanted to try and understand all the weird things floating around in my head before I had to start learning new stuff. Lots of kids hated school, or at least they said they did. Most of the girls spent way more time either in the bathroom or writing notes to each other than they did paying attention to the teacher. Guys said the only things they liked about school were gym and recess, and we wouldn't even have recess anymore in high school. For me though, school made sense. The teacher told you stuff, or you read stuff or researched stuff, and then you had a test and told back what you had learned. It was a simple exchange with no hidden parts. In school if you did what you were supposed to, everything worked out fine. So I was looking forward to school starting, even though I was nervous.

When I got tired of thinking about The Rock and them and what Bert was probably doing, I thought about what had almost happened with Ralph out at the Point, or at least what I thought had almost happened. I hadn't seen him in any of my walks around town, but if I had an eye out for anyone, it was for him. When I did run into him, I hadn't thought it would mean literally. It seemed like some kind of goofy sitcom plot, but it goes to show they don't make up all those stories.

I was walking out of the Portuguese bakery with an elephant ear. I know, I was supposed to be trying to lose weight. I was supposed to be trying to get in shape, but it was hard when I never had been. I didn't know what it would feel like, but I had plenty of practice with what I was, someone who ate when she was unhappy and who chafed at what she looked like every minute of the day. It was a complicated dance, back and forth between the desire to change and the desire to feel comfortable, but one of the things that got me through was sugar. How many calories could a skinny stiff thing that looked like a—

"Boner! Down! Down, boy!" Ralph came running and tried to haul Boner off me. His leash was trailing behind him like a scarf; I could see it well since I was down on the ground, too. I was flat on my ass, arms and legs splayed out, a mountain of dog in between my flaming face and the surging crowd around me. At least I wasn't wearing a skirt, so my not-cute underwear was safely hidden. "Oh, hey, Leticia, I'm so sorry. We've been going to obedience school, but it's not really..." He put down one hand to help me up while he kept Boner cuffed with the other one, a pretty neat trick really.

"Helping?" I took his hand but made sure I did most of the work. Use your legs, that's what they always say about lifting, right? I laughed. "It's fine really. I've wanted to meet the famous Boner, and it looks like he needed that elephant ear way more than I did." Boner was chomping and licking his drooly lips, spewing crumbs on the ground since I was no longer available as his placemat.

"I guess he thought it was a bone. He thinks everything is."

"He's got the right name then, huh?"

"Yeah, he does, even though my mom gives me so much grief about it. My aunt told her she should chill, fair enough since she named him really, but my mom, uh, my mom doesn't..."

"Doesn't chill? Tell me about it. Parents are crazy, aren't they?"

"I heard you just got back from, like, seeing your mom. How was that? I know you kinda wanted to know what she was like now and everything."

"Yeah. I did. Let's just say she's different than I thought she would be." I wanted to get off that subject and fast. "She told me one time to say hi to your dad the next time I saw him."

"She did? I'll tell him. I know he liked her. I know he was sorry when she skipped—damn, I can't say anything right today."

"No sweat. Seriously." I petted Boner's head for something to do that didn't involve looking at how cute and close he was, Ralph not Boner, and how I was being an idiot as usual. "You had a good summer?"

"Yeah, pretty good. I can't believe how fast it's gone. I helped out down at the station, you know, doing a little cooking and cleaning the equipment."

"That's cool. I didn't know you could cook. You think you want to be a firefighter when you..." There must be some better way to say 'grow up,' but I couldn't think what it was.

"Finally get out of this town?" He grinned, and we both knew he meant now we were even.

I'd never finished anyone's sentences or had anyone finish mine (and better than I would have). I brushed some dirt off my shorts for something to do.

"I'm really sorry he bulldozed you. He just gets excited when he sees someone he likes, I mean, something he likes."

"Yeah, no problem. He did me a favor."

"How's that?"

"Well, I'm kinda, like, trying to get in shape. I was out walking, but I stopped for a snack, not like I needed it."

"You kidding? You look great. I hate how girls want to be all skinny. It doesn't even look real, like some kind of magazine person." Right then, wouldn't you know it, Camilla and Justine walked by, each wearing one headphone of a music player. "Like them."

"You're kidding me, right? I appreciate you being nice and everything after your dog bowled me over, but give me a break. You're honestly going to tell me you don't think they're hot?"

"Let's take a walk. You going home?" He checked the snap on Boner's collar, shortened up the leash, and set out in that direction, sure of himself as always.

"Yeah. You didn't answer my question though. Tell me you don't think Camilla and Justine are hot. You'd have to be blind not to." Why could I not keep my mouth from spewing every thought I had?

He walked fast, and I scrambled to keep up. Maybe he was regretting his offer and was actually walking away from me. What the hell was I doing? Here I was walking with the guy I'd liked since forever, and I was talking nonstop about how cute other girls were, that is when I wasn't wiping dog snot off my face. We passed Strangeways, and I hoped he hadn't heard about my last screw-up, that is, the one before the one that got me shipped back return to sender, but he probably had. His dad was a fireman, and his mom worked at the library. What didn't they hear? Ralph didn't say anything though, and amazingly, neither did I.

Ralph was humming, "Let It Be." Was he trying to tell me something, like stop talking, or maybe stop thinking how cute he was and get real? The stop talking I could do, finally, but the stop thinking he was cute was a whole different story. Once he pushed his dark heavy bangs out of his eyes, and I swear I swooned. What I felt like was exactly what that old-fashioned word sounded like, kind of light-headed and warm, and removed from anything bad that had ever happened to me. Luckily I got it together and didn't actually fall down, since I was probably pushing my luck on Ralph picking me up more than once in a day. He was wearing this faded Rugby shirt, green and white stripes, and it looked soft. I'd seen it before. Maybe it was his favorite, it was mine because he was wearing it. Maybe I could find some way to snag it when his mother told him it was too old to wear anymore. Then I could put it under my pillow and have good dreams the rest of my life.

It should have been awkward walking together and not talking, but it wasn't. Maybe it was because we'd known each other our whole lives. Maybe it was because Boner took a lot of concentration, or else he mowed down or licked to death every person coming in the opposite direction. It seemed like Boner was doing Ralph a favor, letting him hold the leash so he'd keep face, but Boner knew who was really in charge. We passed a little blond kid with four teeth eating cotton candy, and for a minute it looked like Boner was going to jump right into the stroller. The kid didn't really seem fazed, surprisingly, maybe kids have some kind of radar about what dogs will hurt them and what ones won't, but the mother's eyes got huge. Then Ralph smiled and apologized, and it was all right. She even smiled back. I knew how she felt.

"That stuff didn't even look like a bone."

Ralph laughed. "Yeah, he's not always so picky. The other day he took this lady's banana. Turns out he's not much of a fruit eater."

"Why? What'd he do?"

"He threw up on her shoes."

"Ugh. Nice."

"Yeah. I offered to pay for her shoes, but luckily for me, she thought Boner was so cute she gave me a pass. Good thing, too, because they didn't look cheap."

I'd give him a pass or anything he wanted. What did he want? That was the million-dollar question. The answer was probably to be friends, same as always.

We made our way to the east end of town where it quieted down. We passed the Art Association and the old Flagship. It had been a whole bunch of other restaurants, but I still thought of it as the Flagship. Most locals probably did. When we came even with the Surfside, I started to turn down Allerton to head over to Bradford, but Ralph took hold of my arm and steered me to the beach. It was late in the afternoon, so the kiddie people were clearing out for early dinner, and the cool people hadn't shown up yet.

When we got out on the sand, we stood there for a minute watching the waves roll in. Ralph let go of Boner's leash even though there were about a million signs saying no dogs between Memorial Day and Labor Day. By late August like it was now, locals got so sick of everything to do with tourists, and that included all the rules about what you could and couldn't do at the beach. The beach was our playground, and it sucked having the rules change because of people who didn't even live here. I'd heard that some guy who lived up Cape hung a banner from the bridge right after Labor Day every year saying, "So Long Tourists." I'd never seen it, but I could understand why he'd do it.

Boner found an old tennis ball and was throwing it for himself. Over and over he whipped his head to the side and flung the ball hard enough that it buried itself. Then he'd dig furiously in the sand with his nose right next to his paws. Little sprays of sand erupted from the hole and then from his nostrils when he sneezed. He was like a toddler, into everything and a danger to himself, only bigger. He was kind of mesmerizing though.

"Leticia."

I turned to look at him. Ralph's eyes were liquid and brown, like Boner's but so much better. "Yeah?"

"All right. I think they're cute. Sure. But not as cute as you." He came close, closer, and then he was kissing me. I was kissing him back. It wasn't anything like kissing Blip had been, no fear, just this thrill running down my spine, past my thighs (I didn't even hate them as it went by), and into my toes. Ralph put his arms around me, and I put mine around him. It was even.

What can I say? Just kill me now before something goes wrong. Or should I try and believe that my life can actually not suck? All right, I'll try.

32 OVERLOOK

'So it's just you and the old man. What do you want to do? Get some dinner?" Joel sneezed one of His trademark they-can-hear-you-in-Canada sneezes and blew His nose in His handkerchief.

"Yeah. That'd be good. You're not working tonight?"

"I switched things around a bit, so this way I got tonight free. I thought we could go by MoJo's, get some of those chips you like, and walk out on the pier. That way my smoking won't bother you."

It seems like He's been trying really hard since I got back. Could He really be going to AA? If so, it's almost too much to take in at once.

"Thanks. Thanks for thinking of that. I might not get chips though. I'm trying to, you know…"

"You're not getting hung up on all that weight crap, are you? There ain't a fat chick anywhere in my family or hers, Gertrude's. Some missin' a few wires on her side, but no hippos. You're gonna be fine. You are fine."

"Yeah, well, I just think that for school and everything, I like want to get in a little better shape. Chips aren't the best for that."

"A few chips won't kill ya. Moderation. That's the way to go, Lettie. I know, I said I'd try with the 'Annie' thing, but I been thinking about that, about how you might not want to go giving away pieces of yourself to get back at her, since most likely it won't phase her one way or the other. She's in her own world. What's that saying? 'Don't cut off your nose to spite your face.' Another way of saying moderation, I guess."

"Huh, I hadn't thought about it that way, like I'd be losing something versus giving something away." I waited a beat, but that's all I had to say about that. "Want to go?"

We got in the truck and drove to the wharf. The lot was full. I braced myself for a round of cursing, maybe a pound or two on the steering wheel, maybe a 'Forget the whole thing,' but He pulled out, crossed over to Bradford, and parked in the lot there. He didn't even say anything about how the rates were f-ing robbery. It was making me a little nervous.

We crossed at the crosswalk with this couple that for sure had to shop in the tent department and their mini-tent kids. They were all licking those giant multi-colored lollipops and squabbling about where to go for dinner.

"They should leave some food in town for the rest of us, maybe go eat in Wellfleet," Joel muttered.

I laughed and breathed a sigh of relief. He was still Him.

We made our way through the crowds in line for the restrooms, only the women's of course, and around to MoJo's. There was a line there, too, but it wasn't the worst I'd ever seen it. A fleet of kites danced in the steady breeze over the kite shop. One of them had a big red lion across its face. Looking at it, it felt like clouds had covered the sun. I shivered even though the sun was actually still about midway down the sky. I tried to think about something else.

His voice cut in while my brain was skittering from one thing to another like a little kid on a trike on the highway. "What do you think Bert's doing about now?"

"Probably looking for something to eat. They're really big on Cuban food down there, and we didn't like it much."

"What's that? Mostly pork, right?"

"Yeah. Pork, rice, and black beans. It'll be fine with me if I never see another black bean."

"They sound all right together, as long as it wasn't too spicy."

""How about for breakfast, on top of your eggs?"

"You are making that up. They did not have that. Did they?"

"They did. It got to be a little much after a while."

"I can see that. Once in a while maybe, that Mexican stuff, but I'll stick to the regular most days. Rather have beef, but that's me."

"A little chipped beef, right?"

"Yes, ma'am. They have that here?" He looked again at the signboard, like maybe he'd overlooked it all the years he'd lived here.

"No. You'd be the only customer for that, I think."

"Don't be so sure. Plenty of people my generation grew up with that."

"Just because you grew up with it doesn't make it good."

"No, it doesn't. And you're not talking about the chipped beef or the black beans anymore, are you?"

I shook my head. It was our turn to order. I ordered the salad pizza, which earned me a look of disgust that I'd passed on the chips (they cut them themselves, and they did smell awesome). He got a foot-long. And the chips. I looked around at the crowds, wondering if we'd see anyone we knew.

"Change your mind? Want to sit in here?"

"No, I'd still rather walk out. It's pretty jammed in here."

"Me, too. Never liked crowds. Funny thing for a bartender, you'd think I'd say the more the merrier and all that, but I'm looking forward to Labor Day as much as the next guy."

Chatty, chatty. Now we were even almost talking about drinking. What was next?

We took our food and walked out to where the sunset cruises left from. He took a seat on a bench, and I sat at His feet with my feet hanging down over the water. I'd forgotten a knife and fork, so the salad pizza was going to be challenging. I started to pick at the salad with my fingers.

"Need these?" He dangled a package of utensils in front of me.

I took them sheepishly. "Thanks."

"You want to tell me what went on down there?"

"What do you want to know?"

Whatever you want to tell me."

I thought about that for a minute, weighing it to see what it was worth. There was so much I couldn't talk about without Him getting all wound up, and I didn't have the energy for that. I knew one thing: I wouldn't be saying anything about all the stuff I stole and stashed under the bed. I could picture it there, the bags collecting dust but the things still with the tags on. I must have not said anything for a while because He started talking again.

"Listen, Leticia, I've been doing some thinking. It sure as hell wasn't perfect here before you left, that business at the music store and such not being a real highlight, but I shouldn't have sent you down there the way I did. I'm sorry about that."

My skin felt all prickly, like He was looking right inside my mind, seeing what I was fretting about.

"But now that I did it, I'm not sorry you saw her for what she is."

This I wanted to hear. "And what is that?"

"A really selfish person. Someone who thinks so much about herself that she doesn't have any room to think about anyone else. Even her kids. Even her husband. Doesn't matter. It's only about her."

"Why would you want me to see that? Couldn't you have just told me?"

"You wouldn't have believed me. I know you. You had this whole picture in your head, this whole fairy tale, about what happened to her. You always liked fairy tales. Well, now you know she isn't some princess locked in a tower looking for you or anyone to rescue her. She likes it in the tower."

"She does have someone though. She has Orlando. And they're so gross, always calling each other these sicky-sweet nicknames and going to take naps." I sneaked a peek at Him to see how He was taking this.

He was staring off toward the sun, smoking, and I didn't think He was looking for the green flash. Did we have that here? I'd have to be on the lookout or think of someone to ask. Ralph, he'd know. I had a warm feeling thinking about Ralph.

"Yeah, well, good luck to him, that's all I can say. I been there, and it'll pass. Something'll come up, and she'll wake up one day and be out of there. Nothing's good enough for her."

"Bert is. She wanted Bert." I had a thought that had been buzzing around in my head ever since Orlando peeled out at the airport. "What if they don't let Bert come back?" My voice was small and uneven.

"Then we'll go get him. He's our boy, and he'll come home where he belongs, one way or the other. Don't you trouble yourself about that. Life's hard enough without worrying about shit that ain't never gonna happen." His speech always got a little hick when He got worked up. Maybe He thought it made Him sound tough. Other days I would have cringed, but that day I held on to the sentiment.

"She didn't care about me at all. Did she ever love me?" My voice was so small now I was pretty sure it was only in my head.

He answered though, and that was something, too. He was answering everything I asked. "She does, in her own way. But I can see that wasn't enough. It wasn't then either. Leticia, here's something you have to see about her, even if you can't see anything else. Some women are only focused on men, or boys, like with Bert, and all other women, or even girls, are competition for that. That meant you, too." His eyes were focused far away, like He was looking back in time. "When you were a baby, she was pretty good with you. Took care of you, seemed to have some fun with it. I was glad to see it. Then you started walking and talking and your hair grew, and everyone said what a pretty girl you were. Well, that didn't go over so good." Joel shook His head. "You'd a thought a mother would be happy to hear that. But not Gertrude. No, sir. She was jealous. When Bert came along, she was different. He was her little man. You though, she didn't want much to do with you once you weren't a baby. I blame him, really."

"Bert? You blame Bert?" I could barely get the words out the way they scratched at my throat.

"No, not Bert. Him. Her father."

"Grandpa? Why?" His startled face was a little scary. I looked down at my salad and picked at it. I hadn't eaten much. He hadn't eaten anything.

"You saw him? Down there?"

"Yeah. We went to Disney World. What's the matter?"

"Disney World. That is fucking perfect. The whole lot of 'em, fucking nuts, and they take you to a nuthouse where grown men dress up like frigging mice. Perfect."

"What? What are you talking about? It was fun."

"I'm glad it was fun. I'm glad you had some fun anyway. You have to excuse me, it's a little too ironic for me."

"Why did you say they're nuts? What do you mean?"

"Was she there, too, the mother, your grandmother?" This word visibly pained Him. It made no sense to me. Our conversation seemed to have changed to some other language without my noticing.

"Yeah. She was there. And Troy and his friend. We went in an RV. Orlando made us eat all our meals in the RV, not even soda in the park." I tried to steer our conversation back to something I recognized.

Joel didn't go for the bait. "Leticia, I'm going to tell you something that will be hard for you to hear. But you are old enough to understand some things. I probably should have told you before you went, but there wasn't time. And I was too mad." He rubbed His hand back and forth over His jaw. "I was asking too much of you, you having to look out for Bert all the time. And me drinking. I was feeling sorry for myself more than I had a right to. I'm sorry about that, too."

This I could understand, and it was like I could breathe a whole new way hearing it. "It's okay. I mean it's not like I did so great." I swallowed hard and said something I should have said a long time ago. "I'm sorry, really sorry, about the things I did. I'm trying to do better now."

He smiled. "Well, we've both got our work cut out for us, eh? And you going to high school in a few weeks. Growing up right before my eyes."

I sat silently, looking at His untouched chips. He followed my eyes and laughed a small laugh, but you could tell the hard things were still there in the back of His throat. I wondered if we'd get to them, or if that was enough for now. I didn't know which way I wanted it to go. "You might want to get fresh ones. These here should be seagull feed about now." Like it was listening to Him, a huge laughing gull swooped down and landed a few feet from us. I tossed it a chip. He scarfed it and let out a huge laugh that definitely said, "Where's the rest?" I began to toss them rhythmically, one at a time, the big bird catching each one in the air. He was attracting a crowd, but he elbowed (winged?) them out. He and I had a thing going, and he wasn't letting anyone else in on it.

"I should have seen it really. But back then when I met Gertrude, she was so classy, this fancy-pants girl slummin' it, looking for some fun. And we had some fun. Don't think we didn't. Don't feel too sorry for me that the fun ended, because I was an idiot not to see that it would. That kind of fun only lasts in the storybooks. In real life everyone has to go back to work and stop partyin', stop being the center of attention, and Gertrude didn't want none of that. Her father made her that way."

This I wasn't sure I wanted to hear. I felt protective of Grandpa, though he probably didn't need it. "I liked him. He was nice to me."

"I'll bet he was. He was nice to her, too, spoiled her so rotten while he stuck her mother away in the loony bin and tried to pretend everything was fine. You know they shocked her silly? Hooked her up to some machine and tried to shock wanting to be a mother to those spoiled brats into her. Of course you don't know that. That's why she's a little fuzzy, because they fried her brain."

I stopped throwing chips even though Big Bird squawked and strutted closer, barely out of range of my arm, and thought about what He'd said. "Does it hurt?"

"I don't know for sure, but I'm betting it does."

"He loves her so much though. You can see he does. I could see it."

"Yeah, she's all fixed up now." Obviously this is where I got the love of sarcasm from; His was so thick I could almost touch it coming out of His mouth. "She does whatever he says, doesn't she? And Gertrude is still fawning all over him, too, isn't she? All is fucking right in his world."

"But the doctor must have said she needed that, right? I mean, you can't just decide your wife needs to have her brain fried like she needs a haircut or something."

"I don't know anything about that, I just know it happened. And Gertrude, well, she didn't have a mother around to teach her things, to show her how to grow up and move beyond being a kid where all you care about is yourself."

"Like me. I didn't have that either—"

"Leticia, you're more grown up than any thirteen-year-old should have to be. You're more like my mother, you remember her, don't you?" I nodded since He so clearly expected that, and I did but not that much. "She was organized like you, liked everything just so, and liked taking care of things. And you've had Dory. She's always looked out for you, and you couldn't ask for a better mother than Dory."

"Dory *is* the best. I've always been jealous of Danny, that she was his mother and not mine."

"Hell, I'm jealous of Danny. Naw, my mother was a terrific lady, but I know what you mean. Maybe one of these days you'll have someone else, too, someone who'd be a real fine mother. I've been meaning to tell you about something, Lettie, but you just got back and I figured you'd been through enough—"

"About Karen?"

"Yeah, about Karen. We've spent some time together since she started over to the Surf Club. She got me back on the wagon, going to the meetings. She's a nice lady."

So it *was* true about the brochure. One Day at a Time, that was their slogan. So far so good, right? "She seemed nice. I liked her dog. Nancy?" I hesitated, not sure how far I wanted to go with this. It was one thing to talk to Him about things that happened far away from here or a long time ago, but it was another to talk about the future. The future was so precious because it wasn't ruined yet. It still had hope. I didn't want to give that up. I hadn't gotten hope that long ago. I'd decided I'd give her back her underwear some quiet way sometime. "She go on dates with you?"

"Nancy? Yeah, like I said when you met her, you ain't gonna see one without the other. I don't know you'd call what we've been doing dates, that's teenage stuff. We've spent some time together, getting to know each other. You though, you're gonna be dating and all that other shit before I know it. I'm not ready for that. You ready?" Joel eyed me through the smoke of His cigarette, but it wasn't accusing, it was more a real question.

I laughed nervously. "I don't have much choice, do I? School starts in like a week."

"You're gonna do great. You're great at school. That's why we got you skipped that year. That's like my mother, too. Did you know she taught school? Kids loved her even though she was tough, wrote to her for years after they left her class."

"That's cool. Do you miss her?" The question surprised me. I didn't usually think about Him that way, like He had feelings, too.

"Sure. She was tough like I said, but I always knew she loved me. Leticia, I wish I could give you that from your mother, but I can't. I can only give you what I have. I know I don't say it much, or probably do a lot of things I ought to do, but do I love you, you and Bert both. You gotta know that."

I looked at Him and looked quickly away so He wouldn't see my teary eyes. I was too slow.

"It's all right to cry, Leticia. Whatever you feel, it's all right. You don't have to keep everything inside. I've done that. I don't recommend it to you." His laugh was bitter, but then it changed somehow, lightened. "Saturday Bert'll be back. The three of us, we're a family. We're gonna be all right." Joel put His hands on my shoulders and turned me to face Him and looked into my eyes for a long minute. I didn't look away. "And now I think we should get some food we're actually going to eat. What do you say?" He put down a hand to help me up, and I took it.

33 WRAP

I was lying on the couch reading when I heard a little bird at the door.

"Hello? Hello?" Dory's voice trilled when she called. "Anyone want to go for a swim? I checked the tide chart; it's going to be perfect in the bay."

I dropped the book and ran over to the door to give her a hug. That's not true. I ran over to get her hug. Her hands against my back gave a little massage before she let go to look in my face. "I heard you were back, and I got tired of waiting to see you. Am I interrupting something?"

I'd thought about Dory so much while I was gone, but once I was back I hadn't gotten motivated to do much besides walk. I knew it would be hard to tell her how things had gone beyond what she had no doubt already heard, and I didn't feel like getting into it. With Joel it was one thing because He thought everything Gertrude did was horrible, but with Dory they had really been friends. I knew Dory still believed they were. I was afraid she'd defend Gertrude, and I wasn't sure I could stand that. "No, I'm just doing my summer reading. *Things Fall Apart*. I'm sorry I didn't come by when I got back. I've been kind of lying low…"

Dory squeezed my hand. "I heard you had a rough time. I wish it had gone better. I was really hoping it would."

I laughed bitterly and recognized it as His laugh. I tried to shift it as Joel had. "Yeah, well, me, too. At least I know her now. That's something, right?" I looked down at my feet. "You want to come in?" I walked into the kitchen for a drink, as much for something to do as anything else. I took two glasses out of the cupboard and got out the iced tea I'd made earlier. I'd tried a mix, but it was lousy, so I had made it from scratch. I held up one of the glasses in Dory's direction.

Dory *mm-hmmed*, and her voice was sad. "Lettie, people don't always act the way we want them to act or even in ways that we can understand."

I scooped out some ice and concentrated on pouring, concentrating harder than the task required because I was trying to think about what I wanted to say. When I had the two glasses ready, I put away the rest and carried them to the table. I plunked myself in a chair, slouching heavily and gnawing on a hangnail. That was another thing I was going to do before school started, quit biting my cuticles. A little drop of blood welled, and I licked it away. "I do understand though. I just don't like what I saw."

"What did you see, honey?"

"I saw that she's selfish, that she only cares about herself and maybe Orlando and her father and a little about Bert. But not about me."

"I can hear how firmly you believe that. Are you really sure it's true though? Sometimes people don't show how much they care because they are afraid of being rejected."

"So now this is my fault, too? You sound like her. That's so unfair!" I banged my glass down on the table and then checked to see if I'd cracked it. Of course I had. I took the glass to the sink and left it there. I wiped up the spill and plopped back down in the chair. "That was stupid."

"You're upset. I don't blame you. I'd be upset too if my mother didn't say anything when some man I hardly knew dropped me at the airport. You have every right to be upset. I hope you can hear me when I say that."

"That isn't what you said before. Before you were defending her, saying I didn't love her so she doesn't love me."

"That isn't exactly what I said, I said that she might not be very good at showing she loves you, but let's work with that."

"So now I'm one of your patients?"

"No, we're just talking, trying to make some sense of what happened to you, Lettie. Annie. I do love your given name. I think it says the truth about you."

"Really? What does it say? Unwanted? Unloved? Leftover?"

"No, actually it means joy and happiness. I looked it up again while you were gone. That's what she, your mother, I mean, wants for you. I know it."

"Does it really mean that? Such an ugly name means those nice things?"

"I've told you, I love your name. I wouldn't give it up so easily, not with all you've lost already. Don't tell me you like those frilly names that are popular now like Ashley and Tiffany. And Brittany. Or maybe those boys' names like Taylor. Now, I'm the one who should be complaining about my name. It means sorrows. What kind of mother names her daughter that?" Dory was joking, I knew from her tone, but still, she had a point. "Your mother chose a lovely name for you. I think you should own it."

"She has a funny way of showing it if she loves me like you say she does. It's more like my name means eat dirt."

Dory gave a small, strangled laugh. "Yes, she does have a funny way of showing it. But you know, sometimes we have to look at things from a different angle to understand them. Maybe it was for the best that she left. Maybe she knew that."

"How can you say that? Every kid should have a mother, or else people shouldn't have kids in the first place."

"You do have a mother, though she may not be what you'd like her to be. But that's true so often in life, that people disappoint us when our expectations are too high or different from what the person is capable of. Maybe she realized that she wasn't cut out to be a full-time mother. Maybe she did you a favor."

"Wow, some kind of favor. I'll have to hope no one does me any more favors. I don't think I could take it."

Dory looked truly surprised. "You have taken it beautifully though. You are a lovely, loving girl with her whole life in front of her, and maybe Gertrude was going to stand in the way of that."

"She's your friend. How come you're saying these things?" I was suspicious that there was a trick in there somewhere, even though Dory wasn't usually someone who tried to trick people.

"She is my friend, you're right. And that won't change. But you, and Bert, too, are very special to Donnie and me. We feel we have been lucky to have such a part in your lives."

My chest loosened a bit, no trick, thank God. "Yeah, well, we're lucky, too. I always wanted you to be our mother instead of her. Did you know that?"

"That's so kind of you, Lettie. But you know, your mother being who she is has helped make you who you are, and I wouldn't change that for anything, any part of it." She got a funny look on her face. "I'll tell you something else. When I had Danny and Gertrude had Bert, they always played together. And Danny told me more than once, when I had said 'no' about something, that he wished Gertrude was his mother instead because she was more fun. And she was."

"Wow. That must have been hard to hear."

"I won't deny it hurt, but some part of me knew a part of her was broken. I didn't know what would happen, I'm not claiming to be a fortuneteller or anything, but I wasn't completely surprised when she left. She had a hard childhood, the little I know about it, and I don't think she ever really recovered."

"People like that shouldn't have kids. It'd be better."

"I can't agree with you about that, Leticia, because then we wouldn't have you. And that is a loss I wouldn't like to contemplate."

It'd be so great if I could put that feeling in a box and save it for later, for when I was feeling down on myself. "So what do I do now? I just want to put it all behind me. I'm starting high school and Ralph—"

A slow smile spread over Dory's face. As for me, I clapped my hand over my mouth, wishing I could take back that one little word. I wasn't ready to share my treasure, my little nugget of warmth that sat right by my heart, even with Dory.

"I can see you don't want to talk about Ralph. He is a darling boy though, one of the best I've always thought. Steady."

I nodded but didn't take up the chance to talk about him in case that would dilute what I had. I smiled to myself, remembering that we were seeing a movie together later. The idea of sitting in the dark with Ralph thrilled me so much I had to force myself back to the conversation with Dory. "So, like I was saying, I want to put it, put her, behind me. I want to start fresh, the new school year and everything, and just be normal." Dory had taken everything else really well, so maybe I should put down my last card, my biggest card. "You know what I really wish?"

"What do you wish?"

I took a deep breath. I wouldn't be able to take it back once it was out there in the air. "I wish she was dead. I know you're going to argue with me, tell me that's horrible, but I do. I wish she was dead. It would be so much easier. Then I could get on with my life and not even think about her anymore."

"Oh, Lettie, I can hear how strongly you believe that, but I don't think you'd find it that way at all. Grief has a way of coloring every part of your life, even when you think you aren't close with the person. Also, you can't reopen that door once it's closed. I'm glad for you that she isn't dead. That way you have the option, the choice to try again later." She must have registered the huge outburst welling in my throat, ready to deny there'd every be another time, because she continued quickly, "If you want. Only if you want. That's the beauty of growing up; you have so many choices in front of you. I'm so glad I'll be here to watch everything unfold." She covered one of my hands with both of hers. Her mother's ring with hers and Donnie's and Danny's birthstones glittered on the top hand. I was jealous my birthstone wasn't there, too, but I tried to be grateful for what I had, Dory, here with me now and into the future.

"Me, too," I took a deep breath and sat up straight, well straighter anyway. "Is that swim still an option?"

"Not an option, my dear, a requirement." Her smile helped my throat relax so I could smile back. "I'll wait while you get your suit on. Make sure you put on sunscreen. It's a hot one."

"Yes, mom," I laughed all the way to my room to put on my new suit. It was a tankini, so it didn't ride up the butt all the time. I was pretty happy with it. Everything was wicked on sale this time of year so I'd gotten it for seventy percent off; even Joel couldn't argue with that. I emerged with my towel slung around my neck and a frown on my face because I didn't have a cover-up. I hadn't done laundry since I'd been back, and my big tees were dirty.

"Have you lost something? Can I help you look?"

"It's what I haven't lost," I admitted ruefully. I pinched up a handful of slack skin from around my waist. "Both my cover-ups are in the wash."

"Maybe I am that fortuneteller I was mentioning." Dory dug in her straw bag and pulled out a square of tie-dyed cloth. "I got this for you. I got one, too, two-for-one. You know how I love a good sale." She showed off her own, what I'd thought was a skirt, and handed me mine.

I unfolded the cloth and looked at it skeptically. It looked like a giant bandana like Joel and Donnie used to blow their noses, though the pattern was cuter. I didn't want to be ungrateful, but I wasn't sure what she meant for me to do with it. "You made what you have on out of this? How did you do it?"

"Oh, it's easy. Look." Dory unwrapped hers with a flourish and held up the square. "See? Yours is the same. You just wrap it around you and tuck in the ends. You try it. You're going to love it: it's so nice and cool." She beamed encouragingly.

"I'm not that coordinated, you know. Like this?" I gave it a try, feeling less the Hawaiian dancer that Dory looked like and more some chump with no thumbs. "Are you sure it's not going to fall off in the street?"

"It might, but will that be any more embarrassing than being flattened by Boner in front of crowds of people?" Her eyes twinkled and told me she already knew all about Ralph and me. Gotta love small towns. "That worked out okay, didn't it? Trust me on this. You look adorable. If it falls off, you just rewrap it, casually, you know, like you planned it."

I took a deep breath. "Okay, I'm ready."

"Let's get going then. I don't want to be stranded on the sand like beached whales because we stood around here chatting all day." Dory took my hand and led me to the car.

"Thanks, Dory. It's great, really."

"My pleasure. Always."

So I had a choice. I could give Gertrude another chance. Or not. It was up to me. There were parts of me that hoped she would come here and apologize at last, beg me to forgive her for leaving, for letting me leave, for everything, but there was another part of me that never wanted to see her again. Which part was on top just depended on the minute, and sometimes even the second. I had Ralph and Joel and Mayes and Dory, and Bert was coming back. Maybe I should and could be content with that. Maybe wanting more than that was just greedy.

34 BREAK

After I tossed and turned for a while and got myself good and sweaty, even down there, which made me think about Ralph and the movies and kissing after, I got up and started rattling around in the kitchen. I made eggs and toast and was wishing we had some bacon when He came in rubbing His jaw. He was dressed in jeans and a flannel shirt even though it was already turning into a real scorcher. He had a cigarette between His lips, but He hadn't lit it yet.

"You're up and at 'em. You cooking for some guests I don't see?" He smiled around His cigarette as He said this.

"I couldn't sleep. I wanted something to do. You want eggs? I've got some." A little practice and I was going to be a pro at laughing at myself.

"I'm going to take a stroll around the lot here, and then I'll be in. I guess those eggs'll still be there. Then we can hit the road."

"Okay." I sat down to eat my eggs and worry some more. It would take a lot of practice to stop fretting about every little thing, and I couldn't work on so many things at once. Dory had said it was good to have goals, but if you had too many it was like having too many sets of directions. Maybe you'd get there, but maybe you'd pull to the side at a standstill. It was kind of like what Joel was always saying now about moderation, something I hoped He was going to take His own advice about, so far so good since I'd been back.

I'd been to Logan more times this summer than I had been in the whole rest of my life, and if I didn't go back there again anytime soon it would be fine with me. Give me a car, okay, but I'd had it with planes. It made no sense to me that people said flying was so much faster, when it seemed like all we ever did was wait.

We'd gotten to the airport early actually, maybe because I'd been up and couldn't go back to sleep. I was thinking about what would happen if Gertrude and Orlando (okay, just Gertrude, Orlando wouldn't keep a kid if you were paying him a fortune) didn't put Bert on the plane at seven like they were supposed to. What if they overslept? What if they didn't get it together? Lots of people would probably be fine with their little brother never coming back, probably everyone I went to school with who had little brothers, and maybe if you'd asked me before this summer I would have said yeah, keep him, but this summer had made me feel that whatever family I had was precious.

We were waiting around outside the Dunkin' Donuts kiosk again. I was trying to avoid looking at the glazed doughnuts, and I was doing pretty well so far. It felt like planes only went in and out of this one gate, and all the rest that I could see out the windows were fakes.

"He's coming, you know. I told you, don't waste your time worrying about that."

"Yeah, I know. I'll just feel better when he's here."

"Me, too. It's been quite a summer, huh?" He ruffled my hair, and it felt good, like Dory's back massage. "High school's gonna be a breeze after all this."

"I don't know about that. It'd be nice if that was true, but I'm still going to be a freshman peon."

"You'll find your place. You'll have to make your way for a while, but you'll get there. I have no doubt."

"I wish I could say the same thing. I—" The loudspeaker startled me and made me forget what I was going to say. I jumped a little when I heard Bert's flight number. "Hey, that's him! He's coming!"

Bert was the last one off the plane, of course. I was betting he'd been in the bathroom. The woman who was his escort did not look like a happy camper. If she could have heaved Bert at us, she would have, but instead she gave a tight smile as she released his shoulder and pivoted on her heel and walked away. As soon as he was free, he rocketed his body at us and held on for all he was worth. He was worth a lot right at that moment.

"Were you in the bathroom?"

Bert nodded, a huge grin on his face. "Look what I made." He pulled a handful of folded paper from a pocket.

I looked closely and started laughing. "You were folding origami on the toilet?"

"They wouldn't let me put that table thing down. Look at this one, pretty good, huh?" He dangled a tiny crane between two fingers.

I looked behind him. "Where's your stuff? And my stuff?"

"They made me park it."

"They made you leave it there?"

"Naw, they stuck it in the plane, you know, with the stickers."

"Do you have the stickers?"

"Um," Bert reached into his pockets again, this time with two hands, and pulled out some crushed and leaking packages of crackers, some gum, unwrapped of course, plane earphones, and a crumpled airline brochure. "This?"

Joel took it gingerly like it might be toxic and tried to unfold it without ripping it. "Could be this." He pointed to a bar-coded number next to the flight number. "Let's go see."

We followed the signs that said baggage claim to some weird racks that looked like escalators tipped on their sides. Lit screens overhead announced the flight numbers. We found Bert's and went to stand with all the poor souls who'd already had to share a flight with him. I expected some of them to flinch when they heard his voice, but people seemed pretty intent on grabbing their stuff and getting out of the airport. I can't say I blamed them. A scattering of bags, mostly black and one red, went around and around without anyone claiming them.

"Where's mine?"

"Have to be a little patient, Bert. Somebody's got to unload all the bags off the plane before they come in here." Joel said this like He flew every day, when actually I didn't know of a time He ever had. "How was your trip? They treat you okay?"

"Yeah, but I'm starving. Can we get some food?"

"Glad to see some things haven't changed. I think you grew while you were down there. And you need a haircut something terrible before school starts, son." He lifted Bert's bangs off his forehead where they hung in his eyes. "You see anything under there?"

"School!" Bert whined. "It's not time yet, is it?"

"You got a few days, and then it's back at it. You got a great teacher, same as Lettie had for fourth grade."

"How come you're calling her Lettie again? Does she mind?" Bert looked up at me, worried.

"It's all right. I'm thinking about it still, but I heard some stuff that made sense, that my name was mine to make something of, and I shouldn't give it away so easily."

"Easy? What's easy about remembering that your sister wants you to call her something else after your whole life? And now you're changing back?" Bert rolled his eyes like Gertrude always did when I said something she didn't like, which was often.

"Don't roll your eyes at me. I hate that. She does that. I'm entitled to change my mind. It's my name after all."

"Well, I'm entitled to some food. What can we have?" Bert gasped and ran forward. "There they are!" I reached out but caught only air. Bert climbed up on the moving belt and grabbed our bags. Guys in uniforms came running.

"Hey! You there! You can't be up there! Whose kid is this?"

Joel laughed and put one hand on my shoulder while He hailed with His other arm. "Bert! Come down from there. Food, remember?"

Bert clambered around and finally jogged over with the bags, eluding his pursuers easily. When the uniforms saw that Bert was claimed, they melted back into the crowd on alert for the next rule-breaker. "That was so awesome! It was like Disney World!"

"You sure took your time coming down," I murmured.

"He didn't have an emergency voice on."

I looked at Joel, and He looked at me. We'd talk about emergencies later, His look said. "They only want bags up there, Bert. Next time wait until I come."

"Airports sure have a lot of rules."

"They don't want to get sued."

"I wasn't going to sue them. I just wanted a ride. I've been sitting for so-o-o-o long."

Joel laughed. "What do you think we take a quick ride into town, walk by the harbor, and let him burn off some energy before we get something to eat? It won't be too late for the drive home, I don't think."

I smiled, liking that He'd included me in the decision. "Sounds good," I reached out and hooked my fingers through my bag's straps. "I'll take that. Thanks for bringing it." I resisted opening it immediately, though I was desperate to know what was in there. It felt about the same as it had months ago when I'd packed it, but I couldn't be sure.

"I didn't do anything. Mommy packed it." That word fell from Bert's mouth so easily. To me it weighed about a thousand pounds and was way too big to fit in my mouth comfortably. "But I found your books. They're in there." His grin was infectious and went a long way to lighten the stone on my tongue.

"Thanks. Thanks a lot. What about…"

"I gave it all to Sammi one time when she came over. I thought she'd know what to do with it. Did I do good?"

"You did awesome. Thanks."

Joel looked from one to the other of us but didn't ask any questions. "Ready to get out of here?"

Bert took off for the nearest door, and we followed in his wake.

It's funny to be writing in here again. It's stupid, but I feel kind of guilty for the days I missed. I am such a geek, like anyone is checking or anything. I'm trying to decide what I want to do with it. It doesn't look like they read it, but who could tell for sure? It's not like they were going to write in the margins or cross stuff out or write back like teachers do at the beginning of the year when they make you keep a journal about your summer reading or your math skills or whatever. She must have though, right? I mean, who could resist if you knew your kid was keeping a journal, and you found it, and you were already pissed at her? I'd like to say I'd honor my kid's privacy, but I'm not sure adults even think kids should have any privacy. So if she read it, does that ruin it? What did she think? Could she even read it, or she did tune it out the way she did whenever I tried to talk to her? That one time I thought I got her, I was out of there the next minute. Maybe I got to her more than I thought; Orlando said I did. Was that a good thing? I don't know. At first I was writing it for the Whopper, like I always do my assignments, and then I was doing it for me, to have someone to talk to, and how pathetic is that? I really needed it at some points over the summer. Now, I don't know, things are kind of looking up. Leave it to me to stress about something that maybe no one besides Bert knows about. I didn't even tell Mayes I started a journal. There was no reason really, I just didn't. She probably keeps one, too, and it's probably a lot better than this one. Oh, well. I'm kind of liking having this, so here goes. I'm back, because I want to be. I'm going to have to get a new book soon. Maybe I can wrangle another few out of the Whopper, you know, so they match and everything. I'm so lame. I don't know the last time the three of us ate out, unless you count us in the Surf Club and Him behind the bar. We went to Legal Seafood, which Joel said Karen recommended, and Bert didn't ask too many questions about her after he heard she had a cool dog. I swear he'd love Dracula if he had a dog. They had this huge blackboard with all the kinds of fish they had that day up there in chalk. Joel said, Look, it's like school, and Bert said, No, we don't have those anymore. He said, Why not? And Bert said, Allergies and stuff. Joel heaved a big sigh but He didn't say anything snide about how pretty soon we'd all be living in little bubbles, but I knew He was thinking it because I was, too. Joel said to get what we wanted, not even off the kids' menu, and I kind of looked at Him funny to see what was up, and He looked back at me like we did this every day. After we ordered, we gawked at all the giant fish tanks. I got chowder, they were famous for that after all, and Bert did, too. Then we split the fish of the day because Bert thought it was hysterical that the fish here were like pets and also dinner. It was pretty good, too, flaky with some kind of cracker crumb crust. Bert said it tasted like French toast, which it kind of did. Joel only had a Coke, and He got some actual food and actually ate it. He didn't even make us sit at the bar where they still let people smoke. You know what? It felt normal.

35 FIX

Here we are, Sunday of Labor Day weekend. It should be called Labor More weekend, since locals on the Cape work more hours this weekend than they do whole weeks in the winter. Mayes is school shopping with her Mom, you know, the mother-daughter bonding thing that I swear I am not bitter about, and Ralph is helping out down at the station. Miraculously, Joel, hmmm, I've been thinking about calling him Dad again, we'll see… anyway, Joel has the day off tomorrow so we're going out to the Point, but today it's just Bert and me. Walking the breakwater out to Wood End is kind of a rite of passage for kids in town. It's one thing to go out there with your parents or whatever, but going by yourself can be tough. For one thing it's pretty far. It doesn't look like it. On a clear day like today, the end of the breakwater is in perfect focus, and the lighthouse stands up against the sky like it's painted there. For another thing it's uneven and some of the gaps between the boulders you have to jump over. And finally, you have to check the tide and make sure you don't get swamped.

"Did you do the sunscreen?"

"Shut up! You're not my mom." Bert cut his eyes at me.

I watched him go, scuttling along like a crab in a bathing suit, and let out my breath long and steady. Bert had been through a lot this summer, too. He hadn't talked at all about what it had been like down there alone, not that I hadn't asked. He didn't seem sorry to be back home with us, but he wasn't overjoyed either. Maybe it was just that school was coming. I walked slowly, enjoying the view. Once you passed the tide line, you couldn't see any buildings in front of you unless you counted the lighthouse, only sand and water and sky. The tide was coming in a little, more on the left than the right, filling in the ridges it had left in the sand when it receded. Then, like it was waiting for me, I saw a perfect pink scallop all by itself on a bed of kelp. I'd have to scale down the side of the breakwater and cross the mussel beds, but it would be worth it.

I looked ahead for Bert and pegged him traveling with this family I dubbed The Perfects: a dad, a mom, and two boys and a girl. The dad and the mom were holding hands, and the kids were skipping. I'm not kidding. I started down.

I was sure it would turn out to be broken or inhabited. Our rule was we didn't take a shell that was someone's house. I picked my way along and crouched down, balancing gingerly. I reached for the shell and palmed it. I said a little prayer and flipped it over, empty but whole. It was kind of like my life, waiting to get filled with whatever the fall was going to bring. I looked up. Somehow I had to climb this sheer cliff holding a highly breakable object. It was slow going, with my feet getting more scraped up by the minute, but when I made the top, I was pretty proud of myself. I caught up to Bert just as he and The Perfects were dodging the poison ivy to climb down onto the sand.

"Oh, you must be Bert's sister. We're the Joneses. I'm Frances, this is my husband Vince, and these are our kids Zoë, Quentin, and Xavier." Wow, they were like a walking Scrabble game. They would so win if you could use proper names.

We trekked across the scorching sand on the narrow path edged with more poison ivy, and we let out a collective gasp when we saw the water of Wood End on the ocean side. It was like God had dropped a million sparkly rhinestones in the waves. All at once we dropped our gear and raced for the water. It had maybe never felt this good, buoyant with salt and a cold bite that tingled and so clear I could see pebbles on the bottom in as many colors as candy rocks.

"Bert! Wait! I have something wrapped up in there!" I raced, knowing I'd never be able to fix it, and my heart raced along with me, back up to the towels. Intact. Phew.

"Lovely. Did you find that on the way out?" Missus Perfect had lunch arranged in perfect piles. "That's so much nicer than any of the ones in town."

"Thanks." I rewrapped it.

"You are lucky to live in such a beautiful place. We're from New Jersey." She said this in an embarrassed way. A Perfect, embarrassed, how could that be?

I looked at the sky, and then I looked around. We were the only ones left on the beach. "We should get going. The tide will be really coming in."

"Is that a problem?" Mister Perfect yipped.

"Well, it gets pretty high when there's a full moon, which there will be, and if there's a breeze in the harbor, well..."

Bert took care of the rest. "Last year three kids got swept off and died."

Mister and Missus started barking at everyone and throwing stuff in bags. We practically skidded across the sand back onto the breakwater. The bay was mostly filled in, and a stiff breeze was making whitecaps on the waves.

"Bert, look out for the poison ivy!" I wrenched my ankle, but that wasn't the part that really hurt. That was my arm that cracked down on a boulder as I fell. I screamed and looked down. My forearm was at a funny angle, and the skin was turning patchy white and red. It seemed like it might have felt better if someone ripped it right off.

"Oh, Lettie! It's broken, isn't it?" Missus looked at Mister for confirmation. The kids' faces shone in a halo above me. I cradled my arm and tried to not to move.

"Shit yeah." He got a glare for that from Missus. "You all stay here, and I'll be back as quick as I can."

"She's my sister. I'm going too." Bert could be pretty determined.

"We're going too! We're going too!" Their kids were clamoring now.

"All right then, forward march double time."

Bert called over his shoulder. "Don't worry, Annie, we'll be back in a flash."

Now he gets the "Annie" bit, figures.

Missus was puzzled. "Annie? Who's Annie?"

"Long story. How about one with a nice happy ending?"

The next time I looked up from my moaning, my own army was coming down the breakwater with Bert at the front then Joel, Martini Tina, Al, Vin, and Ralph. Ralph. Just looking at him made me feel calmer. They had this fireman's rescue stretcher thing, and they gently slung me into it and started toting me back the way they had come, hardly any slower it seemed like but somehow I didn't bang around too much. So maybe we weren't The Perfects, but we weren't a bad bunch.

An ambulance was waiting where we'd left our bikes, and Joel and Bert climbed in after they loaded me. I got a shot for the pain before the attendant even closed the doors. When I woke up, I was in a bed at the clinic, my shell next to me, and Joel was reading the paper.

"Hey, you're awake."

"Yeah, but I'm kind of fuzzy." I looked at my arm encased in plaster. "It figures it was my left arm. Now I won't be able to write."

Joel laughed. "Lettie, I think you're the only kid in America who's sorry when she has to miss school. Now your brother on the other hand, he's thrilled."

"Why? What happened to Bert??"

"Now slow down, he's fine. He's just up to his neck, and I mean literally, in poison ivy. Nurses here say it's one of the worst cases they've ever seen." Joel chuckled. "He says he's missing the start of school, too."

"Oh, no, I'm going to school. I'm so not missing the first day."

"I figured you'd say that." Joel hooked a thumb over His shoulder. "They're all getting something to eat. Someone volunteered to carry your books for you for a while."

"Yeah?"

"Yeah. Nice kid." Joel let that sit a minute. "He tries anything funny, I'm still gonna knock his block off."

36 STAND

I'd been standing on the steps to the cottage watching a neighbor's cat, Spade, stalk through the parking lot toward her usual daytime spot under the never-moving car in front of the Ames's. She would probably get a nice nest going under there. Maybe there'd be kittens in the spring.

A car pulled in, obviously a rental. No one around here had a brand-new car, and certainly not a shiny teal two-door with red pinstripes. The car drove slowly through the small lot, hesitated, and pulled to a stop in front of the cottage next door. I knew no one was home there; I'd seen them go out earlier. The driver, a tall blonde woman, unfolded herself from the tiny front seat and got out. She looked at the empty cottage, maybe looked at the number on the door. She turned and spotted our cottage, its five hanging crookedly from the doorframe, and me standing there. I had barely a second to compose myself.

Holy crap. She actually came. It took her two months, but who's counting, oh right, I am. My heart was beating fast enough to run itself right out of my chest. I felt lightheaded. I thought I was going to throw up. What was she doing here? What did she want? Did she figure out I took some of her stuff? Is she going to apologize? She BETTER be going to apologize for... for EVERYTHING.

Gertrude's steps slowed a bit as she approached, but as soon as she saw me looking, her pace picked up, and she held her chin high. For my part I just tried to look steadily ahead like nothing unusual was happening. I was failing at it, I'm sure. When Gertrude got close enough, I spoke, or croaked, depending on what you wanted to call it, "Bert's inside."

"Hello to you, too. I didn't come to see Bert, though I always love to see him, of course."

Here we go again. The fact that she hadn't bothered to see him for several years clearly still didn't register. Maybe we were more like philosophical children or theoretical children or something like that. Cartoon children, maybe. That kind certainly sounded easier than the kind that needed food and shoes and reassurance.

"I came to see you."

Not so fast. "Huh."

"I thought we could have lunch." Her voice was light and shiny like I'd just won a prize and she was it.

This would be funny if it wasn't so bizarre. "You came here so we could have lunch."

"Yes, I did."

"He eat all the food down there?"

"Engie? No, he was a dream. He missed you though. We all did."

I let that lie where it fell, in the dirt.

"So what do you think? Do you want some lunch?" Her voice was strained now like she couldn't understand why I wasn't jumping for joy.

I decided to stick right to the face value, to not to give her anything she didn't deserve or risk anything I valued. I'd string her out like she'd done to me so many times. "I'm not real hungry. Why don't you ask Bert? Like I said, he's inside."

"I'd like to have lunch with you. That's why I came. I have a few things I'd like to say." She pressed her lips together, hard, so she got a white ring around her mouth.

Nothing I wanted to hear, if what I'd heard so far was any indicator. "I'm watching Bert. As you can see, there's no one else here."

"As it happens, I talked to your father." She was prepared; I had to give her that. Bert chose this moment to come outside. He stood beside me on the step for a minute. He didn't say anything. Then he went over and gave Gertrude a hug. I glanced at him; his heart glowed. Gertrude put her arm around his shoulders and looked down at him. "I'm going to be here a few days, and if it's all right with you, Engie, Joel said he could use a helper shucking clams for the rush. I know how you like that job. I'm trying to convince your sister here to have some lunch with me."

I reached for my handy sarcasm to fend off her chumminess with Bert. "Like I have any choice."

"You have a choice. Let, no, Annie, you're getting so grown up. You do have a choice. You'll have more and more of them to make, as you get older. I'd like you to have lunch with me. If you want, you can just eat and not say anything. As I said, I have a few things I'd like to say. I'd appreciate it if you'd listen to them."

This sounded better. My hopes rose again, as much as I tried to tell them not to. "I don't have to talk?"

Gertrude shook her head no.

"And I can order what I want?"

"Anything you want." Gertrude breathed a sigh of relief now that I was talking about going. "Where do you want to go then? Where do they have a good salad in this town these days? That's what I'd like, that and a comfortable seat far from a car." Her voice was brighter now but still tight.

That reminded me that in a restaurant I'd be trapped if it went badly, which it probably would. I backpedaled. "Nowhere. I'm not hungry."

Gertrude's face fell. "But I thought—"

I had another idea. I wasn't ready to give up on her entirely; she had come here, after all. And I did want to hear what she had to say, why she'd come at least. "I'll go. But I just want to walk. You could take Bert over," I glanced at Bert for confirmation, and he gave a small nod, "and then come back."

"Oh. Couldn't we walk from there?" She made a visible jerk of her head. "All right then. I haven't eaten since five o'clock this morning, but maybe you'll change your mind while we're walking. That can happen, you think you aren't hungry, and then as soon as you see food, you are. Not that it would hurt you to skip a few—" She cut herself off and continued on a new tack. "Well, we'll see. Engie, do you need anything, or can we go now?"

"We can go now, I guess." Bert looked at me, and I nodded and gave him a smile, as much as I could manage anyway. His heart faded a fraction, beet to strawberry.

"I'll be right back. Please be here when I—" Again Gertrude stopped herself. I felt kind of powerful. I was sure it was temporary. "I'll see you in a few minutes."

I watched them walk to the car; Bert ran a finger down the pinstripes as he continued around the car to the passenger side. He opened the door, pulled forward the front seat, and climbed into the back. He turned to wave to me through the back window. I waved back. They drove off, and I considered whether I really did want to be home when Gertrude got back. If I wasn't, if I didn't listen to her, I could just be content with what I had that was good here, and that was a lot. But I realized that was pointless. She said she'd be here a few days; it could be tough to avoid her that long. I sat down on the step to wait. What could she possibly have to say? None of the things I wanted to hear, I was betting. I said a little prayer that I was wrong. I'd certainly been wrong about other things.

When Gertrude pulled in again, this time she parked right in front of our cottage. She got out briskly, tossing her hair over her shoulder and then slapping her hands on her thighs like this was going to be the most fun walk of her life (or else she was calling a dog we didn't have). I didn't know how to take her enthusiasm; me, I was alternating between hope and dread, pretty much in equal parts. "Ready?" When I didn't respond, she continued. "I'm sorry about what I said, you know, about you needing to skip a few meals. It'll come right off. You'll see. The same thing happened to me when I was your age, when I stopped growing."

So right off she was dissing me, even when she said she was apologizing, even when it was true. Couldn't she just love me the way I was? The dread was winning. "Thanks for sharing. I feel all warm and fuzzy now."

She glanced at me to see if I was being sarcastic, which of course I was. There weren't going to be any big Oprah moments on my part, and I highly doubted there were going to be any on hers.

We set out walking, me setting the quick pace and the route from the start. I turned right out of our little lot and strode down Bradford toward town. I swung both arms, my left a little more gingerly than my right even though I'd had the cast off a week now, to 'work the whole body' like they say to do on fitness shows. Gertrude matched my pace easily, her longer legs an advantage, swinging both her arms as she walked, too, like she was also here for the exercise. Neither of us said anything at first, no small talk, no how's high school going, nothing. When we came even with the Surfside Hotel, I stopped.

"Remember this?"

"What, the motel? Sure. A long time ago I used to clean that motel, Leticia. It was called something else then."

"Not that. That." I pointed the other way to the gray and white house set back from the road. "And I told you about a thousand times, it's Annie now." I hadn't decided for sure about this, but I wasn't giving her any leeway.

"Yes, Let, Annie, I remember the house we lived in. Is that what this is going to be, a trip down memory lane?"

I swore she just rolled her eyes at me. Next it would be the shoulder shrug and she'd be off down the road. "Would that be so bad? That would be hard, though, since I don't remember much, and you don't seem to want to fill in the pieces. I just wondered, do you ever think about it?"

She gave a big, aggravated sigh like I was a little kid and had just asked her the same thing over again about a hundred times. "About when we lived there? About your father nearly drinking himself to death? No, I try not to think about it. I try to think about good things."

Okay, so we were bad things. You couldn't accuse her of beating around the bush. "Like what? Like leaving?"

"Is that what you think? You don't know the first thing about it then. Leaving was the hardest thing I've ever done. I've cried every day." Her voice was sharp, like she was mad now, but I couldn't see what right she had to be mad.

I made this weird sound that was halfway between a gasp and a guffaw, love that word. "You don't look like you're crying. And I didn't see you jumping for joy while we were in Florida; mostly you ignored us, me anyway."

"Don't let yourself get hard, Leticia. I'm telling you, it's difficult to come back from that. And don't give me that look about your name. You can't run away from who you are. Believe me, I tried." She laughed this tough laugh, like, I'm so the woman of the world.

"I don't think you're really in any position to be giving me advice, do you? But don't worry, I won't screw up my life as much as you have." I was practically spitting now I was so mad.

"You think I've screwed up my life? Really? I think my life is pretty together now. My art is starting to sell, and I've got a lot of supportive friends, and… well. I tried to show you that in Key West, but you weren't interested."

She sounded a little hurt about that, but no way I was going for it. Plus, it was such a total lie. "No, I meant done screwing up MY life." I didn't mention that I felt like I was getting my life here back now; with the harsh things she was saying, she didn't deserve to know.

"You always looked at things negatively, even when you were little. We'd be at the beach having a great time, and you'd be pointing to the only cloud on the horizon. I only want the best for you, Leticia. I never meant to hurt you."

And yet you have, and you keep doing it. "And when Orlando ditched me at the airport, you thought I was a-okay, huh?"

"I wasn't thinking clearly. I know that now. It was the sex, all of it. When you're older and you're in a relationship with someone, you'll understand." She stated this so baldly that it was clear she really believed it, that it explained everything. She so lived on another planet.

I skipped right over the sex part. I was not getting into that with her no matter what else happened. "I'm so sick of everyone saying when I grow up, I'll understand. First of all, I am grown up, in all the ways that count. Second of all, you're so messed up; I can't believe you can keep a straight face when you lecture me."

"I have made a lot of mistakes. Most people do. I know you've made some, too. Let's not forget what got Joel to agree to your visit in the first place. Now I didn't come here to lecture you, but you aren't perfect either. I am trying to fix one of my mistakes. You could at least give me a little credit. Would that be so hard?"

Yes, yes it would. "Just because you came up here, that's supposed to fix everything? What about all the years that have gone by; where were you then? Why should I care that you came today?" I did, but no way I was giving her that, or anything else.

"Leticia, I'm trying to say I'm sorry. You aren't making this any easier."

Did she really think this counted as an apology like I'd wished for every day for two months, no, make that almost seven years? If she did, it was a good reminder to be careful what you wish for, like in all those stories where people get three wishes and totally screw up their lives because they weren't specific. I should have wished for a really good, meaningful apology. "Why should I? Why should that be my job? Aren't parents supposed to try and make their *kids'* lives easier?"

"Life is hard. I still think the sooner you learn that the better. It's hard. I can't apologize for that."

"Great. You came to apologize, but you can't. Typical."

Gertrude didn't say anything. She seemed to be studying the gray and white house. "What an ugly garage someone built, and right in the front yard."

Clearly nothing was going to come of this. I couldn't see why she'd even bothered coming, unless maybe someone had shamed her into it. Sammi, maybe? Certainly not Orlando. I started walking again down the hill toward the playground in the distance. "So where's your sidekick? He let you off the leash for this little joyride?"

"I'll ignore your tone. The fact of the matter is, he's gone."

I waited for her to say more, but nothing came. I took the bait. "What do you mean, gone? He went on a trip, too?"

"A trip he's not coming back from."

"That's cryptic. Do you *ever* answer a question someone asks you?"

"I know you never liked Orlando. I don't think you really gave him a chance. He tried so hard."

That was really rich. I choked on my own breath I was so mad. "He tried! Was that before or after he almost got us killed on that cute little island of yours? Or maybe it was while he was yelling at us to do stuff for him while he got baked every day, eating every scrap of food there was in the house. Oh, right, you thought he was going back to work after lunch."

"It's funny you picked that."

My eyes bugged out, but she wasn't even looking at me. "I didn't find it so funny. Using your size to scare people smaller than you are isn't funny. It's called being a bully."

"No, not that. He was joking around, trying to have a little fun with you and Engie, but you're always so serious. You know that Engie follows whatever you do."

This was like that movie *Groundhog Day*, living the same scenario over and over again. "So now we're back to you not apologizing. You're starting to make it sound like you think I should be apologizing. Is that what you came here for? I'm the one who spent the night alone in an airport. Not you."

"You don't need to remind me. I stayed awake all night. I was no use at work the next day. Who wants to see a hostess with circles under her eyes halfway down her face? People are on vacation, they go out to eat, and they want someone pretty to seat them."

"La la la, can you hear me? This isn't about you. You said you had some things to say. Are they *all* about you?!" I was yelling now, and I wasn't sure I would ever stop.

"Young lady, I do wish things had happened differently when Orlando took you to the airport, but I did not come here to be insulted. You said some terrible things as well. I felt every one. I have been traveling since early this morning, and—"

I had to shut this down before my head exploded. I needed something else to focus on, something that wasn't making me so mad that I was almost hyperventilating. I did my own version of the shoulder shrug, not that she'd notice. "Right, whatever. Want to walk a little faster? I'd like to get down to the water." We'd reached the center of town. I led the way across Bradford and over to Commercial. I took some slow, deep breaths. The bay beckoned, sun glinting off the little wavelets making their way toward the shore. A stiff breeze made all the flags flap and crack. It was like I was watching my hopes–for an apology, for Gertrude to love me, for a mother–blow away in the wind, blow away like a mirage. The water was grayer now, and the light was different even with the heat of Indian summer. Leisure cruisers of all sizes making their last stops before they headed south crowded the wharf where once a fleet of fishing boats had docked. A few token fishermen still worked out of this harbor, but they hauled mostly shellfish or lobsters or what used to be baitfish. The name Cape Cod didn't really apply anymore. Maybe it should be called Cape Shop, since that seemed like what people came here for now.

"It was one of those," Gertrude murmured.

"What was?" I continued my fast pace out toward the end of the wharf, not stopping for traffic of the foot or wheeled kind. I was a local; I knew my rights. I wasn't really paying attention to Gertrude anymore since there seemed to be so little to be gained or lost. I used to think it would matter so much to me if she actually sought me out, and now here she was, and I just wanted to be done with it, to get back to my life. She was just here to get out of there, off The Rock, for a while. It was about her, like always. She wasn't sorry, she didn't love me, and she never would. What the hell was I supposed to do with that? What kid doesn't want her mother to love her? "You can't always get what you want," that's what The Stones said, and they were so right. My life, Lettie's life, was here, and it wasn't so bad. I should have realized that sooner, but maybe better late than never.

Gertrude pointed. "A fishing trawler. That's what they left in. They thought it would be a good disguise."

"A disguise? What are you talking about?" I was annoyed now. Gertrude seemed to be going off on one of her tangents. These were worse than the self-involved storytelling and made about as much sense.

"Orlando. He was smuggling drugs, drugs hidden in hay bales, from Cuba. He said he was only going on one trip. He was going to make a bundle, set us up. Key West is so expensive." Gertrude paused, frowning. "When the Coast Guard came, the crew threw the bales overboard, trying to get rid of them. You know, fish food, flush them in the world's biggest toilet." A strangled sound that might have been a laugh or might have been the start of a cry came out of her throat. "They floated."

I had no such conflict in me; I shrieked with laughter. It felt good to have some kind of release since I sure as hell wasn't going to cry, no matter what. "They floated! Of course they floated! I guess it was only one trip! He really was as dense as he seemed!" I had a pain in my side now I was laughing so hard. I sneaked a glance at Gertrude.

Gertrude was laughing, too, and crying a little bit. "He's gone to prison in Miami. The lawyer says he'll be denied bail. And he'll get years. Years. Unless he turns on the higher ups, which he'll never do."

Right, that big sense of honor he had would keep him quiet. I sobered up a bit when I registered the word years. That lawyer was probably right, too; he would get years. I was betting Gertrude wouldn't wait around to find out. "Oh. Wow. What will you do?" The words were out of my mouth before I realized they sounded like I cared.

"I don't know yet. I have a lot of friends in Key West. I have my work, but the house, I can't keep the house. My friend Knox—"

Even for her, this was something. Then again, it was just what Dad had said. "You've met someone else. Orlando is in the slammer for five minutes, and you are moving on."

"Knox is my friend. As I was trying to say, he is renovating a hotel with suites, and he says I can stay in one that's nearly done. And it's not like you liked Orlando. You hated him from the first second you met him. I think we can agree on that."

"I don't know what we agree on. I don't even know who you are." I tried to sound chilly and distant; I sounded more like the heroine in a cheesy movie.

"Leticia, don't be dramatic. I am your mother. I will always be your mother. That's it. I'm the only one you get. You've never loved me. I don't know why I bother."

That was it. That was totally it. I wouldn't listen to another word out of her if she got down on her knees begging. "I never loved *you*? You have a lot of nerve. And I don't notice you bothering so much. It's like you want an award for coming here!" I pointed back the way we'd come. "I'm sure you can find your way to your car. You did used to live here. I'm going to see Bert. And Dad. My family. Have a good trip." I turned away from the lapping water and strode toward the Surf Club. My insides felt like they'd been scraped out with a melon baller or maybe even a fork, but maybe that was a good thing, if I could just breathe. I squared my shoulders and stood up straight, really straight, something I hadn't done in so long I couldn't even remember when. My skin slid into place, and it felt like it could be comfortable.

"I'll be staying at Dory and Donnie's for a few days. I hope I'll hear from you."

"You'll see Bert tomorrow. I'll bring him by."

"Will you—"

"Tomorrow."

When I got to the door, I didn't hesitate. I pulled it open and stepped inside. After a few seconds to let my eyes adjust, I headed for Bert sitting at a table with what looked like a burger-fries plate, no pickle of course, and a packet of crayons. He was drawing a dragon and a slew of knights with giant swords definitely heavier than their body weights.

I took a long, ragged breath and tried to smooth out my face. "Seen any buffalo lately?"

He looked up and smiled. "Naw. Just some seagulls."

"This seat taken?" I kept my voice as steady as I could.

"It's all yours." He glanced over my shoulder.

"Nope. It's just you and me. And Dad." I waved over at the bar and smiled, a weak one but still. He was pouring beer at the tap, and I couldn't really see his eyes behind his glasses, but he smiled back and raised his eyebrows questioningly. I gave him a thumbs-up and called out, "Can a girl get something to eat in this joint?"

I was picking at my clam roll when the door opened. You could tell because it got lighter and then darker, but I didn't turn around. My heart tightened up again, and I held my breath then let it out slowly. I had everything I needed right here.

"Leticia! How was your summer? How's high school treating you? I've been thinking about you," Dolores Stopper leaned over our table and whispered, "and your assignment. How'd it go?"

I laughed a kind of demented laugh. When I caught my breath, I managed, "My summer? It was a real learning experience. And about my assignment. Would you believe an alligator ate it?"

THE END, AT LEAST SO FAR

EPILOGUE: MY LIFE IN A BOX, IN A GOOD WAY

Zuzu's been quiet through the whole last chapter, so quiet.

"Well," I say brightly, "some story, huh?"

She looks at me a long while, long enough that I start to fidget under her gaze. Talk about role reversal. Finally, the question comes, the one I've known would come. "Do you forgive her?"

Actually, that wasn't the one I thought would come. That one was more along the lines of, do you miss her? Hers is better though. "Uh, yeah, yes, I do. And you know why? Because Dory, your esteemed great-godmother, was absolutely right. Once I let it go, I could claim my life and get on with it, without that burden. And it's a great life, a totally awesome life. I wouldn't change a thing."

"You didn't want anything more than some postcards and a 'drive-by' once in a while?"

I'd gotten more postcards from Sammi over the years than Gertrude. Honestly, I was sorrier I hadn't seen Grandpa and Grandma again. They'd died while I was still in high school, one right after the other, his heart attack and her heartbreak. I learned this from Gertrude in a postcard of a bowl of fruit. I didn't know Zuzu had ever really taken much notice of those, the postcards or the drive-bys, not in a few years now. Sure, she knew my "real" mother lived in South America somewhere, that collectors the world over bought her art, that I rarely saw or spoke to her, but her focus in that department is squarely on her two sets of grandparents who live right here in town. Mayes and her brood settled in Eastham last year after bouncing around California for a while. The only real out-of-towners in our lives are Bert and his wife Estelle who live in Utah, for the skiing of course, but we'd only been out there once. With their jobs with the airlines, they come east plenty, and we are on the phone or texting pretty much constantly. "Okay, maybe I'd lose ten pounds and some of the gray I'm getting in my hair, but really, nothing."

"Nothing what? Nothing for dinner?" Ralph bellows from the front door. "Oh, no, what will be do? It'll have to be pizza again." He comes into the room, rubbing his hands together with glee. I tilt my head up for my kiss and receive it and return it. Venezuela does the same. He pushes his bangs to the side, longer now to cover the larger expanse of forehead, and my heart beats faster as always.

I still have that green and white rugby shirt in a box of "Ralphabilia." Really I should call it "Lifeabilia." There are train stubs and hostel receipts from all around the world. There are snapshots and tile samples from when we built this house. There are baby shoes and tattered board books from our proudest project that we are pretty sure we started in a tent in the rain forests of Venezuela. We filed almost daily blog entries from wherever we were, and *The Advocate* linked to them to show the progress of its intrepid reporter and her second-grade teacher husband, on leave for a year to see the sites on the thinnest shoestring you ever saw. That was probably the only taste of fame we're ever going to get, when we got back and rode our *papier-mâché* globe float in the Fourth of July parade, people chanting our names and singing that song, you know, "Lettie and Ralph sitting in a tree, k-i-s-s-i-n-g, first comes love, then comes marriage, then comes baby in a baby carriage." Little did they know that baby was already on the way; we barely knew it ourselves. Everyone was great though, pitching in to get us equipped and helping with the house when we got the land in an auction. People here come through for each other, just like family, real family, and I have mine all around me, not an alligator in sight.

LETTIE'S CONTRANYMS

- **Bar** a place grown-ups go to get drunk; a solid rectangular piece of something (soap); to ban or forbid
- **Belt** to sing loudly; to hit; a leather strap to hold up your pants; something that cycles to make something work (like a fan belt on a car); a drink of something alcoholic
- **Block** to keep something from happening or someone from something; a rectangular piece of wood; an obstacle; a part of a street stretching from one intersection to another
- **Bolt** to attach firmly; to flee
- **Bound** going somewhere; tied up
- **Break** a rest; a rip or tear; a stop (like a breakwater); to ruin or make come apart
- **Buckle** to connect (like a belt); to bend or collapse (like knees)
- **Camp** a set up for sleeping outside; silly (campy); to sit somewhere to wait something out
- **Clip** to fasten; to hit; to trot or move rapidly
- **Continue** to keep going; to stop for now (like court)
- **Cross** to go over something (like a bridge or a street); a symbol for Christianity; grumpy; to ask for protection (to cross oneself)
- **Crow** a black bird that is bad luck to some people; to yell in triumph and joy
- **Custom** something usual; something special

a

- **Dike** a wall to stop flooding; a ditch; what some people call a woman who is gay (sometimes dyke)
- **Dump** someplace to leave your trash; when someone leaves you they do this; (take a dump) to defecate; (to dump on someone) to unload verbally, usually unfairly
- **Dust** to add little bits (like confectioner's sugar); to take away little bits
- **Edge** the sharp side of something (like a cliff or a can); to move slowly and carefully toward or away from something
- **Fast** quick; slutty; secure, like a boat tied up; to not eat for a long time
- **Finished** completed; destroyed
- **Fix** to repair; to castrate; to set up the results ahead of time; a bind or bad situation
- **Fly** a little black bug with wings (annoying); to have wings and be able to leave the ground with them (awesome)
- **Fool** to trick; someone who gets tricked
- **Garnish** the frilly part added on a plate (like parsley or orange); to keep back (like money from your paycheck to pay a debt)
- **Left** what remained; to have gone; the opposite of right
- **Lie** an untruth; when a body is horizontal instead of vertical; the direction of something (like a boat)
- **Load** to fill with something; the something that fills something else (load of); drunk (loaded); the force upon something (physics); weighted down (loaded)
- **Off** strange; deactivated (like lights); activated (like an alarm going off)
- **Out** visible (like the stars); empty, gone; openly admitting being gay
- **Overlook** to supervise (like overseer); to neglect; a scenic spot to look at the view
- **Picture** a flat physical representation of something; to form an image in your head
- **Pinch** a tight spot (trouble); a little bit (cooking); when someone takes a fold of your skin and squeezes it until you give in
- **Prone** likely; lying still
- **Put** (out) to extinguish (like fire); to give (like sex)
- **Puzzle** a challenge; to figure out something hard; to confuse
- **Refrain** to not do something; to repeat (like a chorus in a song)
- **Rent** to pay to use something temporarily; to offer something temporarily for money; a hole; torn

b

- **Rock** stone; rhythmic motion
- **Sail** a piece of canvas that can fill with wind and helps a boat move (but often doesn't); to move easily toward a goal
- **Sanction** to approve; to limit (like fishing regulations)
- **Sanguine** cheerful; bloodthirsty
- **Scarf** a long piece of cloth worn around the head or neck; to eat (something) enthusiastically; a joint connecting two pieces so they fit into each other
- **Scream** a yell (usually in fear); to yell (usually in anger); a good time
- **Screen** to analyze (like job applicants or drug tests); to conceal
- **Seed** to plant new plants; to take out the inside of a plant
- **Separate** parts of a whole that are not together; to divide
- **Shop** to go to a business to buy something; to offer something for sale
- **Skin** body covering; to remove a covering
- **Splice** to join; to separate
- **Squelch** the sucking sound when you pull your foot out of wet sand or mud; when someone stomps on you or your ideas
- **Stand** to hold firm; to rise up
- **Stick** to refuse to come apart or give in; a small branch of a tree, broken off
- **Stray** someone who's left behind (a dog or a kid); to leave somewhere you're supposed to stay
- **Strike** to hit; to refuse to participate; to make a bold start (strike out); to end your turn/miss when you try to hit (strike out)
- **Temper** rage or upset; to soften; to make stronger
- **Throw** (out) to get rid of; to suggest or propose
- **Transparent** invisible; obvious
- **Trim** to decorate; to remove the extra
- **Trip** to fall down (which usually hurts); a voyage to another place (which can be fun); a reference to drug usage (good trip, bad trip)
- **Wear** to put clothes on; to break down (like water on stone)
- **Wrap** to cover; to finish; a folded sandwich

ACKNOWLEDGEMENTS

Thanks for taking the time to read my book. Time is precious, and I appreciate that you spent some of yours with me and my work. Thanks, too, to all the nameless people who helped in ways varied and many to encourage me to finish and to make every word my best. That category would include teachers, mentors, fellow writers and readers, coworkers, friends, enemies, and, of course, family. Who else is there?

ABOUT THE AUTHOR

Kirsten Bloomberg Feldman received her undergraduate degree in comparative literature from Brown University and her master's degree in English education from Tufts University. She has written professionally for *The Boston Globe*, the Whitney Museum of Art, Edwin Schlossberg Incorporated, Exit Art, deCordova Sculpture Park + Museum School, and many area print and online publications. She grew up on Cape Cod and the Connecticut shoreline and now lives outside of Boston with her family.

Made in the USA
Lexington, KY
26 April 2014